No, she thought, lov  **her life thus far.**

"Alas, sir," she answered at length, "I must confess I have little enough experience of these matters, beyond facing the prospect of a forced marriage, but that had nothing to do with love."

As the words fell from her lips, Hope was pained to acknowledge that this was the most honest sentiment she'd expressed to Sir Samuel since they'd met. Pained, too, to note the look of earnest sympathy he gave her as she reminded him of her misfortune. An unexpected, unfathomable feeling rose within her, one that made her yearn to tell him more about herself. To tell him truths she'd never uttered to another person. Perhaps even to tell him the truth.

Hope swallowed down the rest of her tea, as though the hot liquid might bring her back to her senses. As benevolent as her rescuer appeared to be, he could not know the truth about her. No one here could. Her entire future likely depended upon it.

Author Note

Readers of *Spinster with a Scandalous Past* will recognize Samuel, the cheerful, sociable opposite of his brooding older brother, Isaac, who is the hero of that story. Readers may also recall that in that novel, Samuel has his hopes of romance dashed. When it came to deciding who to write about next, Samuel was the obvious choice as I really wanted him to have his own happy ending.

A visit to the Cumbrian coast in autumn 2022 led me to explore the area's murkier history, the smuggling and the illegal distilling that went on in the Georgian period. At the same time, I'd been reading a lot about the period's famous actresses, such as Sarah Siddons and Dorothea Jordan, and I knew I wanted to write about a heroine who had the theater in her background. All these elements came together in Hope—a strong, brave and resilient actress with a troubled past.

Samuel and Hope find themselves in close confines at Hayton Hall, and they both have their reasons not to be honest about who they really are. Theirs is a story of secrets, lies and sizzling attraction, and it was an absolute joy to write.

RESCUING THE RUNAWAY HEIRESS

SADIE KING

HISTORICAL

Harlequin® HISTORICAL

ISBN-13: 978-1-335-53967-0

Rescuing the Runaway Heiress

Recycling programs for this product may not exist in your area.

Harlequin Enterprises ULC
22 Adelaide St. West, 41st Floor
Toronto, Ontario M5H 4E3, Canada
www.Harlequin.com

Printed in U.S.A.

Sadie King was born in Nottingham and raised in Lancashire. After graduating with a degree in history from Lancaster University, she moved to West Lothian, Scotland, where she now lives with her husband and children. When she's not writing, Sadie loves long country walks, romantic ruins, Thai food and traveling with her family. She also writes historical fiction and contemporary mysteries as Sarah L King.

Books by Sadie King

Harlequin Historical

Spinster with a Scandalous Past

Look out for more books by Sadie King coming soon!

Visit the Author Profile page at Harlequin.com.

For David

Chapter One

September 1818

A loud cry pierced the cool, still air of the early autumn evening, causing Samuel to startle. He had been enjoying his usual slow promenade around Hayton Hall's fine gardens, appreciating the quiet calm, observing the changing light and admiring the late blooming plants as one season ebbed into the next. Or at least, so he told himself. He found that he told stories to himself frequently these days, as though such works of fiction, if repeated often enough, could eventually embody the truth. He'd tell himself that he was simply a country gentleman, relishing some moments of peaceful solitude before retiring for the night. That he took just as much pleasure in doing his duty as he always had. That he was his own man, in charge of his own destiny. That he did not mind being alone. That he did not spend most evenings walking in that garden, listening to his doubts as they whispered to him, about just how bleak his prospects now seemed.

Samuel looked around him, shaking his head at himself in an uncomfortable acknowledgement of the darker turn his thoughts had taken before that brief, shrill noise had intruded. The gardens of Hayton Hall fell back into silence once more, readying themselves for the impending dark as, above them, the sky's pink hues deepened. His gaze shifted towards the wood beyond, its trees still thick with summer's lush green foliage, the leaves only now hinting at beginning to turn. He stood still for several moments, listening for anything which might betray the origin of such a sound. All he could detect, however, were the occasional caws of the crows as they came home to roost for the night.

'You see, Samuel,' he muttered to himself, 'you've naught but the birds for company.'

Naught but birds, and his servants, of course. Or, rather, his older brother's servants, since it was Sir Isaac Liddell who was the master here. Samuel was merely the caretaker, appointed to look after the family estate while his brother travelled with his new bride.

As Samuel turned his back to the woods and continued his gentle promenade, he found himself counting the weeks since Isaac and Louisa's departure, and considering how much, and how little, had changed since. At first, he'd embraced the responsibility his brother had bestowed on him with his usual cheerful enthusiasm, but although he believed he'd discharged his duties competently, he'd quickly wearied of just how solitary and tedious running a country estate could be. It pained him to admit it, but he resented how it tied him, quite literally, to its acres. He'd never have thought it possible, but he was tired of the sight of his ancestral home. Tired, too, of his own company.

Yet solitude, he'd discovered, was infinitely preferable to being the subject of ceaseless gossip. As happy as he was for his older brother, he could not fail to acknowledge that Isaac had left quite a scandal in his wake, and the news of his elopement with a woman who'd borne a naval captain's child out of wedlock had quickly spread. For the first time in his life, Samuel had become disenchanted with Cumberland society, as he found himself either invited to dinner parties to answer questions about the scandal, or not invited at all. In the end, declining such invitations had been a blessed relief, but it had made his world grow smaller still. It was hard to believe that last year he'd been on the Continent, enjoying picnics on the shores of the Swiss lakes and attending lavish dinner parties in cities like Geneva, Milan and Venice. It was hard to believe that he'd been surrounded by so much culture and good company, and yet now...

A crow cawed again, taunting him.

Resigned to his lonely routine, he sauntered back towards Hayton Hall, to the servants waiting to greet him, to offer their deferential smiles whilst always keeping their distance. They played their roles as well as he knew he had to play his. He'd seen that clearly, the first and only time he'd ventured to suggest that Smithson, his brother's butler, join him for an evening brandy. The ageing man's jaw had just about hit the floor, and Samuel had reddened at his transgression, unable to decide what was worse—the awkward excuses the butler offered as a refusal or the look of pity in his eyes.

Since then, he'd not strayed from his side of the line which divided servants and masters, even though he was not master of anyone—not truly. It was just a part he had to play for a little while longer, until the real master of Hayton Hall returned. Then he would revert to his real role, that of the younger brother, free to do as he pleased, to spend his time and inheritance as he wished. Of the unattached gentleman, untroubled by land or titles.

Or, more realistically, of being the less attractive prospect, the wrong brother. Or at least that was what his rejection by a certain young lady that summer had taught him. As he drew nearer to Hayton Hall he shuddered—at the cooling air, perhaps, or at the memory of her bright red hair, the smattering of freckles across her nose, her broad smile. Remembering her biting words to him that afternoon as they'd walked together and he'd dared to suggest he was fond of her, that he would like, with her father's permission, to begin a courtship.

'Why would you think to even ask such a thing? When I am my father's only daughter, and you are a younger son. When you have no property, no title...'

Samuel grimaced, his mind suddenly filled with the images of her usually pretty face contorted into a look which was part-offence and part-mockery as she quashed his hopes and stamped upon his heart. He held no affection for her now; he'd seen her true fickle nature too clearly for that. But her rejection of him had been thoroughly humiliating and whilst the hurt he'd felt no longer burned his insides, it still stubbornly smouldered somewhere within him, its embers always ready to be rekindled in his quiet, contemplative moments. And, as God only knew, he'd had too many of those during the preceding weeks.

'Pull yourself together, man,' he muttered under his breath, reminding himself that in the coming days his solitude would be over. His friend Charles Gordon had mercifully responded to Samuel's plea that he should visit, gladly accepting and venturing to suggest that he bring his sister with him too. He had much to look forward to, Samuel reminded himself. He'd met Charles during his Continental travels, taking an instant liking to the man's convivial demeanour and outrageous sense of fun. Seeing his friend again would lift his spirits, and he was intrigued about making the acquaintance of Henrietta Gordon, especially since, until Charles had mentioned her in his letter, Samuel had not known about the existence of a sister at all.

Another loud yell breached the silence. It was deeper this time, longer and angrier, almost a roar. Samuel spun around, his eyes darting warily back towards the wood. Up in the trees the crows began to squawk frantically, and it occurred to him then that it could be a fox. He decided he would mention the noise to his brother's steward; the estate's tenants would need to be put on their guard, especially those who raised sheep.

Then, before he could think any more about it, a final cry rang out. This one, however, put paid to any theories he'd entertained about foxes, instead betraying its origins as being unmistakably human. This one, he realised as he ran instinctively towards the trees, was not a scream or a roar, but a plea.

'Help!'

As she lay on the ground, pain pulsing through her as she watched a murder of crows circling overhead, all Hope Sloane could think was how much easier her bid to escape would have been if only she'd had a breeches role. Men's clothing was without doubt far more suitable attire for dashing across the countryside than a flimsy gown of muslin and lace. However, if there was one thing that life had taught Hope, it was that you played the hand you were dealt, and you seized your opportunities when they came. And so she had, running for her life across fields and through woodland, hoping she could get far enough away before falling under the cloak of inevitable darkness.

Unfortunately, the only thing she'd fallen upon was the uneven, branch-strewn ground. She hadn't gone down quietly either, letting out an almighty scream at the pain as it seared through her. Truly, she could not have announced her whereabouts more clearly if she'd tried. She could only hope that her disappearance had not yet been discovered, that there might still be sufficient distance between herself and those who sought to capture her.

Namely her father and the man to whom she'd been promised as though she was nothing more than contraband to be smuggled and traded.

Hope shivered, the short sleeves and thin fabric of her gown doing nothing to ward off the early autumn chill. They'd made her put on this gown, her father and the man. They'd insisted that she should look nice and tidy her hair and make an effort. She was going to celebrate with them, they'd told her, for in a matter of days she would be wed. The following day she would depart for Scotland, where she would smile and make her vows before God, or risk her father's wrath. Then she would go to live with this man, the one her father called George, although she had not cared to even know his name. She would spend the rest of her days on his farm near the Solway Firth, only leaving the place to run whisky over the border and into England by wearing a belly canteen which made her look as though she was heavy with child.

'Except when you're actually having a bairn, of course,' the brute George had said as he leered at her, placing an unwelcome arm around her waist and pulling her roughly towards him.

Both men had laughed and raised their mugs in a toast while Hope had bitten her tongue, resolving to say nothing and to bide her time. Foolishly, after making her change her clothes, they'd left her unbound, instead ordering her to wait on them hand and foot. Recognising the opportunity for what it was, Hope had turned on the charm, forcing a smile on to her face for George's benefit while she'd plied both men with more and more drink. There was no stronger liquor in Cumberland than that which came from her father's stills. All she'd had to do was wait until they passed from stupor into slumber. The moment they did, she'd hurried to escape.

Hope shivered again, wincing as she pulled futilely at the muslin sleeves as though they could somehow be stretched to cover her bare arms. Forcing her to wear that gown had been a form of mockery, she knew that. It was the gown she'd been wearing when they'd grabbed her that night at the theatre, not long after the play was over. It was her Lady Teazle gown, a beautifully embellished but ultimately thin piece of frippery befitting the flirtatious and spendthrift gentleman's wife she'd played in Sheridan's *The School for Scandal*. It was a relic from a life she might never know again, thanks to her own naïve foolishness.

Why had she not tried to excuse herself, when she learned her theatre company were to tour in Cumberland in addition to their usual destinations in Westmorland? Why had she not feigned illness, or injury? She was an actress, after all.

Why had she ever thought that several years of absence and a stage name would be enough to protect her from recognition? Why had she fooled herself into thinking she could slip in and out of Lowhaven, undetected by her father's many spies? Why, on that day five years ago when she'd crept out

of her family's damp cottage for the final time, had she believed that running away to Yorkshire would ever be far
enough?

Hope's teeth began to chatter. And why, she asked herself
for the umpteenth time, had she not taken a breeches role?
She was going to freeze to death in that ridiculous gown! A
potent mix of anger and anxiety coursed through her veins
as she forced herself to sit, desperation and determination
gripping her as she realised she must drag herself, somehow, towards shelter.

Using all the strength she could muster, she tried to pull
herself to her feet, only to fall down once more as a diz-
zying pain in her head overwhelmed her, and her right leg
refused to bear her weight. Furious now, she pounded her
fists into the ground, letting out a loud, guttural cry—at
the pain, made worse by the sudden movement, and at her
predicament. At the unfairness of it all.

She'd run away once before; back then, she'd had more
time to think and to plan, to pack clothing and gather coins
to aid her escape. She'd got on one coach, then another; she'd
put many miles between herself and Cumberland and carved
out a life she could call her own. A life which was not be-
holden to the whims of cruel men, or to the tides of fortune
which dictated whether she escaped the grasp of constables
and excisemen, or found herself in gaol, facing the noose.
A life in which she'd played many different parts, and lived
many colourful lives. A life she could enjoy once again, if
only she could get herself out of this terrible mess.

Above her the crows still circled, their squalls growing
louder and more urgent as though they too understood the
severity of her situation. Hope cast her eyes around, trying
to get some sense of where she was. Trying to ignore the

way pain spread from her head to her neck as well as searing up her leg. Through the trees, she caught glimpses of stonework in the near distance, and her heart began to race at the prospect of having stumbled upon a house, upon the possibility of rescue and shelter.

Play the hand you've been dealt, Hope, she thought to herself as a fresh wave of dizziness threatened to consume her. *Play the hand, even if it means placing yourself at the mercy of fortune's tides once more.*

At the top of her lungs and with the last vestiges of her strength, Hope mustered one final cry.

'Help!'

By the time Samuel found her, the crows had fallen silent, and so had she. Above him, the sky was ink-blue and the sun was long gone, leaving the woodland to languish in the gloomy shadows of its many trees. He bent down at her side, his instincts racing ahead of his thoughts as he tried to assess the situation. The woman before him lay very still, her eyes shut, her arms perishingly cold to the touch. Little wonder really, he thought, since the evening gown she wore was completely unsuitable attire for wandering about the countryside at dusk. She needed warmth, and the attention of a physician. Whoever she was, and whatever had happened to her, it was clear that something was gravely wrong.

Carefully, he lifted her off the ground, simultaneously concerned and reassured by the brief groan which escaped her lips in response to the movement. At least she still lived, although how badly injured she was, he could not tell. Holding her in his arms, he walked back towards Hayton Hall, calling out for his servants once he reached the formal gardens he'd been sauntering around just a little while ago. The noise he made seemed to rouse her slightly, and she began to murmur again—pained moans littered with sobs, and in amongst all that, a few words. Words which seemed to distress her greatly.

'No…not going with him…' she whimpered.

'Hush,' he replied softly, anxious to reassure her. 'You're safe now.'

The woman's eyes rolled and closed once more and, to his horror, he sensed her grow limp in his arms. With increasing urgency, Samuel hurried towards the door of Hayton Hall, from which several servants were rushing towards him, their brows furrowed as they responded to his calls.

'Prepare a bedchamber!' Samuel barked his orders, playing their master once more. 'Fetch some water and light a fire! This lady needs our help.'

Chapter Two

Hope's eyes fluttered open, the brightness of the midday sun immediately overwhelming her blurry vision. She blinked several times, trying to see better, trying to understand where she was. The bed she lay in was large and soft, her head resting upon a pile of pillows as she remained tucked beneath crisp white sheets. She shifted her gaze, wincing at the discomfort that this slightest movement of her head caused as she observed the light streaming through lattice windows, illuminating a room dominated by dark furniture, wooden panelling and heavy tapestries. An old and very fine room, to be sure, but where? And how had she ended up here?

She licked her dry lips, conscious suddenly of feeling desperately thirsty as she tried to remember what had happened. She'd been in some woodland, running as fast as she could. She'd slipped and she'd fallen—she'd felt pain everywhere. She'd cried out, and then...

A voice—deep and reassuring. A tide rolling in, lifting her off the bracken-strewn ground and carrying her away, its undulating waves rocking her, conspiring with sleep to distance her from her pain. Except it hadn't been the sea at all, had it? It had been a man, the one the voice had belonged to, taking her into his arms, offering gentle words to calm her as he carried her away from the woods. She'd been found, but by whom? Where on earth was she? And, more to the point, was she safe?

Or had she been found by yet another of her father's many acquaintances? Had he been alerted to her whereabouts? Was he on his way to take her again, right now?

Hope's heart began to race, and in a sudden panic she tried to pull herself upright. Pain shot through her back and her neck, causing her to cry out. Her head throbbed; she touched the back of it gingerly, wincing as her fingers grazed over a swollen lump. What had she done to herself? Just how badly injured was she? The heat of coming tears burned her eyes and she blinked furiously, forbidding them to fall. Crying would do no good; it never had.

Crying hadn't helped on the day that she'd found her mother's lifeless body strewn across her bed, having finally succumbed to laudanum's charms. Nor had it helped her stop herself from being drawn into her father's underworld of illicit stills and free trading, a world in which she'd never been able to decide whose wrath she feared more, that of her kin or that of the law. Her tears and her pleas had not prevented her father from trying to force her into a marriage, either five years ago or yesterday. The man was immune to tears, and so should she be. The only thing which had helped, then and now, was running away.

She had to run. But first she had to get out of this bed.

Pushing the bedsheets away, she forced herself upright, gritting her teeth as a fresh, sharp agony stabbed at her lower back. Glancing down at herself, Hope was surprised to see that the pretty, thin gown she'd been wearing last night had gone, along with her stays, leaving her wearing only her white linen shift. She felt her cheeks redden at the realisation—who on earth had done that? Not the man who'd carried her, surely? No matter, she decided. She would run across the countryside wearing her undergarments and no shoes, if she had to.

Persevering despite the pounding which grew in her head, Hope shuffled to the edge of the bed and let her toes touch the floor. Her right ankle began to throb and she looked down to see that someone had covered it with a bandage. The rug below her feet felt soft and reassuring as she pressed against it. However, her injured ankle protested, a sudden pain shooting through it and causing both her legs to buckle. Before she could stop herself, she was falling down, landing on the floor with a hard and graceless thud.

'Ow!' she cried out and this time, despite herself, the tears did fall.

Clearly the commotion she'd caused had been heard. Beyond the bedchamber, someone else in the house stirred, and all Hope could do was sit helplessly on the floor, tears flooding down her cheeks as footsteps approached. Quick, frantic footsteps, growing louder by the second. Then, after a moment, the door creaked open and a face peered around it. A man's face, etched with concern, his brow furrowing as he spied her on the floor.

'What the devil are you doing down there?'

He was impeccably dressed; that was the first thing she noticed. As he strode towards her, she drew her first, hurried conclusions about him, taking in his tidy, sand-coloured hair, his high collar and cravat, his immaculate blue coat. A gentleman, certainly, although that was no surprise to her really, considering the fine surroundings she'd awoken in. She stared up at him, meeting his grey-blue eyes for the first time and finding, to her great relief, kindness there. Whatever he saw in her gaze was presumably less reassuring; she watched in confusion as he hesitated, averting his eyes and half turning back towards the door.

'Sir?' Hope croaked, her mouth desert dry.

'Forgive me,' the man said, still looking away. 'I should not have burst in like that. I shall fetch a maid to attend to you.'

A maid to attend to her. Yes—he was definitely a gentleman. Hope glanced down, her confusion clearing like mist as she caught sight of the linen shift she wore once more. Ah, of course. Now she understood his hesitation.

'Thank you, sir. Also, if it is not too much trouble, I would be obliged to you for some water,' she added politely, instinctively slipping into the voice she'd used on stage just days ago—soft and refined, clear and articulate. She didn't know why. Perhaps because she feared that even a word spoken in her own voice, laced as it was with the Cumberland accent, would tell him exactly who she was? Or perhaps because sitting here, in this grand room, speaking to the well-dressed gentleman who'd saved her life, she felt that she ought to smooth over her coarse ways?

She watched as the man glanced at the water jug sitting atop the table. He sighed heavily before turning back around and stepping towards her once more.

'This is ridiculous,' he muttered as he bent down, gently lifting her off the floor and placing her back upon the bed. Despite the discomfort that the movement caused, the brief feeling of his arms around her was warm and strangely reassuring, bringing back those vague, confused memories of the previous night. She did not even need to ask if he'd been her rescuer; instinctively, she knew that he had.

'What is ridiculous, sir?' she asked him.

The man walked around the bed and poured some water into a cup. 'Fetching a maid to help you when I can just as easily do it myself,' he replied, handing the cup to her. 'Anyway,' he continued, 'you did not answer me. What were you doing on the floor?'

'I was trying to get up,' Hope replied between thirsty sips. 'I am grateful to you, sir, but I am sure I have been a burden for long enough. If you could see to it that my dress and shoes are returned to me, I promise I will leave within the hour.'

'The devil you will,' the man replied, frowning at her once more. 'I'm afraid you're not fit to go anywhere right now. Your right ankle is badly injured, and you've suffered a nasty blow to the head. I don't know what happened to you in the woods, but my physician says you're purple and blue with bruises.'

'Your physician?' Hope repeated, her heart pounding once more. She pulled the bedsheets tighter around herself, as though they could protect her. As though anything could protect her.

'Yes, my physician. He attended to you last night. He assures me that your ankle is not broken, and that all your wounds will heal. But he says you must rest.'

Hope, however, was not listening. 'Did you say anything to him about me? Did you tell him where you found me?' she asked, her questions rapid as she began to panic. Did her father know any physicians? Was it possible that this physician knew who she was? Might he betray her whereabouts?

'I told him that I discovered you lying injured in the woods,' the man replied. 'That was all I could say, since I do not know anything about you.' He paused, holding her gaze with his own for a long moment. 'I dare say that's something we ought to rectify. Perhaps you'd like to begin by telling me your name and whether there is someone I should inform of your whereabouts.'

Hope's heart raced even faster, the pain in her head reaching a crescendo as she felt the room begin to spin. 'Someone you should inform?' she repeated.

'Of course,' the man said. 'Surely a lady such as yourself has loved ones who are desperately worried about you? They'd be welcome to stay here too, of course, while you convalesce. Indeed, that would be best, for propriety's sake. I will have to ask them to arrange for some of your clothes to be brought to you. That gown you were wearing last night is unfortunately beyond repair.' He gave her an affable smile, but she could not mistake the curiosity lingering in his eyes. 'I do wonder what you were doing, wandering in the woods by yourself in such a fine evening gown.'

Hope drew a deep breath, trying to calm herself, trying to read between the lines. She thought about the way he behaved towards her—calling her a lady, talking about her fine gown, panicking at the impropriety of being in the same room as her while she wore only a shift. Did he think she was like him? Had he mistaken her for a gentleman's daughter? For the offspring of some grand duke, or of a wealthy merchant?

Hope sipped her water again, buying herself some time as she considered her options. Telling this man the truth about herself was out of the question; the nature of her father's business, such as it was, meant that he was known across Cumberland society. It was well known that Jeremiah Sloane supplied his contraband to many of the fine houses, and many of the magistrates, thus ensuring they happily continued to turn a blind eye to his activities. For all she knew, this was one such house, and one such gentleman. And yet she knew she had to tell this man something. If she had to remain here for the moment, she needed him to understand her requirement for secrecy; she needed him to help her hide. Surely, she reasoned, she could come up with a story which explained why, one which met with the assumptions he seemed to have made about her. Surely she could create a suitably genteel and imperilled character for herself. She was an actress, after all. This would simply be another role for her to play.

She cleared her throat. 'Please understand, sir, that no one can know I am here. Promise me that you will not whisper my whereabouts to a single soul. It is bad enough that your physician and your servants already know…'

Her plea seemed to grab the man's attention and he drew closer, his sympathy evident in his expression. 'Of course, I promise I will say nothing. And please, do not worry— my servants' discretion can be trusted, and my physician is a good man. Besides, no one even knows your name— including me.'

Hope gave an obliging nod. It was the sort of nod she'd cultivated on stage when playing high society types—subtle and reserved. 'My name is Hope…' She paused, searching for a family name. 'Hope Swynford.' Inwardly she groaned; that name was uncomfortably similar to her stage name, Hope Swyndale. She might be a decent actress, but it was already becoming apparent that she was a hopeless playwright.

'Ah! Like the third wife of John of Gaunt,' the man said, a grin spreading across his face. It was a handsome face; she noticed that now, her attention drawn to his blue-grey eyes, sparkling with interest, to his straight nose, his fair complexion, his full lips...

'Oh, John of Gaunt—yes, indeed,' she replied, forcing herself to concentrate on their conversation. She knew that name from a play by Shakespeare, but could not recall which one. Nor could she recall a wife, much less three of them. What on earth had got into her?

The man extended a hand towards her, and she accepted it gingerly. His fingers were gentle and warm, just as his arms had been both times she'd found herself within them. 'Delighted to make your acquaintance, Miss Swynford,' he said. 'My name is Samuel Liddell.'

She offered him a polite smile. 'It is a pleasure to meet you, sir, and thank you once again for coming to my aid. I believe you saved my life.'

'I was glad to be of assistance to you.' He let go of her hand, his expression growing serious once more. 'Perhaps, Miss Swynford, you might tell me what happened to you last night, and why you do not wish for your whereabouts to be known. I would like to help you, if I can.'

The look in his eyes was so genuine that for a brief moment Hope considered telling him the truth. Perhaps this Samuel Liddell really was a good man, perhaps he knew nothing of her father. Perhaps he would be willing to help Hope Sloane just as much as he wished to help Hope Swynford. Yet, as much as she wanted to be honest, she knew that it was not worth the risk. If life had taught her anything, it was that the only person she could really trust was herself.

Hope drew a deep breath, committing herself finally to her deceit. 'I am running away from my uncle, sir,' she began, improvising, the story and her lines unfinished even as she uttered them. 'I am running away from a marriage he wishes to force upon me. From a marriage I do not want.'

Chapter Three

If Samuel's prayers for company had been answered, he could not decide if it was God or the Devil who'd granted his wish. As he made himself comfortable in a small armchair which he'd pulled nearer to her bedside and began to listen to Miss Swynford's sorry tale, he realised that last night in the woods he'd found trouble. Quite literally, it seemed, since by all accounts this uncle Miss Swynford described was a deeply unpleasant character. Hellbent on carving up her inheritance between himself and an acquaintance, he'd concocted a plan to kidnap her and take her to Scotland, where he would force her to marry the co-conspirator, thus transferring her wealth to her new husband, who would then give the uncle his share. It seemed they'd travelled first to Lowhaven, to meet this awful acquaintance off a boat from the Isle of Man, before continuing northwards for the wedding. With her parents both deceased, the poor lady had been powerless in the face of his machinations, until some commotion at an inn had afforded her an opportunity to run away and board a mail coach.

'The coach was bound for Lowhaven, where we had just come from—not that I cared where it was going,' she continued, grimacing as she shifted in the bed. 'I just knew that it was fast, and it would get me away from them both.'

'Did your uncle or this other man see you board the mail coach? Did they try to pursue you?' he asked, trying to ascertain whether she remained in immediate danger.

She bit her lip. 'Unfortunately, I think they did. Two men were fighting in the courtyard, and one landed a blow on my uncle. This distracted them long enough for me to get away from them, but not without them seeing how I'd made my escape.'

She shifted again, clearly uncomfortable. Without thinking, Samuel leapt to his feet, plumping and adjusting the pillows behind her back. This prompted her to let out a nervous laugh, and he realised then just how close he was to her. Just how cream-coloured her bare arms were in that white shift. Just how deep the brown colour of her hair was, how it spilled over her shoulders in thick, wild tendrils.

Truly, he thought, he had found trouble, and not only because of the tale she was telling. He'd realised he'd found it the moment he'd walked into this bedchamber and observed those emerald eyes staring up at him. Something had stirred within his sore, lonely heart then. Something unwise. Something which he could only blame on the long weeks he'd spent in solitude. Something he felt certain this poor lady could do without, given her recent ordeal. He could do without it too, he reminded himself, given his own recent failed romantic endeavours.

'So what did you do, once you got back to Lowhaven?' Samuel asked, retreating to his armchair and forcing himself to focus on their conversation.

'I did not make it as far as that. I'd scrambled atop the coach as it was about to depart, and handed over the only two shillings I had. It turns out that two shillings doesn't get you very far. I've been trying to make my way on foot across the countryside ever since.'

'And where were you hoping to go?'

'London.'

'You were going to walk to London?' Samuel asked, incredulous.

Miss Swynford gave him a sad smile. 'In the circumstances, I had little choice. Anyway, I got thoroughly lost and utterly exhausted, before falling and hurting myself in the woods near to wherever this is. The rest you know.'

'Hayton,' Samuel informed her. 'You're in Hayton, and this house is Hayton Hall. So then, why London?' he continued. 'Is that where you're from?'

She seemed to hesitate. 'No, not really,' she replied evasively. 'But I have a good friend there. A married friend. I was going to go to her and her husband for help, and for protection.'

Samuel nodded, sensing for the first time that there was something she wasn't telling him, but deciding not to press her further. She barely knew him, after all, and could hardly be expected to trust him with every detail of her life, especially in the circumstances. Indeed, given all that she'd endured, she'd be entirely justified in never trusting anyone again.

Samuel rose from his seat, offering her a polite bow. 'You have my promise, Miss Swynford, that you will be well protected here. Once your injuries have healed and you are well enough to travel, I will accompany you and see to it that you reach your friend in London safely.'

He watched as those bright green eyes widened at him, unsure if it was mere surprise or sheer horror he saw in her gaze. 'You do not have to do that, sir,' she protested. 'Please, do not inconvenience yourself on my account.'

'It is no inconvenience. I have thought often about how some time away from Cumberland and a little society would do me the world of good,' Samuel replied, giving her a broad smile. How true that statement was, after so many long, lonely weeks. 'We will travel together, in my carriage. If anyone asks, I will say that you are my sister.'

Miss Swynford pressed her lips together, appearing to accept his plan even if her serious expression told him that she remained unhappy about it. Again, he reminded himself, she was hardly likely to jump for joy at the prospect of travelling with a man she'd only just met. A man who, for all she knew, could prove to be just as much of a rogue as those she'd recently fled from. A man who she had no reason to put any faith in. He made a silent promise then that he would work hard to earn her trust. That by the time they set off in his carriage she would have no reason to harbour any more reservations about Samuel Liddell.

'Do you have a sister, sir?' Her question, softly spoken though it was, pierced the silence which had hung between them.

He shook his head. 'No. We'll have to invent one, I'm afraid.'

She chewed her bottom lip, considering his answer. He found himself staring at her, drawn to the pretty features of her heart-shaped face—her slim pink lips, her small button-like nose and those big emerald eyes which had so taken him aback when he'd first walked into the room. She was, without doubt, uncommonly beautiful. And he was, without doubt, uncommonly ridiculous for entertaining such thoughts about a lady whose only concern was evading her fortune-seeking uncle and finding sanctuary in London.

'What about a brother?' She continued her line of questioning, thankfully oblivious to the inappropriate turn his thoughts had taken. 'Or a wife?'

He chuckled wryly at that. 'I am as yet unwed,' he replied, trying to sound nonchalant. 'I do have a brother, but he is not here at present,' he added vaguely, finding that for some reason he did not wish to talk about Isaac.

'So you live here alone?' She stared at him, incredulous. 'All by yourself?'

'Not entirely alone,' he countered, feeling suddenly defensive. 'My brother will return and...well, there are servants here, of course. Indeed,' he continued, moving away from her bedside and towards the door, 'I think it is past time that I arranged for a maid to attend to you.'

He placed his hand on the door knob, ready to leave, his inner voice giving him a stern talking-to. Why had he not just explained the situation? Why had he not simply told her that his solitary life was only temporary while he cared for his ancestral home and estate in his brother's absence? That the real master of Hayton Hall would return soon and resume his duties, liberating his inconsequential younger sibling to do as he pleased once more.

'Yes, thank you, and please forgive me, sir,' she called after him. 'I did not mean to offend you. I was merely curious.' She glanced around the bedchamber. 'This is a lovely room. I'm sure the rest of Hayton Hall is very fine. Hopefully, when my ankle is strong enough, you will be able to show me.'

He smiled proudly. 'It is indeed a fine country house. A little old-fashioned, perhaps, for modern tastes, but I believe it will stand the test of time. It was built around two hundred years ago, by the first baronet.'

He realised as soon as he said that word that he'd given her the wrong impression. That she'd made an assumption about him, an assumption which he ought to immediately correct. Along with the other assumption he'd undoubtedly led her to—that Hayton Hall belonged to him, that he was the master of a grand house and a vast estate.

And yet, as he looked up and met her lovely green gaze, he found himself unable to say the right words. To tell her that it was Isaac who was the baronet, and Isaac to whom the estate belonged.

'I promise you will be safe here, Miss Swynford,' he said instead, opening the door. 'Safe and well cared for. I'll ask for a tray to be sent up from the kitchen too. You must be famished.'

What in God's name had got into him?

Samuel paced up and down in the library, this same question circling around in his mind. He'd always regarded himself as a very straightforward, decent sort of fellow. He'd travelled all over Europe and mingled with all sorts of people, from country squires to wealthy merchants, to the sons and daughters of earls and dukes, and he'd never once felt any temptation to present himself as anything other than what he was. He was Samuel Liddell, a Cumberland gentleman, a younger son, a man sufficient in both means and good sense to enjoy a very comfortable life. A man who was glad not to have the responsibilities which came with an estate and a title. And yet there he'd stood in that bedchamber, allowing that lady to believe that everything here was his. That he was the master of Hayton Hall, and that he was the baronet. It was unfathomable.

Samuel slumped down into an armchair, sighing heavily and tugging uncomfortably at his collar. Outside, the day had grown dull and blustery, the loss of the earlier sunlight combining with the wind to usher in an autumnal chill. By contrast, however, the library felt stifling, the warm air heavy with the scent of leather-bound books and old wooden shelves. Samuel had no idea why he'd fled in here; this room was Isaac's domain, with everything about it pronouncing the real baronet's taste and temperament—from the dark green leather of its chairs to the decanter of brandy with a single glass and a newspaper placed neatly by its side. It was a quiet, brooding space, and one which had never suited the irrepressible cheer and sociability of the younger brother. Until recently, anyway. Bound by duty to the estate and disinclined towards society, thanks to the whiff of scandal Isaac had left in his wake, it was clear to Samuel that he'd been emulating many of his brother's habits during these past weeks. That glass and that newspaper, after all, were for him.

'None of which makes it all right to let Miss Swynford believe you're the baronet, you foolish man,' he muttered to himself. 'The question is, what are you going to do about it now?'

He had to tell her the truth, of course, before matters went any further. After all, he had not lied to her, exactly. But he had unwittingly misled her, and upon realising he had done so, he had failed to clarify who he in fact was. It was this clarification that he had to now offer, as soon as possible. It would be embarrassing, but by dealing with this swiftly, a simple apology for not explaining the situation to her immediately would suffice. He would not need to offer any further explanation about his reasons for initially misleading her.

What were his reasons, exactly? Why had he not been able to bring himself to utter a handful of simple words, explaining that neither Hayton Hall nor the baronetcy were his? Had these past weeks of effective isolation sent him quite mad? Was he so in want of company that one short conversation with an emerald-eyed young lady was enough to make him lose all reason? It would seem so.

Samuel put his head in his hands, letting out a heavy sigh. Allowing himself to attribute his behaviour to loneliness, no matter how convenient an explanation it was, would not do. There was little point in lying to himself, in failing to acknowledge that the thought of contradicting the lovely Miss Swynford's assumption about him had brought back those painful feelings of the summer. How it had reminded him that he was not quite good enough, that he'd been assessed on society's marriage mart and had been found lacking.

How it had reminded him of the way a certain flame-haired beauty had looked down her nose at him as he confessed his growing affection for her for the first time. The way her words had cut him down and put him firmly in his place—a place which was far below every titled man in England.

'*Mama says I must have a London season, for that is where the very best gentlemen are found. I dread to think what she would say if she knew what you have asked of me today...*'

Samuel shook his head, trying to push the humiliating, hurtful memory from his mind. The fact that he still ruminated upon it was bad enough, but allowing it to cloud his judgement when it came to being honest about himself was ridiculous. Quite apart from anything else, he'd no intentions towards Miss Swynford, or indeed towards any lady. This summer he'd thrown himself wholeheartedly into the turbulent waters of courtship and where had that left him? Washed up, rejected and deserted—quite literally. It was not an experience he was in any hurry to repeat.

He groaned, dragging his hands down his face. He had to put the recent past firmly behind him. And he had to be honest with Miss Swynford—as soon as possible.

His resolve suitably strengthened, Samuel rang for the butler. A moment later the older man arrived, one wiry grey eyebrow raised as he waited expectantly for his orders.

'Smithson, Miss Swynford will remain with us while she recovers from her injuries. Please see to it that she is kept comfortable and please ensure that no one outside of this house learns that she is here. It seems that the poor lady has fled from the clutches of a nefarious uncle who was seeking to force her into a marriage.'

'Poor Miss Swynford,' the butler remarked. 'Of course, sir, I will make sure the staff treat the lady's presence here with the utmost secrecy.'

Samuel inclined his head gratefully. 'As soon as she is well enough, Miss Swynford plans to travel to London,' he continued. 'I have promised to escort her; my absence won't be prolonged, and I'm sure that between you and the steward, the estate will be well cared for,' he added, offering the man an appeasing smile.

'Indeed, sir. Unless Sir Isaac has returned by then, of course.'

The mention of his brother caused Samuel to wince. 'Ah—

yes,' he began. 'You see, Smithson, Miss Swynford seems to have formed the opinion that I am the master here…that, um, well, I am Sir Samuel, I suppose.'

That wiry eyebrow shot up again. 'Miss Swynford has formed this opinion?' the butler repeated. 'Can such things be considered opinions, sir?'

'Perhaps it is more of an impression then,' Samuel replied, grimacing.

Smithson nodded slowly. 'I see. And to be clear, sir, this impression was formed by the lady herself, rather than given to her by someone else?'

Samuel groaned. 'The lady formed the impression and someone else—namely me—failed to clarify matters.' He gave the butler an earnest look. 'I do intend to give that clarification when the appropriate moment arises. However, the lady is vulnerable and her health is clearly delicate, so it is important that the clarification comes from me, rather than a servant, wouldn't you agree?'

He watched as his brother's loyal servant pressed his lips together, his brow furrowing deeply for a moment as he considered his words. 'Just to be clear, sir—you want the household to pretend that you are the baronet?'

Samuel felt his face grow warm. 'I'm not asking anyone to lie, Smithson. I'm simply asking them not to say anything until I can…'

'Until you can clarify matters?'

Samuel nodded. 'Exactly.'

Smithson gave Samuel another tight-lipped look. 'I will ensure everyone in this household does as you wish,' he replied after a long moment. 'I would only caution you, sir, that often what begins as a small deception tends to have a way of getting out of hand. It would be best to be honest, sooner rather than later.'

'I fully intend to be, Smithson.'

The butler nodded, apparently satisfied. 'I dare say you'll need to have clarified matters before your friends arrive, in any case.'

Samuel frowned. 'My friends?'

'The ones due to visit from Lancashire, sir,' Smithson reminded him. 'Mr Gordon and his sister. Are they not arriving next week?'

At this Samuel groaned, dragging his hands down his face once more. In the midst of everything that had happened since last night, he'd quite forgotten about Charles and Miss Gordon's visit. They couldn't possibly come now, not while there was a lady hiding in his home. A lady whom he'd sworn to protect. A lady whose whereabouts he'd promised to keep secret.

'I'll write to Charles and ask him to postpone. I'll tell him I'm unwell,' Samuel replied. 'I cannot possibly entertain guests while Miss Swynford is convalescing in secret. I gave her my word that no one else would know she was here.'

Smithson nodded politely. 'Very good, sir,' he replied. 'Hopefully, the letter will reach Mr Gordon in time.'

Indeed, thought Samuel, it had better. As much as he'd been looking forward to seeing Charles, and meeting his sister, keeping Miss Swynford safe and hidden, and keeping his promise to her, was more important. He might not be a baronet or a landowner, but he was still a gentleman. A foolish, heartsore gentleman, but a man of honour nonetheless.

Chapter Four

The next few days passed in a blur of sleep and soup—the latter served eagerly by a maid named Maddie, who'd been charged with Hope's care. For the first time in her life, Hope discovered what it was like to be waited upon hand and foot, to recuperate in a house which was warm and comfortable, and where no one wanted for anything. As a child, the spectre of illness had frequently cast its shadow over their humble farmer's cottage, taking all of her siblings before they were old enough to help in the fields. Even the merest hint of sickness or injury had spelled danger in a home which was always damp and where there was never quite enough to eat.

If she was being generous to him, she could understand why, in the face of such hardship, her father had turned to more illicit ways of earning a living. What she could not understand, however, was how he'd allowed it to corrupt him so utterly. How he'd allowed it to drag her mother down, her spirit so broken by his cruelty that she'd sought solace in her deadly tinctures.

How he'd been able to face remaining in that cramped cottage near Lillybeck once everyone else had gone. Hope shuddered, her thoughts briefly returning to the night she'd been dragged back there, how it had struck her that nothing about the cottage or him had changed during her five-year absence. The place was still bitterly cold, and so was he—icy and filled with contempt for the daughter who'd disobeyed him and dared to have a life of her own.

Shuffling beneath her sheets, she brushed the memory aside. She could not dwell upon Hope Sloane's difficulties, not when she was meant to be Hope Swynford. After all, the runaway heiress she'd invented had enough problems of her own.

'Can I fetch you anything, miss?' Maddie asked, noticing Hope's discomfort. She was an attentive woman, perhaps ten years Hope's senior, her dark eyes framed by thick brown brows which were drawn together with concern for her charge. Hope tried not to dwell on what Maddie would think if she knew who the woman she waited upon really was.

Hope shook her head, offering Maddie a reassuring smile. 'No, thank you,' she replied. 'Honestly, you have cared for me far better than I have ever cared for myself.'

That much was true. In many ways, life in the theatre had been just as unforgiving as the precarious existence of a farmer turned free trader's daughter. The hours spent rehearsing and performing were long and relentless, while life off-stage presented endless dangers for her to avoid, from gin and opium to men who regarded actresses as little more than harlots. There had been no respite, and little opportunity to either eat or sleep well.

Maddie beamed at her. 'Oh, thank you, miss,' she replied, the colour rising in her cheeks at the compliment. 'I must say, you are looking much better already.'

Hope was inclined to disagree with that. With Maddie's

help she'd managed to wash earlier, and had caught sight of herself and her wounds in the mirror. She was indeed purple and blue, just as the physician had said. Thankfully, her face was unscathed, but her pallor was horribly grey, and her lower back bore a particularly nasty, swollen bruise. In short, she looked anything but better. She had to admit that she was beginning to feel better, though; the pain in her head had largely abated, and while her ankle remained swollen, it was not as sore as it had been. After washing, Maddie had given her a clean shift to wear, which had helped to lift her spirits further.

'It's one of mine,' the woman had remarked. 'It's a bit big for you, miss, since you are so slender, but it'll do until we can sort out some proper clothes of your own.'

Hope had nodded, wondering what Maddie had meant by that. Lending her a shift to wear in bed was one thing, but poor Maddie couldn't be expected to give items of clothing to her indefinitely. In the end, however, she'd decided not to question her further. Since becoming Hope Swynford and pouring out her deceitful tale, Hope had decided that remaining silent and compliant was the best approach. Saying too much, and asking too many questions, risked those around her growing suspicious. Lies had a way of tying you in knots if you weren't careful, and Hope had already told enough of them in the cause of concealing her true identity.

An identity which, thus far, she had successfully hidden. It seemed to be a stroke of incredible luck that she'd not encountered any familiar faces at Hayton Hall. There did not appear to be anyone here who knew who she really was. Perhaps the master of this fine house was completely unacquainted with her father and his unscrupulous dealings. She had no way of knowing; despite being situated mere miles from Lillybeck, she knew nothing of Hayton or its foremost family.

Before running away and joining the theatre, her world had been small, revolving around that damp cottage, household chores and keeping watch over her father's stills, tucked away in nearby caves. A world which only expanded when she was required to accompany her father into Lowhaven, or forced to assist with one of his night-time runs to the coast to shift contraband under the cover of darkness. Hardly a reprieve. Still, she thought, perhaps Hayton was far enough away to offer her sanctuary. Perhaps she had been very unlucky, after all, to have been recognised in Lowhaven.

Hope remained relieved and somewhat surprised too that her hurriedly invented tale had been accepted so readily by Sir Samuel, as she assumed she ought to call him now. When he'd questioned her, she knew she'd been vague and foolish with her answers. Goodness knew why she'd said she was going to London, of all places! Her careless words had not gone unpunished, with Sir Samuel's insistence upon escorting her on her journey south, meaning that she would now have to go there and work out how to survive in a city about which she knew nothing and where she was acquainted with no one. A city which was many miles south of Richmond, of her theatre company. Of her real life.

Her lies, indeed, would tie her in knots. She would have to be careful not to become trapped in a tangled mess of her own making.

A knock at the door broke the silence which had descended in the bedchamber. Maddie gave Hope a knowing look. 'The master again, no doubt.'

Hope smiled, smoothing the bedsheets down in front of

her. It was true that Sir Samuel was a frequent visitor, coming in periodically to see how she fared, or to ask whether she needed anything—which, of course, thanks to Maddie, she never did. Sometimes he'd simply sit by her side for a few moments, talking about nothing much beyond the weather or where he'd been on the estate that day, before apologising for tiring her and taking his leave. She supposed he wished to reassure himself that she was recovering well, that he saw this as his duty, since she was in his home and therefore in his care. Yet she also sensed there was more to his visits, that he did in fact desire her company. She recalled the remark she'd made during their first conversation, about him being at Hayton Hall all by himself, and how that had seemed to offend him. She wondered if, despite his protestations to the contrary, Sir Samuel was in fact lonely.

'Come in!' Hope called.

She raised a brief smile as Sir Samuel entered, although her expression quickly dissolved into one of consternation when she saw the pile of clothing he carried in his arms. She watched as he placed them down gently on the end of the bed, then stood with his hands on his hips, surveying them with a pleased look on his face. He had the most genuine, open smile, one which made gentle creases gather around his grey-blue eyes. The sort of smile which could illuminate a room. The sort of smile which, she reminded herself, she had no business paying quite so much attention to.

'These are for you,' he began. 'I thought you would need something more suitable to wear, once you're well enough to come downstairs.'

Hope glanced down at the clothes, a feeling of panic rising in her chest as she noted the fine lace and muslin on display. 'That is kind of you, sir,' she replied. 'But really, you should not have gone to so much trouble on my account. I cannot repay you at present…'

'Repay me?' Sir Samuel raised his eyebrows in surprise. 'Oh! Heavens, no! I did not purchase these, Miss Swynford. No, in fact, we…er…that is to say, they were already in the house. They belong to my cousin, you see. She stayed here a few years ago, with my aunt as well, of course, until she married. For whatever reason, she neglected to take these items with her, in her trousseau.' He gave a nonchalant shrug. 'So now they are yours—for the time being, at least. I do hope they fit as my…er…cousin is perhaps a bit taller than you, if I recall.'

His awkward acknowledgement of her small stature made Hope laugh. 'I find that most ladies are taller than me, sir,' she replied.

He grinned, apparently too much of a gentleman to comment further. 'Indeed, well, I'm sure Madeleine is more than capable of making any alterations that might be required,' he replied, nodding briefly towards the maid, who gave him a distinctly displeased look. Perhaps, Hope reasoned, she wasn't quite so adept with a needle and thread as her employer believed.

Sir Samuel, meanwhile, had paced over to the window, surveying the view outside with his hands clasped behind his back. Hope found her eyes roaming approvingly over his trim physique, his broad shoulders and slender waist on perfect display in a deep green tailcoat, whilst his fitted fawn pantaloons showed off the strong legs of a man who spent much of his life on horseback. Every impeccably tailored inch of the man announced his wealth and his power, his status as a gentleman, a landowner and a member of Cumberland's elite. A status which was far beyond her own.

Hope swallowed hard, barely daring to contemplate what this man would say if he knew that he'd come to the assistance not of a genteel heiress, but an actress and the daughter of an outlaw.

'Do you think you might feel strong enough to come downstairs today?' Sir Samuel asked, turning back to face her. 'I thought I might show you a little of the rest of the house.'

His question surprised her. 'Perhaps for a little while, although I cannot walk very well, sir.'

He narrowed his eyes, looking thoughtful. 'I may have something which will assist you in that regard, although I will need to go and look for it.' His eyes shifted briefly to Maddie, who hovered beside the pile of clothes. 'Madeleine will help you find something suitable amongst all that, and can let me know once you are ready so I can escort you downstairs. If you are sure you are well enough, that is.'

Hope nodded. 'I am sure, sir.'

Sir Samuel gave her another of his broad smiles, then with a brief bow he took his leave.

Hope watched as Maddie held up each gown one by one, apparently assessing their size and suitability with a keen eye and careful hands. There were more dresses in that pile than Hope had ever owned in her entire life. Most of what she'd worn over the past few years had been costumes; her clothing had belonged to the characters she'd played, not to her. But then, she supposed, so did that pile of dresses. They'd been given to Hope Swynford out of kindness, and to allow her to present herself in a way which befitted her position in society. Gowns like those were not meant for the likes of Hope Sloane.

'It was very kind of your master to fetch those himself,'

Hope remarked, feeling discomfited by the stony silence which had settled in the room. 'I would have thought he'd be too busy.'

'Yes, well, he's very…organised,' Maddie replied. 'Likes to take charge of matters.'

'I suppose that is a good trait to have in a gentleman with an estate to run,' Hope pondered.

Maddie appeared to flinch before answering. 'Suppose so.'

'You don't agree?' Hope asked, her curiosity defeating her resolution not to ask too many questions. 'I did notice that you looked a little displeased with him. Is he not a good master to work for?'

The maid eyed her carefully. 'He's fine, miss, honestly. Except when he calls me Madeleine. I have said that he can call me Maddie, like everyone else does. That's just his way, I suppose—very proper. Very exact. Not a hair out of place, so to speak. He's not at all like…' Maddie paused, pressing her lips together as she made a show of examining a pretty blue dress.

'Not like whom?' Hope prompted. It was clear the maid had said more than she ought to.

Maddie ran a gentle hand down the fabric, brushing away imaginary creases. 'His brother,' she said flatly, avoiding Hope's gaze.

'What about his brother?'

It was clear, however, that the maid was not going to elaborate further. 'I think this one will do very well,' she continued, holding up the dress. 'And I don't think it requires altering, which is a relief.'

Hope nodded, giving the maid a wry smile. The woman really did not like sewing, that much was obvious, but to describe it as a relief seemed a little dramatic. Hope shuffled forward, wincing as she pulled herself out from beneath the bedsheets. Sir Samuel's invitation to come downstairs had intrigued her, and she was keen to see something beyond these same four walls. Nonetheless, she would have to take care not to exert herself too much.

'Let's try it then,' she said to Maddie. 'But without my stays. I'm not sure my bruises could withstand them.'

With a brisk nod, Maddie set about assisting her, and no more talk passed between them—not about brothers, or dress alterations, or anything else. It seemed the maid had decided to hold her tongue, and despite her vow to remain quiet and indifferent, Hope could not help but wonder what it was that the woman was unwilling, or unable, to say.

Chapter Five

Samuel waited at the top of Hayton Hall's stone staircase, clutching his father's old walking cane in his hand. He'd asked Smithson to retrieve it for him, and requested that some tea be brought shortly to the small parlour, as Miss Swynford would be coming downstairs for a little while today. Smithson had given a brief nod of assent, but Samuel had not been able to overlook how the man had pressed his lips together, as though to prevent himself from saying what was on his mind. Not that he needed to: over the past few days, Hayton's butler had left Samuel in no doubt about just how much he disapproved of the situation unfolding in the house.

'The servants are very unhappy about keeping up the pretence that you are the baronet, sir,' Smithson had told him in no uncertain terms. 'Especially Maddie. The poor maid is terrified that she's going to slip up and accidentally say the wrong thing to Miss Swynford.'

'Madeleine's only job is to ensure Miss Swynford is kept comfortable and that all her needs are met while she recovers, Smithson. She hardly needs to discuss my family's history with her and, in any case, I doubt the lady would be interested,' Samuel had replied, conscious of how hollow his protestations sounded. He was, without doubt, making life difficult for his servants. 'I fully intend to explain everything to Miss Swynford,' he'd added. 'When the opportunity arises.'

Smithson had been unmoved, reminding his master of the perils of deception, that even the most banal lies had a habit of getting out of hand. Now, as he waited to escort Miss Swynford downstairs, Samuel found himself reflecting upon just how true this was. Not only had he compelled his servants to join him in deceiving Miss Swynford, but today he'd told her an outright lie, this time about the clothing he'd brought to her. In truth, there had been no cousin who had left her gowns behind; those items he'd gathered up and taken into Miss Swynford's bedchamber had belonged to his brother's beloved and sadly deceased first wife, Rosalind. Since her death two years earlier, they'd remained tucked away in Hayton Hall's old drawers and clothes presses, and Isaac had thus far neglected to do anything with them.

Samuel had agonised over giving Miss Swynford some of Rosalind's old clothes, but ultimately he'd concluded it was the most sensible solution. After all, the lady needed something suitable to wear, and given that she was in hiding from her wicked uncle, he could hardly take her to a dressmaker in Lowhaven. Telling her that the gowns had belonged to the deceased Lady Liddell had, of course, been out of the question—he might be a fool and a scoundrel for allowing Miss Swynford to believe he was the master of Hayton Hall, but pretending that his brother's loss had been his own was a step too far, and so he'd concocted the tale about his imaginary cousin instead. He'd barely been able to meet Madeleine's horrified gaze as he'd laid out the fine garments once worn by her mistress and dared to suggest they might need to be altered. He did not even wish to consider what Isaac would say if he knew. He'd damn him to hell, at the very least.

Feeling increasingly agitated, Samuel began to pace back and forth down the hallway. He'd insisted to Smithson, and to himself, that he'd be honest with Miss Swynford as soon as possible, and yet so far he'd failed utterly to find the right moment. Every time he'd knocked on the door to her bedchamber, and every time he'd sat beside her bed and made polite conversation, he'd resolved to tell her the truth. Then he'd looked at her smiling, welcoming face, at those green eyes regarding him in earnest, and the words had died in his throat. He'd procrastinated, telling himself that she was still weak from her injuries, that the awkward truth ought to wait until she was feeling stronger.

However, if he was honest with himself, he knew it was more than that. There was something about Miss Hope Swynford which had captivated him. Perhaps it was the soft, articulate sound of her voice, or the feeling of her petite form as he'd carried her in his arms, or the way she managed to make a maid's old shift look becoming, but something about her made him want to impress her. He knew that the moment he corrected her assumptions about him, the moment he confessed to being little more than Hayton's caretaker, he would be put back firmly in his unimpressive place.

'I do not mean to be unkind, Mr Liddell. You are very witty, and very charming. Perhaps if you had been born into your brother's position, things might have been different...'

Samuel shuddered as a certain red-headed young lady's words haunted him once more. Like it or not, memories of how it had felt to be rejected not for who he was but for what he was not had thus far rendered him hopelessly silent. That bitter experience had taught him that as soon as Miss Swynford knew the truth she would likely be very disappointed indeed.

Not that he was planning to court her! Of course not. His only role was to protect her, to ensure she recovered from her injuries before seeing her safely to London.

The sound of Madeleine calling to him from down the hallway startled Samuel from his thoughts, and he walked back towards Miss Swynford's bedchamber, twirling the walking cane in his hand with renewed determination. If Miss Swynford was indeed well enough to join him downstairs, then he would delay his embarrassing confession no longer. He would apologise for not clarifying sooner and he would renew his commitment to protect her. He would seek to put the lady at her ease, to make the best out of the situation in which they'd found themselves. To hopefully find enjoyment in each other's company during the short time that circumstances had conspired to bring them together.

When he reached her doorway, however, he felt himself freeze, the cane growing suddenly still in his hand as his gaze came to rest on his houseguest. Gone was the maid's hand-me-down shift, replaced by an elegant cream gown and matching shawl. Her dark hair, meanwhile, no longer hung loose about her shoulders but had been pinned up, except for one or two curls which framed her heart-shaped face. Standing there in the doorway, she looked every inch the refined, genteel young lady he knew her to be. She greeted him with a cautious smile and he found himself swallowing hard before he could return it. She was, without doubt, a thoroughly striking beauty.

Miss Swynford shuffled forward, leaning heavily against Madeleine, and a wave of protectiveness washed over him as he was reminded of what had happened to her. Of why she was here, and what he had pledged to protect her from.

'I want you to have this,' he said, holding out the walking cane. 'It belonged to my father. I thought it might help while your ankle heals.'

She gave him a grateful nod. 'Thank you, sir,' she said, accepting the cane and limping towards him, her steps tentative and unsteady after so many days of being confined to her bed.

Samuel offered her his arm, walking slowly at her side as they made their way towards the stairs. Her hand, like the rest of her petite form, was small and delicate, and he tried not to dwell on how pleasant it felt resting in the crook of his elbow.

'You must tell me if you feel at all fatigued, Miss Swynford,' Samuel insisted. 'I will return you immediately to Madeleine's care. I just thought that you may enjoy some respite from staring at the same four walls.'

'Thank you.' She inclined her head again. 'I will be sure to tell you, sir. I believe the walking cane will make moving around easier. It is fortunate that you still had it.'

He chuckled at that, gesturing around him with his free hand. 'Old family houses like this tend to collect people and their things, storing them within its walls like memories. At least instead of collecting dust, that old cane has come in useful. Alas, I am sure I do not need to tell you that, Miss Swynford,' he added. 'I'm sure you've enough dusty ancestry of your own somewhere.'

He watched as she nodded, her expression suddenly guarded and unreadable. 'Oh, indeed,' was all she said in reply.

Miss Swynford managed the short walk along the hallway well enough, but when they reached the stairs he saw her hesitate, glancing down with trepidation before turning to look at him. 'I'm not sure I can…' she began, shaking her head with regret. 'My ankle is not strong. I am worried I may fall, sir.'

'Of course,' Samuel began. 'Forgive me, it was silly of me to bring you out of your bedchamber so soon. I will return you to Madeleine.'

'No, sir, I am sorry,' she said. 'I admit, I was rather looking forward to seeing some of the house.'

The look of genuine disappointment in those large green eyes did strange things to his insides, and before he could give it due consideration, an idea had come into his mind.

'Then, if you will permit me…' he began, giving her a bashful smile as he scooped her up into his arms. 'I carried you up these stairs days ago. I believe I can carry you back down again.'

The sound of her laughter echoed around him. 'I have only a vague recollection of that, but I do distinctly remember you lifting me back on to my bed after I was unwise enough to try to get out of it and leave Hayton in naught but my bedclothes.'

That memory alone would have been enough to bring the colour to his cheeks, but coupled with the feeling of her wrapping her arms around his neck and clinging to him as he carried her, he was certain he must be glowing scarlet. Samuel tried to focus on taking one step at a time, to pay no heed to the way her alluring form had settled so perfectly into his arms. It was ridiculous to entertain such thoughts, he reminded himself. The lady was only in his home because of the unhappiest of circumstances; his duty was to

protect her, not to admire her. Not to allow his recent loneliness to put ideas in his head which he had no business
entertaining. Ideas which he most definitely did not want
to have, after his recent brush with rejection.

'So where are we going, sir?' she asked softly, thankfully
oblivious to the inappropriate turn his thoughts had taken.

'To my favourite room in the house—the small parlour,'
he replied. 'For tea and cake—in my opinion, two of the
very best things in life.'

Tea, cake, and confessions, he reminded himself silently.

'That sounds lovely,' she replied. 'I feel very safe here,
with you. I do find myself wondering whether, should my
uncle learn that I was here, the risk of offending an important local gentleman such as yourself might dissuade him
from seeking me out.' She paused for a moment, her eyes
wide as they searched his. 'After all, a gentleman in your
position must be closely acquainted with those charged
with upholding the law. That ought to make him think
twice about doing anything…untoward,' she added quietly.

Her words were tentative, laced with fear, and Samuel
felt his blood heat as the need to protect her gripped him.
'I can assure you that the Liddells have always been known
to do what is right, Miss Swynford, and have always main-
tained a good relationship with the local magistrate. Please
do not worry,' he added as he reached the bottom of the
staircase and released her from his arms. 'You are indeed
safe in this house.'

She smiled at him, those emerald eyes brightening with
relief. 'I do believe that I was fortunate indeed to stumble
into the home of a baronet.'

Samuel forced a smile in return, his heart lurching and
descending rapidly into the pit of his stomach. The hopeful

look in Miss Swynford's eyes, and all that it implied, was unmistakable. She believed that his position as the master of Hayton Hall, as a landowner and a baronet, meant that he could protect her better, that he had a standing in society which no wicked uncle could overcome. That his title and his estate could shield her. And in many ways she was right—except neither of those things were truly his!

But how could he tell her that now? How could he tell her that she did not enjoy the protection of a titled gentleman but a mere younger son, playing the master in his brother's absence? How could he, in all good conscience, dash her hopes of receiving the very best protection? How could he knowingly allow her to feel anything less than completely safe with him?

He knew the answer to all of that—he simply couldn't. As they made their way slowly towards the parlour, he almost groaned aloud. Lord help him, but he was going to have to be the baronet for a while longer yet.

Hope sipped her tea tentatively and took a moment to observe the neat little parlour into which Sir Samuel had brought her. She could immediately see why he liked this room, with its compact size and good number of windows making it both warm and bright. Her gaze fell briefly upon the fireplace around which the sofa and chairs were arranged, and she found herself imagining how cosy it must feel to sit in front of the fire on a cold winter's day.

She doubted she'd ever experienced such comfort in all of her life; even with the hearth lit, her childhood home had always felt so cold and damp, whilst the wages of an actress had only ever afforded her the most meagre accommodation, invariably shared with other women who made their living on the stage. She pushed the thought from her mind, reminding herself who she was now. Or at least, who she was pretending to be. Hope Sloane might sit in awe of a simple parlour, but Hope Swynford never would.

'Do you have everything you need, Miss Swynford?' Sir Samuel asked.

The master of Hayton Hall had sat down opposite her, leaning forward slightly as though anxious to ensure she was well before he would relax. Upon bringing her into the room he'd placed her gently upon the sofa, then set about fetching cushions for her back and a footstool upon which to rest her injured ankle. Truly, his attentiveness was rather endearing, and she found herself struck by how pleasant it was to be treated thus by a gentleman. She found herself thinking too about those few moments she'd spent in his arms as he'd carried her down the stairs. How she'd found the courage to broach the subject of his acquaintance with local men of the law, looking for even the merest hint of crookedness or, God forbid, of dealings with her father. How Sir Samuel had not hesitated to tell her what she'd already begun to suspect—that the Liddell baronets were decent, upstanding men.

How reassured she had felt, in that moment. How relieved to be in his home, to enjoy his protection. And how safe she had genuinely felt as she'd wrapped her arms around him and clung to him for dear life.

It was a disconcerting idea, and one which she pushed swiftly from her mind. No doubt she was simply in awe of this gentleman, of his grand home and his impeccable kindness to her. The gentlemen she'd encountered in theatres were usually very different—at best, drunk and unintelligible by the final act, and at worst, downright lewd and trying to procure the sorts of services she absolutely did not offer. She felt herself begin to blush at the thought of it. She was quite sure Hope Swynford would never have to put up with such humiliation.

'Miss Swynford?' he prompted her, and Hope realised she had not answered.

'Yes, thank you, sir,' she replied, offering a smile which she hoped would be reassuring. She glanced out of the window, spying the view to the front of the house. Neat gardens, stone walls and fields as far as the eye could see. From this aspect, Hayton Hall felt remote. But was it remote enough to keep her hidden? She had to hope so.

'So what is Hayton like?' she asked him. If they were going to drink tea and converse, she reasoned that she might as well learn a little more about exactly where she was.

'It's a small village, just a short walk away,' Sir Samuel replied. 'It has an old church, and a single inn. It is a quiet place. Not a great deal happens in these far-flung corners of England, Miss Swynford,' he added with a grin.

'It sounds lovely,' she remarked, thinking how like Lilly-beck it sounded. Thinking too how small places so often appeared sleepy and innocent on the surface. Peel back the layers, though, and there was always some darkness to be found.

'And what about…wherever it is that you are from?' Sir Samuel asked.

Hope hesitated. She had not yet managed to invent a satisfactory explanation of where exactly she'd come from. In truth, her knowledge of England was piecemeal, confined largely to Lillybeck, Lowhaven, and the handful of northern towns she'd visited whilst travelling with her theatre company. She could not risk claiming to be from any of them; if Sir Samuel happened to know any of the prominent families from those areas, her story would quickly come unstuck. The south, meanwhile, was unknown to her; she could not convincingly claim to be from any part of it. Perhaps, she reasoned, it was best if she did not explain at all.

'If you will forgive me, Sir Samuel, I would prefer not to speak of home,' she said quietly, her heart beginning to thud in her chest. She avoided his gaze, hoping he would not press her further. Hoping he would not somehow sense the truth among the lies, that the last thing she ever wanted to tell him about was Hope Sloane's life in Lillybeck with a free-trading father and an opium-eating mother.

He held up his hands. 'Of course, of course. It was thoughtless of me to ask, after all you've endured of late,' he replied. 'Although if you'd said you were from Lancaster, I'd have definitely grown suspicious about your connections.'

Hope frowned, her stomach lurching as a wave of anxiety gripped her. 'What do you mean, sir?'

Sir Samuel grinned at her. 'I was referring to Katherine Swynford,' he replied. 'I am sorry, it was a terrible joke. An inaccurate one too, since the lady was likely from Hainault.'

Hope shook her head, still not understanding. 'Forgive me, I…'

'John of Gaunt's third wife,' he reminded her. 'I was referring to a remark I made when you first told me your name. You share the same name as the third wife of John of Gaunt, who was the Duke of Lancaster. As I said, a terrible joke.'

'Oh, yes,' she replied, recollecting now. Recollecting too the play from which she knew the name. 'John of Gaunt, from the play by Shakespeare *The Life and Death of King Richard the Second*,' she added, allowing herself a brief indulgence in her memories. Her company had performed that play during her first year in Richmond. She'd had only a small part as one of the Queen's ladies, but it had not mattered. Newly liberated from her father's clutches, everything about her life then had seemed so fresh and new. So full of possibility.

Sir Samuel nodded enthusiastically. 'Indeed, from Shakespeare and from history, of course. John was a younger son of Edward III. The story goes that John fell in love with Katherine, but he was already wed and so took her as his mistress. Together they had several children, and after the death of his second wife, he married her.' He regarded her carefully. 'Forgive me, I am perhaps telling you something you already know.'

Hope pressed her lips together, unsure if this was something which a genteel lady like Hope Swynford ought to know. Hope Sloane did not, but then what Hope Sloane knew had been learned from books and plays, from observation and conversation. It was knowledge grasped during a colourful and chaotic life, not the result of orderly tutoring or instruction.

'It is quite the love story, is it not?' she observed after a moment, choosing words which would neither suggest knowledge nor convey ignorance.

Sir Samuel chuckled. 'I suppose it is. Alas, neither of them lived many years after their marriage. And, of course, their offspring's descendants, the Beauforts, went on to be thoroughly embroiled in the quarrel between the roses, as Mr Hume called it.'

'Of course,' Hope replied, feeling thoroughly lost now. 'A love story with unintended consequences, then,' she added thoughtfully.

'Ah—yes, very good,' Sir Samuel agreed. He paused, finishing his tea. When he met her gaze again, she saw his blue-grey eyes seemed to have darkened. 'I don't know about you, Miss Swynford, but it seems to me that there are always consequences when it comes to matters of the heart.'

His words, though smoothly delivered, seemed raw, and Hope found herself wondering at the cause of such an observation. During the short time she'd known him, Sir Samuel had seemed to her to be a kind and gentle sort of man. The sort of man who would be generous with his affections, and perhaps the sort of man whose own feelings were easily wounded.

By contrast, she had always guarded her emotions closely; grim experience had taught her that she had to be the master of them, that feeling anything too deeply was unwise in a life dominated for so long by crime and cruelty. And as for love—that was something others traded, whether it was her father making her his part of a bargain with a fellow outlaw or the actresses she'd known, selling their affections for little more than trinkets and the whispers of gentlemen who made empty promises of a better life. No, she thought, love had played no role in her life thus far.

'Alas, sir,' she answered at length, 'I must confess I have little enough experience of these matters, beyond facing the prospect of a forced marriage, but that had nothing to do with love.'

As the words fell from her lips, Hope was pained to acknowledge that this was the most honest sentiment she'd expressed to Sir Samuel since they'd met. Pained too to note the look of earnest sympathy he gave her as she reminded him of her misfortune. An unexpected, unfathomable feeling rose within her, one which made her yearn to tell him more about herself. To tell him truths she'd never uttered to another person. Perhaps even to tell him the truth.

Hope swallowed down the rest of her tea, as though the hot liquid might bring her back to her senses. As benevolent as her rescuer appeared to be, he could not know the truth about her. No one here could. Her entire future likely depended upon it.

Chapter Six

After that first afternoon they spent together in the parlour, something of a routine was quickly established at Hayton Hall. Sir Samuel would spend the morning attending to his duties on the estate, leaving Hope to rest in her bedchamber. Around noon, Maddie would serve her luncheon in her room and then help her to dress before Sir Samuel arrived to collect her and carry her down to the parlour for tea.

If Hope was honest with herself, she'd already begun to look forward to their meetings, perhaps more than she should. After all, every conversation they had carried a risk—a risk that she might accidentally reveal some detail about her real self, or a risk that she might say something to provoke Sir Samuel's suspicions about the authenticity of the story she had told him.

Despite these risks, Hope did her best to immerse herself in the role she had created, allowing herself to enjoy the fine dresses she wore, the comfortable sofa she sat upon and the quality tea she sipped while getting to know her host better. Sir Samuel seemed to understand that she did not wish to talk much about herself. Since she'd politely refused to answer his enquiry about where she was from, he had not asked her anything specific about her life at all.

Instead, he engaged her on less contentious topics, everything from the minutiae of the day to discussions about favourite pursuits. Hope learned that he'd travelled widely, that his knowledge of the Continent, of its different countries and cultures, was second to none. She found his descriptions of all that he'd seen fascinating; from lakes flanked by towering mountains in Switzerland to crowds of boats on the Venetian lagoon, it was as though he was revealing new worlds to her through words alone.

'You are fortunate to have seen so much of the world,' she'd mused one afternoon as he concluded one of his tales. 'Especially with an estate to manage.'

'Well, of course, all of this took place before I had such responsibilities,' he'd replied, giving her an odd, strained look.

Realising he must have been referring to the time when his father still lived, she'd glanced at the walking cane she'd placed beside her, suddenly struck by all that had passed from father to eldest son. 'It must be a strange thing to inherit all of this,' she'd remarked, waving a hand delicately about her. 'For all the security it surely brings, it must also place limitations upon a gentleman. You cannot freely do as you please when you have duties to your family, your land and your tenants.'

Sir Samuel had given her a tight smile. 'I hardly think any gentleman born into comfort and wealth has any right to complain about his lot, however much he might wish to.'

His reticence had made Hope grin. 'Surely everyone has the right to complain sometimes,' she'd replied. 'It strikes me, sir, that running an estate well is very hard work.'

'Indeed it is,' he'd agreed, 'and not only for gentlemen, as you may discover, should you one day marry and find yourself the mistress of some grand house with many acres attached to it.'

Her smile had faded quickly at that. 'That seems unlikely,' she'd replied, grappling for the right answer, the one which Hope Swynford would surely give. 'My uncle all but dragged me to the border to wed a stranger,' she'd reminded him. 'He might not have succeeded, but I hardly think that detail will matter. I am doubtless ruined in the eyes of society.'

She'd half expected Sir Samuel to argue, but instead he had agreed. 'Polite society is apt to condemn, and apt to make ill-founded judgements upon others,' he'd remarked with such resignation that Hope could not help but wonder if his words had been provoked by more than her retort.

'Oh, I almost forgot,' he'd said, swiftly changing the subject as he lifted a pile of books off the nearby table. 'All that talk about John of Gaunt and Katherine Swynford the other day prompted me to remember these books. Mr Hume's *A History of England*. I thought they might help you to pass the time while you convalesce. That is, if you have not already read them.'

Hope had shaken her head, accepting the six volumes as Sir Samuel handed them to her. 'No, I confess I have not read them,' she'd replied as casually as she could manage. Again, she'd no idea if a woman like Hope Swynford would be expected to have read such books or not.

To her relief, Sir Samuel had seemed not at all perturbed by her admission, which was just as well because Hope had felt unsettled enough for the two of them. As much as she enjoyed Sir Samuel's company and conversation, it was moments like that which reminded her of all she was pretending to be, and all that she was really not. Sir Samuel was a learned gentleman, well-tutored and well-travelled. By contrast, Hope was fortunate that she could read at all; as a girl, she'd been taught her letters by her mother, but they had not owned books like the ones Sir Samuel had given to her. As a woman, she read broadsides and chapbooks, and perhaps the occasional well-thumbed novel which had been passed between the actresses.

Life had taught Hope most of the lessons she knew, and latterly, the theatre had been her schoolroom. Indeed, the theatre was the one area in which she could perhaps match Sir Samuel's knowledge, albeit whilst implying that she'd become acquainted with Shakespeare's plays from a seat in a box at Covent Garden or Drury Lane, and not because she'd spoken his words on stage at Richmond's Theatre Royal.

Unfortunately, it seemed to Hope that fate had more discomfiting moments in store for her. Today, as they rose to leave the parlour, Sir Samuel suggested that they dine together in the evening for the first time. Hope was reluctant; until now she'd eaten her evening meal in her bedchamber, under Maddie's watchful eye but with no expectation of displaying the proper manners or refinement. She knew enough about the habits of the wealthy to know that dining formally with Sir Samuel would be an entirely different matter, and one which she was not confident she would manage. Indeed, the thought of sitting at his fine table, completely lost in the face of all those dishes and all that cutlery, made her feel quite sick.

'I'm afraid my appetite is not as it should be,' she explained, trying her best to thwart him as gently as she could. 'I do not think I could manage it.'

'I do not propose we get through a pile of game and a

mountain of jelly by ourselves,' he replied. 'Indeed, most evenings I sit down to a bowl of soup followed by a small plate of fish and vegetables.'

That admission caught her by surprise. 'That is what I am served most nights, in my room.'

'That's right, because that is what my cook has made for us both,' Sir Samuel answered with an amused smile. 'You look startled, Miss Swynford.'

She shook her head. 'I do not know why, I just had not imagined you were eating the same meal as me.'

He began to laugh. 'Oh, heavens! Now I'm concerned you must have imagined me dining downstairs upon fifteen courses while Madeleine served you meagre soup and fish. I'm a country gentleman, Miss Swynford, not the Prince Regent.'

Hope felt her cheeks begin to flush. 'I can assure you, sir, I did not think that. It is just that I have found my meals very restorative and I assumed they had been served to me for that reason.'

Sir Samuel nodded. 'Yes, and what is good for you is also good for me. I prefer simple, hearty fare. I am not a great enthusiast for rich sauces or heavy puddings.'

'Except cake,' she countered. 'One of the two best things in life, if I recall.'

He grinned at her. 'That's right. Now then, on the promise of a small, simple meal, will you dine with me this evening, Miss Swynford?'

Hope felt her hesitation melt in the face of his convivial persuasion. That was something else she'd observed about Sir Samuel—what he had in learning was easily matched in charm and good humour. She found herself reflecting momentarily upon his qualities, his affability and aptitude for conversation, and contrasted that with what she knew of his life at Hayton Hall, alone and unwed. She wondered why that was, wondered too if it had anything to do with the remark he'd made just days ago about matters of the heart and their consequences. Then she pushed the thought aside, deciding it was none of her business.

Instead, she returned his smile, knowing that whatever misgivings she still had, there was only one answer to his invitation that she could possibly give. 'That sounds lovely, Sir Samuel.'

Samuel took a mouthful of his evening meal, believing it to be the best mackerel he'd ever tasted. Weeks of dining alone had led him to become largely disinterested in what was on his plate, the business of eating having become a mere necessity rather than a pleasure. This evening he was reminded just how much he enjoyed dining in company. He'd been delighted when Miss Swynford had agreed to join him, although acknowledging this delight had made him feel instantly guilty as he was forced to remember that he was enjoying her company under false pretences. That he was allowing this lovely young lady to believe she was dining with Hayton's baronet. Swiftly he had buried the thought, reminding himself of the reason for his ongoing deception. It made Miss Swynford feel safe and protected. That alone made the lie a worthy one, didn't it?

He'd wrestled with that question, and his conscience, ever since that moment at the bottom of the staircase when he'd made the decision to hold his tongue. He'd wrestled too with the uncomfortable knowledge that as honourable as his intentions were in keeping the truth from her, maintaining the deception had also saved him from seeing her evident disappointment when she learned who he truly was. He had to admit to himself that whilst his desire to make her feel secure with him was paramount, he was still allowing his wounded pride to rule his head, at least in part.

Across the table, Miss Swynford caught his eye and he offered her a smile. Like him, she'd dressed for dinner, the cream day dress she'd worn earlier now replaced by a very becoming periwinkle blue gown. Several times his gaze had been drawn to how the colour contrasted so sharply with her dark hair, how the silk fabric flattered her slender form, before he reminded himself that he had no business admiring her. Especially not when it was another of Rosalind's dresses that she wore.

Miss Swynford returned his smile shyly, before taking a tentative sip of the fine claret he'd had Smithson fetch from Hayton's cellars. She seemed on edge tonight, surveying the food and drink before her with wide eyes, consuming them slowly and deliberately, as though she was unsure of herself. As though she was unsure of him.

Samuel felt his smile fade, gripped now by the worrying thought that he might be responsible for her apparent discomfort, that perhaps dining together like this had been a step too far. However compelling the reasons were for her to remain in his home at present, she was nonetheless an unchaperoned, unmarried woman, convalescing in close confinement with an unmarried man. Perhaps she'd been able to countenance tea and cake in the afternoon light of a parlour, but the presence of claret and candles as day faded to night felt too intimate. He had not considered it like that before but, now that he did, he could see how dining like this could be construed in that way. How it might give rise to concerns about his intentions, and just how dishonourable he might in fact be. He reminded himself again of all that she'd endured of late. Certainly, her wicked uncle and his equally dreadful conspirator had given her no reason to trust a gentleman.

'I hope you will forgive me for asking you to join me this evening, Miss Swynford,' Samuel began, possessed now by the urge to say something, to explain himself.

She looked up from her plate, fork poised. 'Forgive you?'

'Indeed, it was very selfish of me. I occupied you for much of the afternoon in the parlour, and ought to have left you to rest this evening.'

She wrinkled her brow at him. 'Do I look tired, sir?'

'Well, no, of course not…'

She gave him another of those small smiles. 'Then all is well. I will be sure to say, if I wish to retire.'

'Yes, of course, very good.' He paused, momentarily unsure how much more he wished to say, before swallowing his pride and adding, 'I would just like to assure you that I have only the most honourable and gentlemanly intentions in inviting you to dine with me. I merely felt it would be nice for us both to have some company during dinner, that is all.'

Miss Swynford sipped her wine again, lingering somewhat over it, and he could tell that she was considering his words. Inexplicably, his stomach started to churn, and he began to regret eating that mackerel quite so enthusiastically. He would have to ask Smithson to have the cook prepare for him some of that sweet ginger drink she always swore aided digestion.

'I am relieved to hear it, Sir Samuel,' she replied at length. 'I cannot tell you all the wild thoughts I had been entertaining since we sat down to our soup.'

Samuel felt his heart skip a beat. 'Really?'

The horror on his face must have been comical, because Miss Swynford began to laugh. 'No, of course not,' she said between chuckles, clearly trying to retain a modicum of self-control. 'I cannot think why you would even feel the need to clarify your intentions, sir. I know we have only known one another for a matter of days, but you have given me no reason to think of you as anything other than the very best of gentlemen.'

He raised a smile at her compliment, even as it made him feel utterly wretched. Would she still think that if she knew he was not really Hayton's baronet? 'I only wished to put you at your ease,' he said after a moment. 'I am sorry to observe it, but you looked uncomfortable from almost the moment you sat down to dine.'

In the dim light offered by the candles and the coming dusk outside, Samuel was sure he saw her expression darken. 'I am not used to dining in this manner,' she replied quietly, 'with such fine food and drink, such civilised company.'

He frowned. 'What do you mean?' he asked, a furious heat growing in his chest as his mind raced to contemplate all that her words might imply. 'What happened to you, Miss Swynford? In what manner was this uncle of yours keeping you?'

She shook her head gently, declining to answer. When she looked up, her expression had brightened once more. She reached for her glass again. 'The wine really is very good, sir,' she remarked, taking a sip and, he suspected, collecting herself. Something was amiss, but he was damned if he could fathom what it was.

He nodded, lifting his glass in agreement. 'A Bordeaux wine, and one of my particular favourites, although I only indulge when in company. Drinking such fine wine alone always seems rather a waste,' he added.

'I must confess to wondering why you are alone here, Sir Samuel,' Miss Swynford replied, meeting his eye. 'Forgive me, but you must surely be one of Cumberland's most eligible gentlemen.'

Her directness took him aback. 'I'm not sure about that...' he began, before realising that he had no idea what to say. How could he possibly explain himself? He did not want to let yet more falsehoods fall from his tongue, to portray himself as some sort of humourless baronet, so committed to managing his estate that he had not yet troubled himself to find a wife. Yet he could not bring himself to tell her the truth either, that he was a lesser prospect, a younger brother, a recent reject on Cumberland's marriage mart because he had not quite passed muster. That final fact, in particular, was too humiliating an admission to contemplate.

It was clear from the expression on her face that Miss Swynford had seen his discomfort. 'I am sorry,' she said softly, before he could settle upon an explanation. 'It is none of my business. In any case, I dare say it will not be long before I hear of your marriage to some well-connected society beauty with a large fortune.'

Samuel gave a wry chuckle. 'She sounds...intimidating.' His smile faded. 'To be frank, I think I'd prefer genuine companionship, Miss Swynford. Wealth and connections might matter a great deal to some people, but not to me. If I marry, I would rather it was for love than status.'

Miss Swynford's eyes seemed to search his, as though she was surprised by this admission, as though she was trying to determine if he was in earnest. Truly, she must have

only ever been acquainted with the most dreadful gentlemen if she could be so astonished by his heartfelt confession. Then again, hearing those words fall from his own
lips had come as something of a surprise to him too. He'd
heard the sharp edge in his own voice as he'd spoken about
other people's considerations, and the frankness when he'd
confessed his own.

He had not meant to be quite so blunt, to speak of marriage and love—two things he'd sworn off for now, and for
very good reasons. Truly, what had come over him lately?
Clearly, those smouldering embers of the hurt and humiliation he'd experienced had been given cause to reignite. Or
perhaps, he considered, they'd never quite ceased to burn
in the first place.

Samuel shook his head at himself. 'Forgive me...'

The sound of the door opening caused them both to startle and Samuel turned to see Smithson burst into the dining
room, somewhat breathless, his cheeks flushed.

'Sir, I am sorry to disturb you at dinner,' the butler began.
'But I need to speak with you urgently.'

Samuel pushed back his chair impatiently, nodding an
apology to Miss Swynford before turning to regard the older
man. 'What on earth is amiss?' he asked as he strode towards him. 'Has there been some accident? Is it one of the
servants?'

'No, sir.' Smithson spoke in a hushed tone, giving Miss
Swynford a worried glance. 'No accident. But I must tell
you that there is a carriage coming up the drive. A carriage
I do not recognise. Someone is coming to call at Hayton
Hall, sir. Tonight.'

Chapter Seven

Samuel hurried towards Hayton Hall's grand entrance, his heart hammering in his chest. Usually, he left the business of answering the call of visitors to the butler, but he'd instructed Smithson to escort Miss Swynford and find somewhere for her to hide. Besides, he reasoned, he was damned if he was going to put any of his servants in harm's way. In his brother's absence, he was the master of the house; dealing with unwelcome visitors was ultimately his responsibility. If, indeed, that was who awaited him in the carriage outside. It was possible that both he and the butler were jumping to the wrong conclusion, that this unexpected evening call had nothing to do with Miss Swynford's presence here, that her whereabouts had not somehow been discovered by those who sought her. That it was not the uncle coming to claim his niece, or the would-be groom coming to claim his unwilling bride.

But if it was not them, then who else could it be?

At the door, Samuel paused, pressing his eyes shut momentarily as he collected himself. As he prepared himself for the worst. Since Isaac's elopement and Samuel's retreat from society, Hayton Hall had received no visitors for weeks and, in any case, there was not a single person of his acquaintance who would consider calling uninvited at this late hour. Suppressing a groan, Samuel turned the door-knob and opened the door with trepidation. The chances of whoever waited outside being here to pay him a friendly call seemed vanishingly small.

Outside, the light was fading fast, and Samuel found himself peering at the carriage which had drawn to a halt before Hayton Hall's front steps. A driver had dismounted, opening the door for the person or people sitting within, and Samuel felt his breath catch in his throat as he watched a man step out. An imposing man, very tall and thickset, wearing a greatcoat and a conical hat.

A man, he realised immediately, who he did in fact know. A man whom he'd invited to visit before circumstances in the form of Miss Swynford had prevailed upon him. A man to whom he'd written and asked not to come at present, but who had apparently come nonetheless. Samuel felt his mouth fall open, his stomach lurching as his relief at see-ing a familiar face came into conflict with his awareness of the other difficulties this unexpected arrival presented.

'Charles?' Samuel called out, hurrying down the steps to greet him.

'Hello, Sammy,' Charles replied with a hearty chuckle. 'I am sorry we are so late. The roads rather wreaked havoc with this dear old thing. Father let us take the family coach— I suppose it is well suited to long journeys but I do so pre-fer the landau.'

'Oh, I see, yes, very good,' Samuel stuttered, still col-lecting himself.

Charles reached back into the carriage and Samuel watched as a gloved hand accepted his. A young lady stepped out, immaculately dressed in a deep blue bonnet and matching pelisse. Samuel watched as she brushed a swift hand down her long coat, keeping her eyes fixed on the ground as she stood dutifully beside Charles and awaited the necessary introduction.

'Sammy, this is my sister, Miss Henrietta Gordon. Sister, this is Mr Samuel Liddell.'

Finally regaining his composure, Samuel inclined his head politely at Miss Gordon, who mirrored his gesture but did not lift her eyes to meet his. She was uncommonly tall, much like her brother, but, unlike him, she was extremely slender, a fact which leant her stature a willowy, almost fragile air. Samuel found himself rather unwittingly contrasting her with the diminutive Miss Hope Swynford, a thought which prompted him to remember that poor Miss Swynford was still hiding somewhere in the house, fearing her imminent discovery. A thought which also reminded him that he was now going to have to find a way to explain that young lady's presence in his home to his unexpected guests.

A young lady who still believed he was the master of Hayton Hall. At that moment, Samuel could have groaned aloud. What on earth was he going to do?

Charles regarded Samuel with a half-amused, half-puzzled expression on his face. 'You look rather astonished to see us. Had you forgotten our little visit this week?'

Samuel shook his head. 'Of course not. Only…only I had written to you, to ask if we could perhaps postpone for a few weeks. I presume you did not receive my letter.'

At this, Charles laughed, patting Samuel playfully on the back. 'Doubtless your letter arrived at Shawdale, but Henrietta and I have not been there for almost three weeks, have we, sister?'

Miss Gordon shook her head, still not meeting Samuel's eye. 'We have been in Buxton, taking the waters.'

'Why did you wish to postpone?' Charles asked, glancing up at Hayton Hall. 'Is something amiss? Are you unwell? You do not look unwell.'

'I am fine,' Samuel replied, bristling as he recalled that it was illness which he'd used as an excuse to postpone in his letter. 'It is just that…well, I have a guest already. She arrived rather unexpectedly several days ago and…'

'She?' Charles interrupted him. Samuel watched as his friend's gaze shifted briefly to his sister. 'Is this conversation suitable for a lady's ears, Sammy?'

'Of course it is—it is nothing untoward. The lady was injured…she needed somewhere to stay, to recover, and… listen, I will explain everything when there is more time. Poor Miss Swynford is inside; I need to go and tell her that all is well, that she can come out of hiding.'

Charles frowned. 'And who exactly is Miss Swynford? Why is she hiding? What the devil is going on?'

'I will explain everything in good time,' Samuel said again, wringing his hands in front of him.

He was anxious to return to Miss Swynford now, but that was not the only reason he felt so on edge. Determining what to tell Charles about how Miss Swynford had come to be in his home was difficult enough, but the thought of owning his deception of her caused panic to rise in his chest. Smithson's words of caution rang in his ears. Lies did indeed have a way of getting out of hand. Certainly, this one was entirely out of his hands now; Samuel had no choice but to place it into the keeping of his friend, and hope that he would understand or, at the very least, that he would keep the knowledge of it to himself. In that regard, he was cautiously optimistic—for all that Charles was loud and enjoyed a good piece of gossip, Samuel knew that he could be relied upon when it mattered most.

Besides, what choice did he have? The alternative was to risk Charles bursting into his home and unwittingly revealing Samuel's deceit to Miss Swynford. The notion of her learning the truth from someone else was unthinkable. No—it had to come from him. If he could ever find the right moment, the right words to explain…

The right words to reassure her that she would always be safe with him, whether he had a title or not.

Samuel stood in front of his guests, his back momentarily turned to Hayton Hall. 'I need to ask for your co-operation in one matter, though,' he began, lowering his voice.

The furrow in Charles's brow deepened. 'Sammy?' he prompted.

'If Miss Swynford refers to me as Sir Samuel, please do not contradict her,' Samuel blurted, detesting the words as they fell from his lips.

A mischievous smile spread across Charles Gordon's face and he glanced up at the grand house once more. 'The lady thinks all this is yours, does she, Sammy?' he asked. 'Good grief. Just what sort of trouble have you gone and got yourself into?'

Hope shuffled on her chair, grimacing at her ankle as it throbbed in protest at the evening's exertions. The imminent arrival of that carriage had thrown Hayton Hall into a panic, and Smithson had worked quickly to find her a suitable hiding place. She'd followed him down into the servants' quarters at a pace which had been far from comfortable, leaning heavily on the walking cane as the butler swiftly placed a chair inside a pantry and instructed her to wait inside. There she'd sat ever since, feeling sore and restless in equal measure as her mind reeled with a myriad of discomforting thoughts.

Guilt possessed her first of all—guilt at acknowledging that, unlike Sir Samuel and his butler, she did not fear that those arriving in that carriage were looking for her. Guilt at realising how her deception had made her host fearful of an uncle and a co-conspirator who did not exist, whilst keeping him in the dark about the menacing spectre of men who definitely did.

If her father or indeed the man she'd been meant to marry were seeking to find her, they would not come in a carriage. They would not call at the front door and announce themselves. Men who lived as they did, who were involved in the sorts of things they were involved in, were never so conspicuous. Men like them worked under the cover of moonless stormy skies or in the deep black of Cumberland's caves; they drew their power from the places where shadows and chaos reigned. If they ever came for her then, without doubt, they would have her in their possession before Sir Samuel even knew anything about it.

Hope suppressed a groan, dragging her hands down her face in despair as the evening's events forced her to consider just what a tangled web she'd woven with her deceit. Moments before that carriage's arrival she'd been sitting at that fine dining table, sipping wine, allowing its potency to blur the lines between the real and the imagined, between who she really was and who she was pretending to be. She'd let her mask slip too many times; she'd allowed the veil of ladylike refinement she'd worked hard to draw across herself grow too thin. Hope reddened to recall her response to Sir Samuel's efforts to reassure her about his good intentions, how she'd teased him quite wickedly about wild thoughts, and, worse still, how she'd met his observation of her discomfort with something alarmingly approaching the truth. Why had she not simply said she was tired, or out of sorts? Whatever had possessed her to all but admit that she'd never dined like that before? Why did she seem so intent upon allowing glimpses of Hope Sloane to be seen?

Because she did not like lying to him, that was why. Because since the moment she'd arrived at Hayton Hall he'd been unfailingly kind and candid, and the knowledge that she'd repaid him with nothing but deceit gnawed at her. Worse still, the guilt she felt seemed only to grow with every passing day and every conversation. With every new thing she learned about him. With every growing doubt that the master here would be the sort of man to have any acquaintance with her father or his business dealings. She had not known what to do with herself tonight when he'd spoken so honestly about his desire for genuine companionship over more worldly considerations.

'If I marry, I would rather it was for love than status...'

Hope straightened herself and forced her mind to cease lingering upon those words. Indeed, she'd had no right to draw them from him in the first place, to ask him such searching questions about his life. She definitely had no right to be impressed by them, no matter how heartfelt or genuine they had seemed. Not when she was deceiving him. Not when those words had been intended for Hope Swynford, and not for the ears of Hope Sloane.

The door to the pantry swung open, causing Hope to startle. Her alarm, however, quickly dissolved into relief when she saw that it was Sir Samuel who had come, presumably to collect her and take her back upstairs. Drawing a deep breath, she reached for the walking cane and got to her feet, resolving to set aside all that she'd spent these past interminable minutes mulling over. There was little point in dwelling upon her guilt or fretting over what she'd said or done. There was nothing she could do about that—there were only the consequences of choices she had already made. Those choices, she reminded herself, had left her with a role to play.

'Is all well?' she asked him. 'Was it my…my uncle? Did you send him away?'

Sir Samuel sighed. 'Not quite.'

Hope watched with growing confusion as he glanced over his shoulder before stepping into the pantry to join her and closing the door behind him. She became aware, quite suddenly, of the confined space around them, of the shelves crowded with jams and grains. Of his close proximity to her, of the soft rhythm of his breathing, of the lemon scent of his cologne.

'The good news, it was not your uncle,' he began. 'The bad news, a friend of mine has arrived, along with his sister. Their visit was arranged prior to your arrival here, after which I wrote to Charles and asked to postpone. It seems he did not receive my letter.' Sir Samuel shook his head. 'Suffice to say, I cannot simply send them away now.'

'No, of course not,' Hope replied quietly. 'I am only sorry that you felt you had to cancel their visit on my account. If I had known how my presence here would inconvenience you…'

Sir Samuel reached out, placing his hand on her arm. 'You have not inconvenienced me,' he insisted, his grey-blue gaze holding hers. 'Please, do not think that.'

Hope nodded her assent, conscious of the warm reassurance of his fingers against her bare skin. 'Then what are we to do?' she asked. 'I suppose I could pretend to be a servant here.'

'No.' He retracted his hand, leaving her feeling oddly bereft. 'Regrettably, we cannot do that, Miss Swynford.'

She frowned. 'Why not?'

'Because I am an utter blockhead,' he replied with a heavy sigh. 'Charles turning up like that had me in such a panic and I…well, I may have told him that I already have a guest staying with me.'

Hope felt her heart begin to race. 'I see. Does he know anything else about who your guest is?'

'Only your name, and that you arrived unexpectedly and are staying here while you recover from some injuries.'

Her eyes widened at him. 'You promised you would not tell a single soul about me…' she began. 'You may as well put up posters in the nearby village telling everyone my whereabouts and have done with it, sir.'

Sir Samuel met her eye, and she watched as he pressed his lips together as though he was trying to collect himself. It was an odd change on a face which was usually either serene or cheerful, and it irked her to observe that he wore a grave expression just as well as he wore a happy one.

'You must know that I would never deliberately put you in harm's way, Miss Swynford,' he said. 'My words to Charles were careless but he is a good man and, besides, he does not know the whole story. I am sure we can come up with something. Indeed, we must tell him something…'

Hope shook her head, feeling the heat of tears prick in the corners of her eyes. Not more stories. Not more lies piled upon lies. She could not countenance it. She huffed a breath then moved to step past Sir Samuel, suddenly possessed of an urge to leave that cramped little room, to retire to her bedchamber and put some distance between herself and this man. To envelop herself in dark silence and try to reconcile the conflict currently raging in her weary mind between her angry disappointment at Sir Samuel's momentary indiscretion and the guilt-ridden knowledge that he'd done little more than repeat a small portion of her tall tale. And she would have done all of that, had it not been for the walking cane she leaned on. Instead, the perfidious thing seemed to catch against the uneven stone floor. She jolted, losing her footing as her weakened ankle failed to bear her weight, and fell forward.

Straight into Sir Samuel's arms.

He caught her—of course he did—raising her slowly back to her feet, his gaze intent upon her own. She felt her breath hitch, felt her hands pressed against his chest, apparently powerless to move. Felt the furious beat of his heart through his white shirt, felt his hands remain gently upon her waist just a moment longer than was necessary. Felt the closeness, the sheer heat of him. She'd never stood like that with a man before. It was strange, intoxicating, and not at all unpleasant.

Then Sir Samuel cleared his throat and took a step back. 'Forgive me.'

'No…yes, of course,' Hope said, giving him a tight smile and doing her best to compose herself. She moved to step past him again, this time successfully. 'Excuse me. I think I shall retire for the night.'

'Indeed, you must be exhausted,' he replied with a brittle nod. 'I will need to go and attend to my guests. We can save formal introductions for tomorrow but, in the meantime, what would you like me to tell them about you? I'm afraid Charles is surely going to ask.'

Hope pushed the pantry door open, letting out a resigned sigh. 'Tell him the rest of the story,' she said, her head still spinning with the odd intensity of what had momentarily passed between them. 'I dare say that there's little else to be done about it now.'

Chapter Eight

'Well, Sammy, that's a fine mess you've made for yourself.'

Charles Gordon sat back in his chair and sipped his brandy as Samuel nodded glumly, finding it hard to disagree with his friend's assessment. Miss Swynford had retired some time ago, without so much as casting another word or glance in his direction, leaving him to entertain his new guests. After a hasty supper of whatever the cook could cobble together at such short notice, they had retired to Hayton Hall's largest and finest room to converse. Predictably, Charles had pursued the matter of Miss Swynford, and Samuel had rather uncomfortably answered his questions, acutely aware of just how much having her story told would displease his other guest. Although, of course, there was little for him to tell, since he knew only the barest details; she'd refused to tell him where she came from, and he knew neither the uncle nor the other man's names. Clearly, the lack of meat on the bones of the story dissatisfied Charles, and before long he'd returned to marvelling at his friend's pretence of being Hayton Hall's baronet.

'I simply cannot fathom it—Samuel Liddell, lying to a lady,' Charles continued, shaking his head slowly. 'I would never have thought you capable of it.'

'Unlike you, brother,' Miss Gordon interjected. 'As I witnessed for myself in Buxton.'

Samuel raised an eyebrow in surprise. Charles's sister had had little to say for herself during supper, and since sitting down in the drawing room she'd apparently preferred to sip her tea and stare rather vacantly at the fire which roared in the grate. The nights were growing colder, and in the larger, infrequently inhabited rooms of Hayton Hall the chill was particularly notable. He watched as Miss Gordon adjusted her shawl across her thin frame, tearing her eyes finally from the fireplace to meet the discomfited gaze of her sibling.

'Please, do tell, Miss Gordon,' Samuel prompted her, relieved at the opportunity to turn the conversation away from his own shortcomings.

Miss Gordon raised a tight smile. 'We attended several balls at the Assembly Rooms during our stay. I cannot say if it was the strength of the punch or the sheer quantity of eligible young ladies which made my brother dizzy, but something possessed him to tell some really rather tall tales about himself. By the end of our stay, several had been led to believe that Charles had been closely acquainted with the late Duke of Devonshire himself.'

'It is not so unbelievable, is it?' Charles replied, an unbecoming shade of scarlet creeping up from beneath his cravat. 'The duke has only been deceased for a handful of years and, as everyone knows, he took a keen interest in Buxton and its improvement. It is entirely possible that I might have known him or…or met him, at the very least.'

Samuel chuckled, shaking his head at his friend. 'I thought you would have learned your lesson during our travels, Charles. As I recall, you came unstuck on more than one occasion when a young lady discovered you were not the son of an earl or a duke as you had claimed to be.'

Miss Gordon's eyes widened and she leaned forward before saying, 'Did he, indeed?'

Samuel nodded. 'They were all most disappointed to learn that Viscount Faux-Title here had no aristocratic connections at all.'

Charles let out a heavy sigh. 'Alas, where some men shall inherit castles, I shall inherit calico printworks.'

Samuel let out another amused chuckle. 'To listen to you, anyone would think you were not from one of the wealthiest families in Lancashire. Perhaps if you spent more time telling young ladies about that and not pretending to be someone you are not, you would have more success.'

He watched as both his guests stared at him, mouths identically agape as the irony of what he had just said sunk in. He suppressed a groan as wearily he rubbed his brow, his mind wandering to the lady sleeping upstairs, the one who did not have the faintest idea who he really was. The one whose company he had been enjoying once again just hours ago, as they'd dined together, as they'd talked. The one who'd fallen into his arms in the pantry, and whom he'd relished catching more than he cared to admit.

Samuel gulped down the last of his brandy, flexing his free hand against the arm of the chair, still feeling the ghost of her waist against his fingers. After the abject misery of confessing his deceit to Charles, he'd gone down to the pantry, resolved to tell Miss Swynford the truth there and then. However, his resolve had wavered in the face of how panicked she'd been at the thought of his guests knowing even the barest facts about her, and how rightly upset she'd been with him over his poor judgement and loose tongue. He was reminded at once that she already had enough to worry about, that she was in very real danger. A danger which she believed that he, and the title and status she believed him to have, could shield her from. His duty, first and foremost, was to protect her, not to burden her with any further worries.

A duty which certainly did not involve letting his thoughts linger on the feeling of holding her in his arms, he reminded himself. No matter how pleasant such thoughts were.

'I realise I have no business lecturing you, Charles,' he said after a long moment. 'Please, forgive me.'

Charles shrugged. 'There's nothing to forgive, Sammy. I can be a complete cork-brain and I know it. But you, my dear fellow, are not. What I do not understand is why you told Miss Swynford that you were a baronet in the first place.'

Samuel hesitated. 'I did not tell her exactly…she assumed, and, to my great shame, I did not correct her. I've been torturing myself with exactly why that was ever since—foolish pride, I suppose. I've been either a younger son or my brother's heir all of my life and, God willing, now that he's wed again, I will not be his heir for much longer. When Miss Swynford presumed I was more than that, I suppose I just got a little carried away.' He paused, deciding that was all he was prepared to say. Charles was his friend but, even so, he was not about to confess to him just how much of a wounding his pride had suffered of late. Or indeed how much of a role his humiliating rejection in the summer might have played in his willingness to be the baronet.

Charles grinned. 'So it is not because you want to court her, then?'

'Hardly.' Samuel bristled at the suggestion, alarmed to

note the image of her looking up at him, her hands pressed against his chest, returning to him once more.

'In that case, why don't you simply tell her the truth?'

'I was on the cusp of doing so,' he replied miserably, 'but then Miss Swynford told me how safe she feels here, how protected. It's clear she attributes this protection in no small part to my title and standing in Cumberland—or at least the title and standing she believes me to have. How could I undermine that when she is in my home, alone and vulnerable? How could I knowingly allow her to feel unsafe? And what if I confessed all and she felt so unsafe that she left Hayton Hall before she had properly recovered and ended up back in harm's way with her uncle?'

'The Sammy doth protest too much, methinks,' Charles replied, chuckling.

'Shakespeare—yes, very good,' Samuel grumbled. He slumped back in his chair. 'Perhaps I should just tell Miss Swynford the truth, whatever the consequences.'

'No, I think you're right.' Miss Gordon spoke up, nursing her tea thoughtfully. 'Miss Swynford is here in your care, and as you've no intentions towards her beyond offering her comfort and shelter while she convalesces, then I'd leave the situation as it is rather than risk her fleeing and coming to harm.'

Samuel inclined his head at Miss Gordon's interjection. She was an odd lady, carrying herself with such an air of disengagement, of disinterest, and yet it was clear she was listening to everything that was said, weighing it up and drawing conclusions. There was a cold clarity, a steeliness about her which her loud, affable brother had never possessed. How different two siblings could be, but then,

Samuel already knew that. He'd grown up with a far more sombre, far more reserved older brother, after all.

Samuel found himself wondering about Miss Swynford's family then, about who had been there for her before her uncle had her in his clutches. Her parents were dead, he knew that, but had there ever been any brothers, any sisters? He reflected on that strange remark she'd made at dinner, about how unused she was to enjoying good food and drink, and civilised company. How long had it been since anyone had truly cared for her? A heavy feeling settled in his stomach as he found himself contemplating the possibility that no one had, that apart from her wicked uncle she was all alone.

'Well, if Henrietta agrees, then who am I to argue?' Charles said, placing his glass upon the table and rising from his seat. 'I will go along with it, Sammy.' He grinned. 'Or, should I say, Sir Faux-Title?'

Hope sat up in bed, the first volume of Mr Hume's *History of England* perched upon her lap. She'd awoken some time ago but, oddly, Maddie had not yet come to attend to her, and Hope suspected this had much to do with the arrival of the other guests. Proper guests, she thought, feeling her heart sink. The sort who were accustomed to maids and butlers, to grand houses, large dining rooms and lavish meals.

An uncomfortable feeling settled over her then, as she recognised that the familiar routine she'd hitherto enjoyed at Hayton had come to an end. There would be no more mornings spent with Maddie fussing over her; the maid simply would not have the time for that. There would be no more parlour meetings with Sir Samuel either, no more afternoons of cake and conversation. That particular thought bothered her most and she fidgeted, trying to cast it from her mind.

'You're just out of sorts, Hope, that's what's the matter with you,' she muttered. 'You just don't want to go and meet these new guests.'

That was true, certainly. Playing the role of Hope Swynford was challenging enough in front of Sir Samuel and a handful of servants; adding two further scrutinising pairs of eyes to the audience of people she had to convince was the very last thing she wanted. She looked down at her book again, forcing herself to concentrate on its lofty prose about a queen called Boadicea and her battles with the Romans, and trying not to think about last night. The way she'd allowed candlelight and fine wine to loosen her tongue at dinner. The way she'd reacted when she'd learned that Sir Samuel had told his visitors about her presence there. The way she'd fallen into Sir Samuel's arms in the pantry.

Hope felt the colour rise in her cheeks as she recalled how her senses had seemed to heighten, at once acutely aware of the muscular solidity of his chest beneath her hands, of the warmth of his arms as they circled her waist, of how his blue-grey eyes had searched hers, as though trying to discern the answer to a question which had not been put into words, as though…

As though he might kiss her.

Hope sat bolt upright in bed, pushing the book to one side in growing irritation at herself. What a fanciful notion to entertain! Of course a gentleman like Sir Samuel had not been about to kiss her, and nor had she wanted him to. Nor could she want him to—not when she was a guest in his home, enjoying his faultlessly kind and considerate hospitality under false pretences. Her ankle throbbed, giving her a timely reminder of the consequence of her clumsiness, and of the reason she was here at all. Hayton Hall was a place of refuge and its master had been a Good Samaritan to her, but there was nothing more to it than that. Indeed, she reminded herself, if he knew who she really was, and if he knew just how fundamentally she'd lied to him, he might not be so hospitable.

A knock at the door startled Hope from her thoughts. 'Come in,' she called, smoothing the sheets down in front of her and placing the book back in her lap. It was almost certainly Maddie, come at last to ask her what she would like for breakfast, and to help her dress. The poor maid must have been run ragged by the other female guest in the house if she had been detained until now.

'I am in no hurry, Maddie, so please…'

Hope's words died in her throat as Sir Samuel walked in and closed the door behind him. Immediately, thoughts of their close encounter in the pantry ran unbidden through her mind and she felt the heat rise inexplicably in her cheeks.

Stop it, Hope, she told herself. *Stop thinking about it. You're being ridiculous.*

She watched as Sir Samuel took a couple of steps into the room, then seemed to freeze. He stared at her, his eyes wide, his lips parted in surprise.

'Oh, you're not…' he began, waving a flustered hand in her direction. 'Erm, where is Madeleine?'

'Waiting upon your friend's sister, I expect,' Hope replied.

Sir Samuel gave a slow nod. 'I see. Perhaps I should go, then. We can speak once Maddie has been to help you dress.'

Hope frowned. 'Why? You sat by my bedside and talked

to me when I was most unwell.' She pulled irritably at her shift. 'This is nothing you have not seen before.'

Sir Samuel coughed. 'No, indeed, but…there are others in the house now. Others who may think thoughts which ought not to be thought if they…' He faltered, the expression on his face one of excruciating embarrassment.

'If they observe you slipping into my bedchamber in the morning before I am dressed. Or, I suppose, if they observe you coming in here at all,' Hope said, perhaps more bluntly than she should. After all, she doubted Hope Swynford would speak so plainly about such matters. In Hope Sloane's world, however, gentlemen being caught alone with actresses was of very little consequence. Certainly not something that anyone would bother to tiptoe around.

'Indeed,' Sir Samuel replied. 'I should not be here.'

Hope inclined her head in polite acknowledgement, before making a point of turning her attention back to the book on her lap. She could not explain why, but all that talk about the need to behave properly in front of the other guests troubled her. Almost as much as the realisation that Sir Samuel had probably sat them down last night and told them all about the poor runaway heiress sleeping upstairs. The thought of them all chewing over her concocted tale made her feel quite sick.

'Miss Swynford?'

Hope looked up from the pages, surprised to see he had not yet moved. 'Yes?'

'I came only to ask if you wish to come downstairs today. I realise that yesterday must have been quite a trial for you, so if you do not feel well enough then I understand.' He took a step closer, peering at her book. 'Is that Mr Hume's book you are reading?'

She nodded. 'It is. I have just reached the part where the Romans are leaving Britain. I have not managed to read very much of it yet.'

He smiled meekly. 'Of course, and gentlemen bursting into your bedchamber will hardly be helping.'

'Not gentlemen,' she replied. 'Only you.'

Sir Samuel laughed. 'I'm not sure whether I should feel complimented or affronted by that remark.'

'I'll leave that up to you to decide, Sir Samuel,' Hope quipped, trying and failing to suppress a smirk.

To her surprise, however, Sir Samuel's smile faded. 'Call me Samuel,' he said, his voice low and sincere.

Across the room, their eyes met and Hope found her thoughts straying to that odd moment they'd shared in the pantry once again. 'As you wish,' she answered him, trying her best to sound nonchalant. 'And I suppose you should call me Hope, rather than Miss Swynford.'

He inclined his head politely. 'I would like that very much, Hope.'

The way he said her name made the most disconcerting heat grow deep within her stomach. Hope looked down at her book once more. He needed to leave now, and not only because they risked the scandalous remarks of the other guests with each passing moment.

To her relief, Sir Samuel—or, rather, just Samuel now—moved back towards the door. 'I'll ask Madeleine to attend to you,' he said. 'You have waited long enough.'

'It is fine,' Hope replied, waving her hand. 'I am not in a hurry and, besides, it must be a lot of additional work, having all these people in the house who are not usually here.'

Samuel raised his eyebrows as though this was the first time that the extra burden having guests placed upon his servants had crossed his mind. 'Yes, you're right about that,' he conceded after a moment. 'You're right too to be cross with me for telling them about your presence here. I should have spoken to you first, to agree the best approach.'

'What's done is done,' she replied with a small shrug. 'I suppose they know all about me now, do they?'

'I have explained how you came to be here,' Samuel replied. 'I have also stressed how important it is that your presence at Hayton Hall remains a closely guarded secret.'

'Thank you. What did you say their names are? And where are they from? I'm afraid I cannot recall.'

'Charles and Henrietta Gordon, from Lancashire,' Samuel replied. 'I believe their home is called Shawdale, on the edge of a town called Blackburn, where their father does very well in trade.'

'Trade?' That all too familiar word made Hope look up in consternation. 'What sort of trade?'

'Calico printing, I believe.'

Inwardly, Hope breathed a sigh of relief. A proper sort of trade, and perfectly legal—of course it was. She was too quick to think the worst, to jump to the wrong conclusion when, realistically, she probably had nothing to fear. She'd never known her father to have dealings with anyone in Lancashire, much less those involved in calico printing. It did not seem likely that Mr Gordon or his sister would know who she really was.

Samuel's expression darkened. 'Why? Is that a problem?'

'No, of…of course not,' she stammered. 'Why would it be a problem?'

'Because, to some, the idea of associating with anyone who comes to wealth and prominence through means other than inheriting land and a title is offensive,' he said pointedly.

'Oh,' Hope replied, feeling as though Hope Swynford would probably have known that. 'Well, I assure you that I only asked out of curiosity.'

Samuel inclined his head, apparently appeased. 'So, you will come down to meet them today?' he asked hopefully.

Given the offence her questions had almost caused, Hope knew she had little choice. She knew too that meeting them was inevitable; she could hardly avoid them for the duration of their stay. The Gordons' visit was not ideal, but they were here now and that was that. This was the hand she'd been dealt, and she'd simply have to play it, and her role, very well indeed.

'Of course,' she replied, painting on a smile.

Chapter Nine

Samuel sat back in his favourite chair, trying his best to relax. He'd arranged to have tea with all of his guests in the small parlour, and hoped that the cosy familiarity of the room would put Hope at ease when meeting Charles and Miss Gordon. She'd seemed anxious when he'd met her in the hallway to escort her down, and for the first time since arriving at Hayton she'd refused to let him assist her on the stairs.

'I dread to think what your guests would say if they saw you carrying me,' she'd pointed out in a hushed tone. 'Besides, I am feeling much stronger. I managed to go upstairs by myself last night, and I am sure I can manage to walk down them today if I use the walking cane.'

Samuel had acquiesced, but nonetheless he'd remained close by her side as she'd made her way, somewhat unsteadily, down each step. Several times he'd observed her grimace in discomfort, and he suspected her ankle was not as healed as she'd suggested. But she was right; he could no longer be permitted to lift her into his arms, not when there were others in the house. An unexpected wave of regret had gripped Samuel then. Regret that his visitors had turned up as planned, that his letter had not reached them. Regret that his time alone with his unexpected guest had passed. Immediately he'd chastised himself for it. Hope was living in his home under his protection, not so that he might, quite literally, sweep her off her feet. That was something he had absolutely no intention of doing, especially not when he was being so untruthful.

The introductions over, their group had settled into some pleasant, if a little stilted, conversation. To Samuel's surprise and relief, Charles appeared to have decided to be on his best behaviour, engaging Hope in only the gentlest of enquiries about her convalescence and whether she was enjoying her time at Hayton Hall, notwithstanding the circumstances.

'This is the first time I have visited Sammy's home,' he said, looking all about him. 'And I must say that I have never laid my eyes upon a finer country house than this.'

'It is very lovely,' Hope agreed demurely.

Samuel, however, rolled his eyes. 'I am sure I recall you saying the same about almost every house we visited on the Continent,' he replied. 'And I am equally certain that Shawdale can compete with them all.'

Charles made a face. 'Shawdale is very grand, but it is not a country house. It is on the edge of a town and is barely ten years old. It does not have the depth that Hayton has, or indeed that any old family seat has when it has stood long enough to store the centuries within its walls.'

'You must forgive Mr Gordon,' Samuel said, turning to Hope. 'He has an unhealthy preoccupation with having an ancient noble lineage and a castle to keep it all in. You'll have to marry a duke's daughter, Charles,' he added, addressing his friend once more. 'Then you can ask your father-in-law if you can borrow one of his.'

Samuel was amused to see Hope splutter on her tea at that. She seemed to have relaxed a little now, and her laughter had made the colour rise in her cheeks, giving her a healthier glow. He found his gaze lingering upon her as he considered how well she looked in her cream day dress, her dark curls framing her face, her emerald eyes sparkling with merriment. Perhaps, he considered, their little group of four would not be such a bad thing, after all.

'He mocks me, Miss Swynford, but I am going to build my own castle,' Charles continued.

Hope's eyebrows shot up. 'Oh, like the Prince Regent? He builds castles for himself, does he not?'

Charles shook his head. 'The Prince Regent builds mansions and palaces. I shall build a castle which William the Conqueror himself would be proud to live in.'

Samuel chuckled in disbelief. 'You're going to build yourself a Norman castle?'

'Another of my brother's wild schemes,' Miss Gordon interjected drily. Until now she'd sat quietly, so much so that Samuel had quite forgotten she was there. 'When he inherits our father's fortune, he plans to knock down Shawdale and erect his monstrosity in its place.'

Samuel regarded his friend, aghast. 'And what does your father say about that?'

'He does not know.' Charles shrugged. 'Nor shall he.'

'You speak of legacies, Charles, yet you'd readily demolish what your father has built?' Samuel shook his head, unable to fathom it. 'And what about your mother? Or your sister?' he added, inclining his head towards Miss Gordon.

'Oh, I care not,' Miss Gordon said. 'When our father is gone, Charles can do as he likes, and so shall I.' She gave a self-satisfied smile then turned to Hope. 'I presume you had parents at one time, Miss Swynford?' she asked.

Samuel watched as Hope met his eye cautiously before answering, 'Yes, of course.'

'And have you committed yourself entirely to guarding their legacy?'

Hope sipped her tea, and Samuel saw that she was considering her answer. In truth, he was intrigued as to what it might be. In their time together, she'd said so little about herself, about her history. He knew nothing about where she'd come from, in terms of either location or heritage. He wondered now if Miss Gordon's rather abrupt questioning might yield more information than he'd thus far managed to gather.

At length, Hope shook her head. 'I confess I'm not sure I've ever thought much about it.'

'Well, what did they bequeath to you?' Miss Gordon put up her hand. 'And, before you think me impudent, I am not speaking of money. What I mean to say is, do you have happy memories of them to treasure, or would you too be happy to tear down the ancestral home?'

'Sister...'

Charles spoke gently, but the warning contained within his voice was all too clear. Samuel found himself wondering what on earth was going on, how a convivial conversation about Norman castles could have taken such a dark turn. Still, though, he was curious as to how Hope would answer. If she would answer.

He watched as Hope looked up, meeting Miss Gordon's gaze squarely. 'I dare say that, like many people, I can confess to cherishing some memories, while wishing to cast away others like stones.'

'And the ancestral home?' Miss Gordon pressed.

Hope gave a grim smile. 'It can remain standing, but I shall never set foot in it again.'

'I am sorry to hear that,' Samuel interjected quietly, glancing around him. 'I feel fortunate that I can look upon my family's home with such fondness.'

'Ah, and that is why Hayton is such a haven,' Miss Gordon answered, her tone lighter now. 'The perfect place to convalesce, I am sure. Well, except for Buxton. Its waters always do me the world of good, don't they, Charles?'

Charles might have answered but, in truth, Samuel was no longer listening. Instead, he found himself mulling over what Hope had said, trying to discern its meaning. He'd wished to know more about her, but what Miss Gordon's enquiries had revealed had only provoked more questions in his mind. What were the memories she wished to cast away? Why would she never return to her ancestral home? Did any of this have anything to do with the uncle from whom she was currently hiding?

Miss Gordon had spoken of guarding legacies. Well, Samuel thought, Hope was guarding something about her past, he felt sure of it. Something, he suspected, that was painful. Something she'd much rather forget.

Hope wasn't sure if she felt better or worse after her first meeting with the Gordons. Mr Gordon had seemed pleasant and good-natured enough, and she'd enjoyed the affectionate teasing which was clearly central to his and Samuel's friendship. Miss Gordon, however, was a different matter entirely. Frankly, the lady unnerved her, bestowing those dark eyes upon her as though she was peering into her soul, and asking questions in a way which seemed to suck the life out of the room.

Her behaviour had already caused consternation among the servants too. When Maddie had finally arrived in Hope's bedchamber that morning, she'd been flustered, explaining that it had taken several of the female servants to rouse Miss Gordon, such was the depth of her slumber.

'When, finally, she awoke, I thought she was unwell,' Maddie went on. 'She seemed weak and listless, and her eyes kept rolling back as though she was struggling to remain awake. I was ready to send for the physician, but she insisted nothing was amiss and ordered me to help her dress. Rather curtly, I might add.'

Hope had thought little of it at the time, reasoning that Miss Gordon was likely exhausted after her long journey to Hayton. Now, having met her, and having noted the sharp edge to her questions and the brittle way she spoke of family and legacies, Hope realised she would need to be on her guard. There'd been some pain and turmoil in that near-black stare, she felt sure of it. There'd been a story, barely concealed and threatening to spill forth, driving a tendency to want to unravel the stories of others. Hope knew her sort; the theatre had been packed with just such haunted individuals, taking to the stage to escape themselves. Hope wondered now what Miss Gordon's escape was, and whether it had anything to do with her difficulty in waking that morning. That was something she'd witnessed before too.

After tea, they took a walk in the beautiful gardens which sprawled to the rear of Hayton Hall. To begin with, Hope had hesitated about joining the group on their afternoon promenade. The walls of Hayton Hall, she realised, had become a fortress for her. Inside, she felt hidden away, protected from those who might be roaming the countryside, looking for her. The garden, by contrast, felt dangerous and exposed. Instinctively, Samuel had seemed to understand this.

'I can ask Madeleine to fetch your book and some more tea to the parlour, if you'd prefer to stay here,' he'd suggested. 'Although the gardens are very secluded, and we will not venture far from the house.'

Hope had felt the eyes of the other two guests upon her as she'd considered her options. Her gaze had wandered towards the window where, outside, a bright autumn day awaited. She did so long to feel the warmth of the sun on her face again. Surely, she reasoned, the risk of briefly venturing into private gardens, tucked between a large house and sprawling woodland, was not so great.

'I will come,' she'd said in the end. 'The fresh air will do me good. Although I'm afraid that my ankle means that my pace will be painfully slow.'

'There is nothing painful about a gentle promenade,' Samuel had replied, offering her a reassuring smile. 'I find it allows plenty of time for quiet reflection or, if in company, some delightful conversation.'

Equipped with the walking cane and a wide-brimmed bonnet sufficient to shield her face, Hope limped along the orderly paths which wove their way through beds thick with plants and bushes. She clutched Samuel's arm tightly, partly for support and partly, she realised, for reassurance. He had not left her side since they'd walked out of Hayton's rear door, nor had he spoken much, apparently preferring companionable silence to conversation.

Hope told herself that she ought to be relieved; she was still reeling from Miss Gordon's questions in the parlour.

Though her answers had been suitably vague, they had also contained much truth about herself—her real self. In light of that, the chance to keep her own counsel for once should have been welcome, yet instead Hope found herself wishing that Samuel would engage her on some topic, however ordinary. Wishing too to rekindle something of those short few days they'd spent together, prior to the Gordons' arrival.

'Is everything all right?' she ventured to ask in the end, finding herself unable to tolerate the silence any longer.

He gave her a bemused look. 'Of course, why would it not be?'

'You seem unusually quiet, that is all. I thought perhaps something was amiss.'

'I was just thinking about the last time I walked in these gardens.' He smiled at her. 'About hearing a scream coming from the woods. About finding you.'

She nodded. 'I am glad you did. Who knows what would have become of me?'

'I am glad that I did too.' He regarded her thoughtfully. 'You have made a remarkable recovery in…how long has it been? A little over a week?'

Hope drew a deep breath. 'It's odd—it feels as though I have been at Hayton Hall much longer than that. I agree, though, I am feeling much better. I have you to thank for that, sir.'

'Just Samuel,' he reminded her.

'I have you to thank, Just Samuel,' she retorted with a grin.

He chuckled at that. 'I dare say it's actually Madeleine you should thank. She has cared for you, after all.'

Hope inclined her head in agreement. 'It's Maddie,' she corrected him. 'She prefers to be called Maddie.'

He glanced at her again, a frown gathering between his eyes. 'Er...yes, you're right, I do recall her once suggesting that I call her Maddie.'

'Then why do you insist upon calling her Madeleine?'

'I do not know... I suppose because that is her proper name.'

'Well, it vexes her, Samuel. For whatever reason, she does not care for her proper name. Just as you do not care for being called Sammy by your friend,' she observed.

He gave her a quizzical look. 'How do you know that?'

'Because you flinch every time Mr Gordon says it,' she replied. 'However, Mr Gordon is your friend and your equal; if you really wanted to, you could insist that he call you Samuel. But Maddie is your servant—she can hardly challenge you over what you call her.'

Samuel cleared his throat, his countenance shifting into something less jovial, less comfortable. Hope saw that her words had struck a chord. 'Yes, quite,' he replied. 'I did not realise that it bothered her. But you are right, of course.'

She raised her eyebrows at him. 'Yes, I am right. Perhaps I shall begin to call you Sammy too. Perhaps I will do so until you start calling her Maddie.'

'All right, all right,' he said, a smile breaking on his face as he glanced at her. 'You are very direct—do you know that? Very plain-speaking.'

Hope felt her heart begin to thrum faster at his observation, conscious that she'd allowed her true self to be glimpsed once again. 'Miss Gordon seems to speak her mind too,' she retorted, nodding her head towards the siblings, who were now some distance away.

'Miss Gordon speaks in riddles,' Samuel replied, shaking his head. 'Quite what her conversation in the parlour was about, I cannot fathom. She even had Charles looking uncomfortable, and nothing usually ruffles his feathers.'

'I dare say all is not well at Shawdale,' Hope observed. 'Perhaps that is what lies beneath their stay in Buxton, and their visit to you.'

'I think you may be right about that.' Samuel regarded her carefully, his grey-blue eyes holding her own. 'It occurs to me now that when we were on the Continent, Charles never seemed inclined to return home, and he never said much about his family. Indeed, until he wrote to me to accept my invitation to visit, I did not even know he had a sister.'

'That is odd,' Hope mused. 'Although I suppose people have their reasons for not wishing to discuss their families.'

'Like you, you mean.'

Hope realised they'd stopped walking, standing instead in the middle of the path. When had that happened? She felt suddenly and acutely aware of her arm still resting in his, of his proximity, of his eyes fixed on hers. Of the weight of meaning in his observation. Of all that separated them, of the chasm wrought by his wealth and status. Of everything he did not know about her, and everything he could never know.

'Yes, like me,' she said quietly, looking away.

If she had expected an inquisition, it did not come. Instead, Samuel reached over, placing his free hand over hers, which remained in the crook of his elbow.

'Whenever you wish to talk about it, I am ready to listen,' he said.

The gesture was so tender that she could not bring herself to meet his eye. Instead, she simply nodded, not quite trusting herself to answer. Not quite trusting herself not to blurt out her story, and lay the unpalatable facts of her life at his feet.

Chapter Ten

'I am heartily sick of this interminable rain.'

Samuel looked up from his newspaper, suppressing his irritation at Charles's complaints, which were as endless as the biblical torrents falling outside. In the days since the Gordons' arrival the weather had indeed taken a turn for the worse, a fact which Charles seemed to have taken as a personal insult. Samuel had lost count of the number of times Charles had wandered over to the window, only to sigh heavily at the sight which greeted him. He knew from past experience that his friend was like a caged bear when confined to the house; a particularly wet few weeks spent in a villa by Lake Geneva had taught him that. Charles was a man who needed to feel the sun on his face and sense the world at his feet. It was a wonder, Samuel reflected now, that he'd ever returned to the damp confines of north-west England at all.

'There is nothing to be done about the weather, Charles,' Samuel said, chuckling. 'You'd be best to find yourself an occupation—the rest of us have. The ladies both look very content to sit with their books.'

He noticed Hope raise a brief smile at his remark, before returning her attention to the page in front of her once more. They'd retired to the library a little over an hour ago, after Miss Gordon had declared rather brusquely that she had nothing to divert her and Samuel had felt obliged to offer the opportunity to find some reading material. Hope had almost immediately taken the seat nearest to the fire, which burned brightly in the grate and kept the autumnal chill at bay.

His heart had warmed to observe that she'd brought one of Mr Hume's volumes with her and although there was plenty within his newspaper to occupy him he'd found his gaze wandering towards her more than once. He'd watched with some amusement as her upright, ladylike posture had dissolved into something more relaxed, sitting back, her chin resting on her hand, the book balancing on the arm of the chair. Once or twice he'd even seen her move to tuck her feet up beneath her, before remembering either the constraints imposed by her healing ankle or the requirement for decorum—he wasn't sure which. Whatever the reason, he found watching her forget then remember herself rather endearing. The distraction of a good book, it seemed, could make Hope Swynford almost drop her guard. In the end, he forced himself to avert his gaze. His eyes, and his thoughts, lingered upon her far more than they should.

'What do you do for enjoyment in this wet little corner of Cumberland, then?' Charles continued, still complaining. 'Are there no assembly rooms, no theatres?'

Samuel noticed Hope's eyes flick up briefly at Charles's question. 'We have both in Lowhaven,' he answered.

'And where the devil is Lowhaven?' Charles asked.

'A few miles away, on the coast,' Samuel replied. 'It is a busy port town, and has everything we need.'

'Then let us take the carriage there,' Charles suggested.

'We can enjoy a drive around the town. It will pass the time and we may discover what is on at the assembly rooms or the theatre.'

Hope's eyes flicked up again, for longer this time. Samuel met her gaze, saw what looked like panic rising within it.

'You forget that Miss Swynford cannot leave Hayton Hall,' Samuel reminded his friend. 'She is still convalescing and, besides, we cannot run the risk of encountering her uncle.'

'Oh, of course. Well…perhaps Miss Swynford could remain within the carriage?' Charles asked. 'Surely the chances of her being spied through a carriage window are vanishingly small and, anyway, I dare say this uncle has given up searching for her by now. It's been, what, more than a week since she fled from his clutches?'

'Nearly two weeks,' Samuel replied. 'Nonetheless, Charles, we cannot be certain, and I will not take any risks when it comes to Miss Swynford's safety. Take the carriage into Lowhaven if you wish but, regrettably, we cannot join you.'

'Neither of you have bothered to ask Miss Swynford what she wishes.'

Miss Gordon's interjection startled both men. Samuel turned to regard her, observing that she had made her remark without so much as troubling herself to tear her eyes from the pages of her book. She'd selected Walpole's *The Castle of Otranto* from the library's shelves, and clearly the dark and supernatural novel held her interest. How unsurprising, Samuel thought wryly.

'Miss Gordon is right,' Samuel said, returning his mind to the matter at hand. 'Forgive me, Miss Swynford,' he continued, addressing Hope now. 'I dare say you've had quite enough of gentlemen making decisions for you of late—decisions which they've absolutely no right to make. What do you want to do?'

Given the earlier look of panic he believed he'd glimpsed, he expected Hope to decline outright. Instead, however, she appeared to be giving the outing some consideration, chewing her bottom lip thoughtfully as she apparently weighed up her options.

'You have not asked Miss Gordon what she'd like to do either,' Hope replied after a moment, glancing at the other woman.

'Oh, I care not,' Miss Gordon replied airily. 'I find that it is best to remain indifferent, Miss Swynford, when your desires will not be taken into account in any case.'

Samuel saw Charles flinch at his sister's cutting remark. 'Then it is up to you, Miss Swynford,' he said, smoothing over whatever was amiss between the Gordon siblings. Frankly, he could not care less about that right now. 'If you would prefer to remain here, then I will stay with you.'

He watched as she looked towards the window, the rain still running like tears down its old panes. She bit that lovely pink lip once again, and he found himself wondering what she was thinking, if she was as taken with the idea of remaining at Hayton as he suddenly was. If it had occurred to her, as it now had to him, that they could sit together in the parlour and enjoy tea and cake, just as they had before the Gordons had arrived. That they could talk—really talk. That she might bring herself to confide in him, that she might answer some of the questions which had been whirling around his mind about her family, about where her home was and why she would not, or could not, return to it. About exactly what had happened to her to leave her at the mercy of such a wicked relative, and why it appeared she had no one except an unnamed friend in London to turn to.

Not that he had any right to expect such confidences, he reminded himself. Not when he was still deceiving her about who he really was.

At length, when Hope delivered her answer it came as quite a surprise. 'I will come,' she said plainly. 'But I will remain out of sight within the carriage, as Mr Gordon suggests.'

Charles clapped his hands with delight as Samuel mustered an obliging nod in Hope's direction. She met his eye but her expression gave nothing away. Nothing about what had informed her choice to venture out when she'd thus far been so cautious. Nothing about whether cake and conversation with him had even occurred to her and, if it had, why she had rejected it in favour of a rainy carriage ride with the restless Charles and his prickly sister.

'As you wish, Miss Swynford,' Samuel replied, forcing a smile.

Hope shrank back into her seat, her heart beating hard in her chest as the carriage rattled along Lowhaven's bustling streets. She kept her head bowed, allowing the wide-brimmed bonnet she wore to keep her fully in shadow. She'd barely dared to look out of the window, convinced that the moment she did she'd be immediately recognised by some keen-eyed, wicked associate of her father and dragged back to Lillybeck. That had happened to her once before, after all.

She suppressed a shudder at the memory of being hauled away from the back door of the theatre, a coarse hand clapped over her mouth, stifling her screams. Of how powerless she'd felt as they'd dragged her along a lonely alley-way before binding her hands and feet and bundling her into a cart.

These past weeks at Hayton, she'd found sanctuary, and not only from the very real dangers she faced. She'd found sanctuary from her thoughts too, and from her memories. By inhabiting the role of Hope Swynford, she'd put some distance between herself and Hope Sloane's troubles. Now, in the midst of this busy port town, it all returned to her, running unabated through her mind. The confusion. The fear. The desperation.

In her lap, she squeezed her gloved hands together. Why had she come here? Why had she not simply said she'd pre-fer to remain at Hayton Hall?

Because Samuel would have remained with her, that was why. They would have been left alone, and that was something Hope feared she could no longer countenance. Ever since that tender moment they'd shared in the garden, Hope had come to believe that she could no longer trust her-self around him. The way she'd reacted when he'd touched her hand and spoken to her so earnestly…the temptation she'd felt to surrender to the truth, to admit everything—it would not do.

It was bad enough that she was clearly in awe of his good looks, his fine house and his gentlemanly manners. It was bad enough that she'd allowed her thoughts to linger too often on how it'd felt to be in his arms as he carried her down the stairs or broke her fall in the pantry. It was bad enough that she'd entertained ludicrous ideas about him kissing her. Now, was she seriously contemplating placing her trust in him and telling him the truth? What good did she think could possibly come of that?

No good—that was what.

Sir Samuel Liddell was hardly likely to greet the news that she'd lied to him, that she was no heiress or gentlewoman but an actress and the offspring of an outlaw, with anything other than horror and disdain. For all that he'd shown himself to be kind and decent, such qualities had limits, and a gentleman in his position could surely not countenance allowing a woman like her to remain under his roof. She was the lowest of the low—a common criminal's daughter who'd only managed to escape her father's grasp by taking a profession which, in the eyes of many, made her little better than a harlot. And she had lied about it—she'd dined at Samuel's table, slept in his guest bedchamber and socialised with his friends under false pretences. That, she realised now, was perhaps the most unforgivable part of all.

She had to hold her tongue, she reminded herself, and if that meant avoiding being alone with Samuel and using the Gordons as a shield, then so be it. As soon as they left, she would make plans to leave too. She would allow Samuel to escort her to London as agreed and she would begin her life anew from there, even if that meant making her home in the Rookeries and acting on the makeshift stages of the city's many penny gaffs. This time, she vowed, she would put as many miles between herself and her father as possible. She tried not to consider that the same distance would then exist between herself and Samuel. There was, after all, no point in dwelling upon that.

Hope was so lost in her thoughts that it took her several moments to realise that the carriage had drawn to a halt. She looked up to see Mr Gordon hurry out of the door, before reaching back in to assist his sister as she too disembarked.

'We shan't be long, Sammy,' Mr Gordon called, his tone so cheerful that Hope was sure he'd almost sung the words.

Behind them the carriage door clicked shut, concealing Hope from the outside world once more, and leaving her with the master of Hayton Hall once again. So much for avoiding being alone in his company, she thought wryly. Clearly, fate had other ideas. Across from her, Samuel attempted what looked like a reassuring smile, but it quickly dissolved into an exasperated sigh.

'Goodness knows if either of them will find anything at the assembly rooms or the theatre which will please them,' he said, shaking his head. 'I fear Buxton has spoiled them both. Lowhaven's meagre entertainments and lack of pump rooms can hardly be expected to compete. Do you know, Hope, that we have only seawater here? Appalling.'

Hope smiled at his witty remark. 'I dare say Buxton's plays differ little from Lowhaven's. They're all put on by touring provincial theatre companies, after all.'

'Very true,' Samuel replied, raising his eyebrows at her observation. 'You are quite the theatre enthusiast, I think.'

Hope shrugged, trying to ignore the way her stomach lurched. Once again, she'd forgotten herself. Forgotten who she was meant to be. 'I do enjoy a play from time to time,' she replied, doing her best to sound nonchalant. 'Although, of course, I will not be able to join you and the Gordons at the Lowhaven theatre, should they find a play they wish to see one evening.'

She watched as Samuel knitted his brow. 'No, of course, but as you cannot go, I shall not join them either.'

'But you must,' she protested. 'They are your guests…'

'They know the situation,' he insisted. 'They will understand. I promised that you would remain under my care until I escort you to London. I would be remiss in my duty to you if I left you alone and went to Lowhaven for the evening.'

'I would not be alone. I would have Maddie, Smithson and all the other servants there with me...'

'And what if that blackguard of an uncle were to come for you under the cover of darkness?' He held her gaze, his blue-grey eyes seeming to darken. 'What would my poor old butler or my maid be able to do about it then? I can see that you are fearful of your uncle, Hope. You have looked terrified all the way here, even though Charles is correct—there is little chance of him spying you in a carriage with us, if he even remains in Cumberland at all.'

'Trust me,' she replied, lowering her gaze. 'He will still be close by. He will not give in until he has found me.'

Samuel frowned. 'If that is the case, what difference will going to London make? Does he know you have a friend in the city and, if he does, isn't it possible he will find you there? Can this woman and her husband protect you, or are you simply going to be running for ever?'

'I do not know.'

Beneath her lashes, Hope felt a tear slip out. That was the truth, of sorts: Hope Sloane had as little a notion of what the future held for her as Hope Swynford apparently did. Beyond that, Hope was at a loss for what to say. Her story was quickly coming apart under Samuel's growing scrutiny; the tangled web of deceit she'd hurriedly woven together was disintegrating, and she could not even bring herself to attempt to repair it, to tell yet more lies.

'Forgive me, I have upset you.' Samuel leaned forward, placing his hand over hers, which remained folded in her lap. 'Tell me how to help you, Hope. Tell me what more I can do.'

'You have done enough already, Samuel,' she replied, attempting a watery smile.

'Clearly that is not the case, if I am to deliver you to London so that you may spend the rest of your life living in fear. And what sort of a life will you have there? Can you support yourself? Can you access your inheritance?'

'Please, do not concern yourself...'

'But I am concerned,' he insisted. 'I am very concerned about exactly what this nasty and ruthless individual has done to you. I am very concerned that you do not appear to have any family except him, that there is no one to care about your welfare...'

'You are right—I have no one,' Hope conceded, her tears continuing to fall. 'You have been very kind to me, Samuel, and I thank you for it, but you are not my father or my brother, or my...'

Husband.

She stopped herself, just before she could say the word.

Hope sniffled, trying to regain her composure. 'As I said,' she concluded quietly, 'it is none of your concern.'

At that moment the door to the carriage swung open once more, causing them both to flinch. Swiftly, Samuel withdrew the hand which had been resting over hers and, despite herself and all that had occurred in those past moments, Hope could not help but feel bereft at the loss of his touch. She watched as Miss Gordon climbed back in, followed in quick order by her brother who, judging by his broad grin, was very satisfied with his findings indeed. The air which blew in behind them was crisp and laced with salt, and Hope found herself wishing she could go outside and take a swift, restorative lungful of it. Right then, she needed something—anything—which might help to get her thoughts in order.

'Well, that was very enlightening,' Mr Gordon began. 'There is a ball each month at the assembly rooms, and the place has a card room, which suits me very well. And the theatre has a performance of *As You Like It* every evening, although it is finishing its run very soon so we must be quick to catch that one.'

'But that is not the most interesting thing we learned,' Miss Gordon interjected. 'Brother, tell them what we heard about the previous play.'

Hope felt her heart begin to beat faster as Mr Gordon leaned forward conspiratorially.

'Oh, yes,' he said. '*The School for Scandal*—one of my favourites. Apparently, an actress went missing on its penultimate night in town. Disappeared right after the show, it seems. No one's seen or heard anything from her since.'

'Really?' Samuel asked, furrowing his brow. 'The poor woman. I do hope she's not come to any harm.'

'I dare say that actresses absconding from the stage is not all that uncommon,' Mr Gordon scoffed. 'Such is the sort of life that many of them lead—or so I hear. Courtesans at best and harlots at worst, in many cases.'

'All right, Charles,' Samuel replied, making a face. 'I do not think that is a suitable topic of conversation with ladies present.'

By now Hope's heartbeat had grown so fast and so loud that it was a wonder the whole carriage could not hear it. Her cheeks burned as she looked down at her lap once more, wringing her hands together and praying that no one would spot her sheer mortification. Of course these people thought that—didn't everyone? Of course Samuel thought that. Whilst he had not said the words himself, he had not contradicted his friend either. Further confirmation, if it was needed, of exactly why he could never know who and what she really was. Confirmation too of exactly why he could never know just how profoundly true her words had been when she'd told him that she was none of his concern.

Gentlemen like Sir Samuel Liddell concerned themselves with high-born heiresses, not lowly actresses with criminal connections. As the carriage set off for Hayton once more, Hope decided that she would do well to remember that the next time she was tempted to be truthful with him. The truth, she realised, would only injure them both.

Chapter Eleven

Samuel cantered along the coastline on his horse, a salt-laced mist dampening his face to match his mood. He'd gone out a little while earlier with Charles, sensing his friend's characteristic restlessness might be best served by some fresh air. He'd been reluctant to leave Hope, but she had insisted that she would be fine sitting in the small parlour with Miss Gordon, who had no more wished to ride than it appeared she wished to do anything at all. Samuel had thought about protesting, about reminding her of his promise to protect her from the threat she faced, but something about the adamant look in her eye dissuaded him.

'I shall not be gone long, and we shall not venture far,' he'd sworn instead.

Hope joining them, of course, had been out of the question; even if she could countenance straying so far from Hayton Hall, her ankle was not yet strong enough to either ride or walk such a distance.

As he'd headed to the clifftops, Samuel had increasingly found himself wishing that she was there; indeed, that they could ride together, alone. That he could show her the wild and rugged parts of his county, and the sheer remote beauty of places where it was possible to ride for miles without seeing a single soul. He had quickly instructed himself to stop being ridiculous; the lady was convalescing in his home, not visiting for pleasure. His duty was to care for her, not to seek to impress her. Not to seek time alone with her.

Not to interrogate her.

He winced, thinking of their conversation in the carriage, how tense it had become. He'd been wrong to press her about her family, and to call into question the plans she had made. She was right; it was none of his concern what she did, or who she sought help from once she was in London. It was none of his business what had happened in her past, or what her terrible uncle had done to her. His questions had damaged the trust which had been building between them—a delicate trust, he reminded himself, which already rested upon the creaky foundations wrought by his lie about who he was.

Since their drive into Lowhaven, Hope had seemed to withdraw from him, burying her nose in her book every time he so much as glanced at her, and staying firmly by the side of Miss Gordon, whose conversation suddenly seemed to hold a great deal of her interest. Samuel understood her need to keep her distance, and had acted accordingly by keeping his. He knew that he'd crossed a line with his intrusive questions, and that he'd upset her. He'd taken too much of an interest and he was not, as she'd pointed out, her father or her brother, or…

Her husband.

She'd been about to say that, hadn't she?

Samuel stared vacantly out to sea, listening to the waves crashing below and wondering why that word felt so odd to him as it rattled around in his mind. Wondering too exactly why he had grown so interested in what the mysterious

Hope Swynford's tale truly was, and why he felt the heat of anger rise within him at his increasing suspicion that she was all alone in the world, left to face some malevolence which she could not bring herself to name. Anger was not an emotion which came readily to Samuel Liddell, and yet that was how he felt. He could feel it in his racing heart, in his blood as it boiled and coursed through his veins.

He tried not to consider that there might be other feelings at play, other reasons for this visceral physical response. Reasons connected to the sight of her emerald gaze, to the sight of her sitting abed in her shift, her dark hair tumbling in waves over her shoulders. To the feeling of her slight frame nestled in his arms, and the feeling of her slender waist beneath his hands. If she was so adamant that his concerns for her welfare were unwanted, he did not wish to contemplate her horror if she knew how often his mind lingered on thoughts such as those.

'I never had you pegged as the brooding type, Sammy.'

Charles brought his horse to trot alongside Samuel's and gave his friend a mischievous grin. Samuel braced himself for an onslaught of Charles's customary teasing.

'I'm not,' Samuel retorted. 'I believe that the reputation for brooding belongs to my older brother, not me.'

'Well, since you've borrowed his title, I dare say you can borrow his character traits too.'

Inwardly, Samuel groaned at the reminder. His continued deception of Hope was something else which increasingly preyed upon his mind. He would remind himself of why he kept up the pretence, of the need to make Hope feel safe, but that did not stop the lie looming like a spectre over every moment he spent in her company, and over every day that she remained within the sanctuary of Hayton Hall. He'd had the audacity to seek and enjoy her company, to express concern for her and to ask questions about her story, when he was not even being honest with her about who he was. The guilt of it was becoming intolerable.

'Do you know what I think?' Charles continued, undeterred by his friend's silence. 'I think you're a little bit smitten with Miss Hope Swynford. That's why you're pretending to be a baronet, and that's why you won't just admit your folly to her.'

'Nonsense!' Samuel declared, shaking his head.

Charles eyed him suspiciously. 'Is it? She's a pretty young chit, as I'm sure you have not failed to notice. And if the uncle's reckless actions in kidnapping her are anything to go by, I'd say she's wealthy too.'

Samuel bristled at his friend's observation. 'You know that such considerations are no inducement to me, Charles.'

'Which part—her uncommon good looks or her large fortune?' Charles teased.

'Both,' Samuel replied. 'Miss Swynford is in my home under my protection, Charles, not so that I can take advantage of her. That is not my way—you know me well enough to know that.'

Charles nodded. 'You were always a finer gentleman than me. I would be thoroughly dishonourable, if only I was better at it,' he added with a roguish grin.

'Just as long as you are not minded to be dishonourable towards Miss Swynford. The poor lady has been through quite enough,' Samuel lectured him.

'First brooding over the chit, now defensive of the chit— are you quite sure you're not pining for her?' Charles asked.

'Absolutely certain,' Samuel snapped back, although even he could hear his words lacked conviction. Her fortune—

large or otherwise—was of no particular interest to him. Her striking beauty, however...

'We should return to Hayton Hall,' Samuel continued, turning his back to the sea. 'We've neglected Miss Swynford and your sister for quite long enough.'

'I doubt Henrietta will mind,' Charles replied. 'She seems to quite enjoy Miss Swynford's company.' He shook his head in mock disbelief. 'Rich, beautiful, and capable of lifting my sister's sullen spirits. The Sammy I knew on the Continent would have been the first gentleman in the room to try to woo a woman like that.'

Samuel grimaced at his friend's words. The 'Sammy' Charles knew would not have allowed such a woman to believe he was someone he was not. But then, that Samuel had not yet had his pride dented by rejection. That painful experience, he acknowledged yet again, was part of what had driven his deceit. What prevented him from ending it was altogether more complex, and was just as attributable to the potent mix of protectiveness and affection he felt whenever he looked at her as it was to his residual feelings of shame and humiliation whenever he so much as contemplated explaining his lie. But he had to contemplate it, he knew that, even if it risked losing her respect. Even if it meant an end to the way she seemed to regard him, as though he was a knight who had come to her rescue. That was nothing less than he deserved.

If only he could find a way to tell her which would not cause her distress. If only he could be certain that the knowledge that she was not living under the protection of Hayton's baronet wouldn't cause Hope to panic, or to flee back into harm's way. The thought that it might was unbearable, and was another reason why he continued to wrestle with his conscience. And another reason, no doubt, why his blood heated with that overwhelming desire to protect her, to envelop her in his arms and not let go…

Where in damnation had that thought come from?

'I am not wooing anyone,' Samuel replied after a moment. 'And certainly not Miss Swynford. That is a ridiculous idea, given the circumstances.'

Impatiently, he cracked his whip, unable to stomach the sound of his own hollow protests any longer. Unable to abide the maelstrom of whirring thoughts as his honour, his conscience and his pride warred with each other in his mind. Instead, he raced back towards the home of which he was not truly master, to the life and title which were not truly his, and to the woman who, to his great shame, believed him to be in possession of all of it.

'Courtesans…and harlots…'

Hope sat alone in the small parlour, forcing her mind to focus on the book which rested on her lap, to absorb the information contained within Mr Hume's dense prose. Her mind, however, had other ideas, returning continuously to those injurious words which Mr Gordon had uttered. Words which Samuel had not refuted as accurate descriptions of actresses. Words which Hope had been smarting over ever since.

'Courtesans at best and harlots at worst.'

The irony of the insult was not lost on her since she was, without doubt, thoroughly unqualified to be called either. During her time in the theatre she had steadfastly refused to succumb to the easy virtues expected of those in her profession, rebuking many a man for his unwanted advances. Indeed, the only experiences she'd ever had of the opposite sex were in the form of those who'd tried to kiss or to touch her without invitation. She'd never experienced any welcome intimacy; she'd never been embraced by a man who made her heart race or kissed by one who stirred the heat of passion within her. These were feelings which she knew existed—she'd heard enough of the coarse chatter of other actresses, after all—but they were not experiences she'd had for herself.

Indeed, she realised, the closest she'd ever been to a man was when she'd unwittingly fallen into Samuel's arms in the pantry, or when she'd allowed him to carry her down the stairs. Encounters which she found herself replaying in her mind, picking over their details, reliving the feelings such closeness had evoked in her. She'd felt comforted, re-assured, safe, but something else too. The heat of something which she could not find words for, but was there none-theless, rising within her as her eyes met his, as his arms held her momentarily, tantalisingly close. Another irony, she reminded herself, forcing her mind to cease from lin-gering over those memories once more. Regardless of the feelings Samuel's proximity might provoke in her, in every respect that mattered—in status and in wealth—she could not be further apart from him.

Hope sighed heavily, putting the book to one side as finally she admitted defeat. Having grown weary of the Anglo-Saxons and the Normans, she'd jumped ahead, seek-ing diversion in the story of John of Gaunt and Katherine Swynford, which Samuel had briefly yet so tantalisingly re-counted. In this, however, she was ultimately disappointed, finding only the smallest reference to their union, and even then it was to discuss how it was believed to have injured the dignity of the Duke of Lancaster's family. As a learned gentleman, no doubt Mr Hume had little time for mistresses who become wives, Hope had thought wryly. Just as baronets could not be expected to have any regard for actresses.

She fidgeted, kicking off the ill-fitting slippers she wore—another item borrowed from Samuel's cousin—and carefully stretching her legs out across the sumptuous fabric of the sofa. At least this unexpected time alone had afforded her some respite from playing her role of the society heiress. Samuel and Mr Gordon were still out riding, and Miss Gordon had retired to her room some time ago, claiming she was in the grip of yet another headache. She had seemed to suffer from a great many of those of late, excusing herself at least once daily on the insistence that she needed to rest awhile. Several times, Hope had observed her brother's brow furrow as his gaze followed her out of the room. It was a look which spoke of his concern, but it was knowing too.

Hope had spent more time with Miss Gordon these past days, feebly shielding herself from the possibility of further questioning by Samuel. Thankfully, the lady had largely desisted from asking Hope any more leading questions about ancestral homes and the like. Nonetheless, between her frequent headaches, clipped conversation and general aloof air, Hope found the unease she'd experienced when first meeting the lady to be fully vindicated. When it came to Miss Henrietta Gordon, it was clear that there was more going on than met the eye.

Then again, Hope thought, Miss Gordon was not the only one at whom such a charge could be levelled. She might be under no illusion as to exactly what Samuel would think of her if he knew who and what she truly was, but that did not stop her guilt at her deception of him continuing to gnaw at her. Moreover, after the way he'd questioned her as they'd sat together in his carriage in Lowhaven, Hope felt that the risk of him unravelling her story for himself was becoming very real.

If he continued to pick over the vague information she'd offered, if he continued to press her for more detail than she was willing to give, then a gentleman as learned as he was could not fail to grow suspicious, and then what would she do? Tell more lies and hope to assuage his desire for knowledge? Tell him the truth and watch the anger and disappointment cloud his usually cheerful countenance? Neither option held any appeal. She regarded him too highly to deepen the deceit, yet she feared the consequences of honesty—she feared losing his good opinion and she feared hurting him. She cared too much to do that.

She cared too much about him, didn't she? And that was the problem. That was the root of her current predicament. Because, as it turned out, deceiving someone so kind, so open and likeable as Samuel caused her pain, far worse perhaps than any of the injuries she'd sustained mere weeks ago. It made her heart sore, and her stomach ache.

Tentatively, Hope glanced at her ankle as it rested on the sofa. The acute discomfort was gone now, as were the bandages. Indeed, the only evidence of injury which remained was the bruising, which had gradually turned from an angry purple to a deep greyish brown. It was not strong enough to walk far yet and it still hurt if she spent too long on her feet but, to all intents and purposes, it had healed. She had healed. Perhaps, she reasoned now, the answer to her growing set of problems was not to choose between honesty and deceit, but to escape. Hayton Hall was only a temporary sanctuary, after all, offered to her while she convalesced. Well, she had recovered, at least well enough to travel. Perhaps it was time to make arrangements to leave.

The sound of horses cantering up the drive caused her to startle, and out of the window she saw Samuel and Mr Gordon approach. Quickly, she sat up straight, sliding her feet back into the slippers as she composed herself and resumed her role. It would only be for a little while longer, she told herself now. She would speak to Samuel about making arrangements for her journey south as soon as possible. He would remain ignorant of her deception and they would part on good terms. In time, his acquaintance with the enigmatic heiress would become nothing more than a strange, brief interlude in his life. Surely her swift departure was necessary. Surely it was for the best.

Hope picked up her book once more, determined to appear absorbed as, out in the hallway, the rhythm of approaching footsteps rang out. Determined too upon her chosen course and determined above all not to dwell on how the prospect of leaving had made her heart ache even more.

Chapter Twelve

'Is everything all right? Where are the Gordons?'

Hope limped into the dining room, feeling the absence of her walking cane with every tentative step. She'd left it upstairs after dressing for dinner, determined to demonstrate that she was fit enough to walk without it and prove she was well enough to leave Hayton Hall. She had not managed to speak to Samuel about that yet; indeed, she'd barely spoken to him since he'd returned from his ride with Mr Gordon yesterday. He'd seemed unusually subdued last night at dinner and had retired early, and today he'd spent much of his time locked away in his library, ostensibly dealing with estate matters. No doubt he was—as a landowner and a gentleman he would have business which required his attention and could not be expected to entertain guests all the time.

The Gordons, however, had not seemed quite so understanding and, after enduring quite enough of Mr Gordon's fidgeting and Miss Gordon's sullen temperament, Hope had excused herself and spent the remainder of the afternoon resting in her bedchamber. Now she'd returned downstairs at the appointed dining hour to find the house quiet, the table bare, and Samuel hovering beside it, leaning on the back of a chair.

'I thought we could take supper in the library this evening,' he said, offering her a small smile. 'I don't know about you, but I've rather wearied of formal dining of late. Too many courses, too much fuss.'

Hope gave a brisk nod. 'As you wish. Will Mr Gordon and his sister be joining us?'

'Afraid not,' Samuel replied, shaking his head. 'They've decided to go to the theatre. Apparently, it's the very last night for *As You Like It* in Lowhaven and Charles cannot countenance missing it. Miss Gordon seemed less enthused, but has done her duty and accompanied her brother,' he added with a wry smile.

'Did you not wish to go with them?' Hope asked.

'My duty is to remain here, with you,' he replied firmly, giving her a look which reminded her at once of his words in his carriage that day, when he'd spoken of his promise to protect her. When he'd acknowledged the look of fear he'd seen in her eyes.

'There will be other opportunities to go to the theatre,' he continued. 'Now, aren't you going to ask me why we're taking supper in the library and not the parlour?'

The mischievous grin he gave her piqued her interest, and she pushed all thoughts of invented nefarious uncles and all too real and threatening fathers to one side.

'All right,' she replied, raising a smile to match his. 'Why?'

'I thought, since we cannot go to the theatre, we would bring the theatre to us.'

Hope frowned. 'What do you mean by that?'

Samuel chuckled as he walked towards her, taking her by the hand. 'You'll see. Come on.'

The feeling of his gentle fingers holding hers made her thoughts scatter, and willingly she allowed him to lead her out of the dining room and down the hallway to the library. Once inside, she saw that a table had been laid with bread, cold meats and a healthy decanter of red wine set between two glasses. Nearby she spied another, smaller occasional table, bearing several leather-bound books. She turned to Samuel then, raising an expectant eyebrow as she awaited an explanation.

'I know it is a little unorthodox,' he said, relinquishing her hand. 'I can assure you, I don't make a habit of dining in the library, but it seemed like the most suitable place.'

'The most suitable place for what?' she pressed him.

'To read some Shakespeare. And to show you something rather precious, which I think you will appreciate, given your enthusiasm for the theatre.'

Samuel beckoned her over to the smaller table, where carefully he lifted up a very thick and apparently very old brown book. 'Shakespeare's Comedies, Histories and Tragedies,' he said as he passed it to her. 'A collection of his plays, printed in 1623.'

Hope gasped, gently opening the book to see the title page, where the Bard's famous image gazed back at her. 'It's almost two hundred years old,' she marvelled.

Samuel nodded. 'It's also very rare. I believe only seven hundred or so copies were ever printed. And we are fortunate enough to have one of them here, at Hayton.'

'Fortunate indeed,' she mused, still staring in disbelief at the treasure she held in her hands. 'I have never seen anything like it. The only scripts I have seen have been...'

Hope pressed her lips together, remembering herself just in time. Her heart raced at the knowledge of what she had almost unwittingly revealed. She'd felt herself—her real self—bubbling to the surface once more. This was becoming too difficult—to hide in plain sight, to suppress her true identity beneath polite speech, fine clothes and a character with the vaguest of histories. To keep lying to Samuel, to repay his unfailing kindness and generosity with deceit. This, she reminded herself, was exactly why she needed to leave. Perhaps she ought to speak to him about that this evening, if she could find the right moment, the right words…

'Oh, I am sure you must have one or two priceless heirlooms tucked away in a dusty family library somewhere,' Samuel remarked, apparently oblivious to her inner turmoil. 'Perhaps in that ancestral home which you've vowed never to set foot in again,' he added pointedly.

Despite herself, Hope found her mind drifting the several miles across the countryside to Lillybeck, to that damp stone cottage tucked on the hillside. She doubted her father kept so much as a broadside in that barren, cold place.

'Perhaps,' she replied, regretting now that piece of information which Miss Gordon had managed to draw from her at their first meeting. At the time she'd thought it an evasive enough answer; now she suspected Samuel had caught the scent of truth emanating from it. 'Here,' she continued, passing his book back to him and hoping to swiftly change the subject. 'You'd better take this and put it somewhere safe.'

Samuel accepted the book, placing it back on the table as he shook his head in disbelief. 'You are really not going to tell me anything, are you, Hope? About your past, about your life before you stumbled into that woodland that day.'

Unable to bear his consternation, she dropped her gaze, momentarily lost for words. Deep down, she'd known to expect this conversation, ever since that carriage ride. This was why she'd avoided being alone with him, why she'd stuck closely by Miss Gordon's prickly side. But sensing what Samuel wanted to say and knowing how to answer him were two different matters. What could she say that would not cause yet more harm? Lies were damaging, but the truth was damning.

Instead, she lifted her eyes to meet his, trying not to dwell upon how their grey-blue depths seemed to swirl with concern, with sadness. 'I thought we'd come to the library to read Shakespeare, not to talk about me,' she replied obstinately, folding her hands in front of her to stop them from trembling. She glanced over at the larger table, still laden with food. 'Perhaps first we should have some of that bread and meat, before it spoils.'

Samuel walked over to the table, lifting the decanter and pouring two glasses of wine. The only thing which was being spoiled, he thought to himself, was their evening together, and the fault for that was entirely his. He'd set out to make the most of their unexpected time alone, to indulge in something which he believed would interest her, to recapture some of the easy companionship they'd enjoyed before Charles and his sister had arrived. And, most importantly, to grasp the right moment to tell her the truth about himself, to offer his heartfelt apology and hope that she would accept it. To reassure her that whilst she might not have the protection of a baronet, she would always have the protection of Samuel Liddell.

Instead, he'd fallen right back into the same trap and had overstepped the mark with his questions, just as he had that afternoon in the carriage. Her life really was none of his business, he reminded himself, especially when he was still not being honest about his own. The problem was, not knowing the details of her story made his mind run wild, imagining the worst possible scenarios until his need to protect her felt quite overwhelming. He'd never been gripped by feelings like this before—burning, unpredictable emotions which made him feel quite out of kilter.

'Forgive me,' he said, handing her a glass of wine and forcing a smile. 'You are right, of course. We should read some Shakespeare, as I originally proposed. Although not from the 1623 book—I don't think future generations of Liddells would forgive me for that. There is a newer, smaller volume of his works on the table.'

He watched as Hope walked back towards the books he'd fetched out earlier.

'Do you have a particular play in mind?' she asked. 'A favourite, perhaps?'

He shook his head. 'To be honest, I like them all. Why don't we let fate decide? Open the book and see which play finds us.'

Hope did as he suggested, putting her wine glass down before picking up the book and opening it at random. He watched as those emerald eyes briefly scanned the page. 'Oh, goodness,' she said with a wry chuckle. *'Romeo and Juliet.'*

Fate, Samuel thought, was clearly laughing at them. Or at least it was laughing at him, given some of the thoughts about Miss Hope Swynford which his errant mind had entertained of late.

'Goodness indeed,' he replied, his throat growing unfathomably dry. 'The star-crossed lovers in fair Verona—which he never visited, or so I believe.'

'"Two houses, both alike in dignity, in fair Verona where we lay our scene,"' Hope recited, apparently from memory, since she was not reading from the book. *'"From ancient*

grudge break to new mutiny, where civil blood makes civil hands unclean."'

Samuel grinned at her. 'Very well remembered. A favourite of yours, perhaps?'

She shrugged, closing the book before retrieving her wine glass and taking a considered sip. 'Not particularly—I have watched it a few times is all. If anything, I find it very disheartening.'

'You find a play about love disheartening?'

'Is it really about love?' she countered. 'Surely it's about the thwarting of love—first by the hatred between two families, and then by death. If anything, Shakespeare is telling us that sometimes love is impossible. Circumstances make it so. Fate makes it so. No matter how much two people want to be together, sometimes there are just too many obstacles. There is too much to keep them apart.'

'All right,' Samuel conceded, relishing the opportunity to debate. 'Although you must surely admit that there is beauty in the play too. The love between Romeo and Juliet is genuine, pure and heartfelt, is it not?'

'Of course it is, but therein lies the tragedy because ultimately it is not enough. It does not even serve to end their families' feuding—it takes them both dying to do that. As I said, disheartening.'

Samuel nodded. Her argument was persuasive and her knowledge impressive. She was more than a theatre enthusiast, he decided. It was very apparent that she was acquainted with at least some of Shakespeare's work inside and out.

'You would have enjoyed some of the dinner parties I attended on the Continent,' he remarked. 'Packed with scholars and intellectuals, brimming with opinions on the best and worst that English literature has to offer.'

He watched as her brow furrowed. 'You're teasing me.'

'Not at all—I am in earnest. Some of the best evenings I had while travelling were spent in the company of such people. Poets, writers, artists, philosophers, or simply avid readers. I think you would have liked talking to them too, and I think a great many of them would have liked talking to you.' He reached out, taking her hand in his. 'This evening with you has reminded me of some very happy times, Hope, and I must thank you for that.'

She nodded obligingly, her expression softening. 'That is kind of you to say,' she replied. 'Alas, I am unlikely to ever find myself moving in such circles, never mind on the Continent.'

'You could travel, Hope, it is not impossible. Now that you are free of your uncle, and as long as you can access the means…'

'Believe me, it is impossible,' she interrupted, refusing to meet his eye. 'My life has been very different to yours, Samuel. You do not understand. You cannot understand.'

'Then explain it to me.' Instinctively, he stepped towards her, still clutching her hand with his. Her fingers felt so small and delicate beneath his touch. 'You can tell me about it, Hope,' he said quietly. 'You can trust me, please believe that.'

'I cannot…' She was shaking her head vehemently now. 'I need to leave. I need to…'

'What do you mean, you need to leave?'

She did not answer, and the fear he saw swirling in her eyes was too much to bear. Before he could think about what he was doing, Samuel stepped forward, pulling her towards him and enveloping her in his arms. Instinct overcame thought as he held her and, to his surprise, she allowed him, her head coming to rest against his chest as her arms looped tentatively around him. The feeling of her warm hands against his back made his blood heat and, before he could stop them, his own hands had reached for the near-black curls of her hair, his fingers running unbidden through them, teasing them from their pins, then diving under them to find the soft skin at the nape of her neck...

Against him she sighed, before looking up at him, her green gaze no longer filled with anguish but something else, something he could not name.

'What is it, Hope?' he whispered. 'Please, tell me.'

She shook her head again but did not break eye contact, nor did she recoil from his embrace. Every sinew of his body was alive with awareness of her petite, alluring form pressed against him, rendering rational, gentlemanly thought impossible. Instinct continued to rule him as he leaned down, his lips gently touching hers. His heart sang as she welcomed his kiss—indeed, she kissed him back hungrily, pulling herself ever closer to him, sending shivers down his spine as she ran her fingers over his broad shoulders then through his hair. She kissed like she spoke about Shakespeare—passionately and with conviction. With her encouragement his own passion grew, sending his lips on a quest to find the soft flesh of her ear, then her neck, then the swell of her breasts which hinted at the neckline of her gown...

Good God, what was he doing? He was meant to be confessing to her, not kissing her!

'I am so sorry,' he blurted, pulling away. 'Forgive me.' He swallowed hard, shaking his head at himself in disbelief. 'I should not have done that. Not when there is so much

I need to say. Hope, I must tell you that I am not who you think I am. I am not...'

His words died in his mouth as the door to Hayton's library burst open. He heard Hope gasp as, like him, her eyes flew to see who had intruded so unexpectedly. He was stunned to see Smithson standing in the doorway, looking uncommonly rumpled, a serious expression etched on his heavily lined face.

'I am sorry to disturb you, sir,' the butler began, sounding a little breathless. Samuel watched as the wily old man's gaze flitted between the two of them, no doubt noting Hope's mussed hair and burning cheeks. 'Really—very sorry.'

'Well, what is it, man?' he demanded, his customarily gentle tongue abandoned. Now really was not the time. Not when he'd just kissed Hope. Not when Hope had just said she was going to leave.

Not when he'd been on the cusp of telling her the truth.

'It's Miss Gordon, sir,' Smithson continued, still regarding them both carefully. 'I'm afraid Mr and Miss Gordon have had to return from the theatre early. Miss Gordon has been taken ill.'

At that moment Samuel could have groaned aloud with frustration. The news about Miss Gordon's health was concerning, but the thought of leaving the unspoken truth hanging between himself and Hope was unbearable. However, there was nothing he could do. Duty called—his duty as Charles's friend, and his duty as Hayton's caretaker master.

'I'm sorry,' he said, turning back to Hope. 'I promise that we will talk soon.'

'Of course,' she agreed, regarding him just long enough for him to see the concern and confusion swirling in her green gaze. Then she turned away from him, striding purposefully towards the door. 'I think we should go and assist Miss Gordon, shouldn't we?'

Chapter Thirteen

'What on earth has happened, Charles?'

Samuel followed Smithson into the small parlour, where the broad frame of his friend loomed large, wringing his hands and pacing tirelessly. His sister, meanwhile, had been laid out on the sofa, her eyes closed as Maddie sat beside her, dabbing her forehead with a cool cloth. Hope, who'd followed behind him, immediately joined Maddie at Miss Gordon's side, tucking the loose tendrils of her dark hair behind her ears as she bent down to examine the patient. Realising he was staring at her, Samuel tore his gaze away and focused again on Charles, trying to force himself to focus on the matter at hand. Trying not to dwell on the memory of her lips pressed against his, of the feeling of her in his arms. Of how those heady, intoxicating moments had brought his guilt rushing to the fore. He'd been so close to telling her, so close to explaining everything…

'The physician has been sent for, sir,' Smithson informed him, answering when it was clear, after a long moment, that Charles would not.

Samuel nodded. 'Thank you, Smithson. Charles,' he said gently, trying again. 'Do you know what happened? Do you know what ails her?'

Charles shook his head, his face growing paler by the moment. 'She was fine until after the interval,' he replied. 'Then she began to behave in the most odd manner, calling out the strangest things, then laughing so much that she did not seem able to stop. People were staring at her like she was mad.' His friend paused, clearly collecting himself. 'I decided we ought to leave and got her back into the carriage. She fell asleep on the ride home and I have not been able to rouse her since. I do not know what the matter is with her, Sammy.'

Samuel glanced down at Miss Gordon. 'Is she feverish?' he asked Maddie.

'No, sir,' the maid answered.

'And she was absolutely fine all day, before you went out?' he asked Charles.

His friend nodded. 'She was her usual self, Sammy, warts and all.'

Samuel shook his head. 'Then I am at a loss. We will have to hope that the physician can offer further insight.'

'If he comes tonight,' Charles replied fretfully, glancing towards the window, which had been shuttered against the darkness outside. 'It is rather late, after all. What can we do in the meantime?'

'Keep her comfortable,' Samuel replied, staring glumly at Miss Gordon, who remained unresponsive. 'And keep watch over her, in case there is any change in her condition.'

His eyes shifted once again from the patient to Hope, who seemed to be observing Miss Gordon closely. He watched as she leaned forward, as though listening for something. Then, to his surprise, she reached over, lifting Miss Gordon's eyelids to open her eyes one at a time, frowning at whatever it was she saw.

'What is it, Miss Swynford?' Samuel asked, stepping towards her.

Gingerly, Hope stood up, turning to face him. Her expression, he noted, remained grave. 'I believe I might know what is wrong with Miss Gordon,' she replied, flashing Charles a wary look. 'If I may speak plainly, Sir Samuel.'

Samuel winced at her use of that blasted title. How he wished he could banish it for good! How he wished he could tell her the truth, here and now. But of course he could not—not in front of Charles and his servants. Not when Miss Gordon was plainly so unwell...

He nodded briskly, pushing his swirling thoughts aside. 'Of course. You may always speak plainly to me, Hope,' he replied, venturing now to use her first name in company and hoping she would do the same. In truth, right now, he was not sure how many more 'Sir Samuels' he could stomach.

'I believe Miss Gordon is suffering the effects of having taken laudanum,' Hope replied quietly. Those emerald eyes of hers met his again for the briefest moment before she turned to address Charles. 'Mr Gordon, I wonder if you can confirm whether your sister has been taking this, perhaps on the advice of your family's physician?'

Something about Hope's tone told Samuel that she suspected Charles was well aware of what was going on.

'No, well, indeed, she may have taken a tincture once or twice...' Charles prevaricated.

'This is important, Charles,' Samuel urged him. 'We cannot help your sister if we do not know what is amiss.'

Charles's eyes seemed to widen like saucers. 'For headaches,' he said after a moment. 'Yes—I remember now. She took laudanum on our doctor's orders, for headaches.'

'Took?' Hope repeated. 'Forgive me, sir, but it seems to

me that your sister continues to take laudanum, presumably for the headaches which, as I'm sure you've also observed, she continues to suffer.' Samuel watched as carefully Hope sat down at Miss Gordon's side once more. 'Her pupils are like pin pricks,' she explained, briefly opening one of the lady's eyes again. 'Her breathing is shallow. And the behaviour you described at the theatre sounds very much like the sort of delirium which laudanum is known to induce. In short, sir, if you check your sister's reticule I believe you will find a bottle of what has poisoned her within it.'

'Poison?' Charles said, aghast.

'Yes—poison,' Hope replied emphatically. 'Laudanum relieves suffering but if she has taken too much then... surely, sir, I don't have to explain to you how dangerous that may be.'

Samuel's mouth fell open at the bluntness of her warning. 'What can be done for her, Hope?' he asked.

'She must be watched over, as you suggested,' Hope replied. 'In my experience, we need to keep her propped up, as she is right now on the sofa. It is better for her breathing and better if...well, if she expels anything. And we should try to rouse her, if we can. Beyond that, we can only await the physician's advice.'

Samuel nodded dumbly, her words still sinking in. Knowing, confident words spoken, as she'd just admitted, from experience. Despite the severity of the situation, Samuel found himself wondering about the nature of those experiences, about what Hope might have faced in her past which had taught her how to handle something as dire and life-threatening as this. He wondered too if it was this very sort of experience that caused Hope to guard the story of her past so closely.

Now, however, was not the time to ask her questions such as that. Giving himself a mental shake, Samuel sprang once again into action.

'You heard Hope,' he said, addressing the room. 'Let us pray that the physician's journey here is swift and without delay. In the meantime, Miss Gordon shall not be left alone for a moment.'

Groggily, Hope opened her eyes, grimacing at the aching she felt in her neck and limbs after being curled up on a chair for goodness knew how long. She looked towards the window, relieved to see daylight hinting at the edges of the shutters, which were still closed to the world outside. It had been an endless night. The physician, it had transpired, had not been at home, having been summoned to an emergency elsewhere, leaving Hope and the others to care for Miss Gordon alone and without guidance.

Having checked his sister's reticule and found a small bottle of laudanum tucked within it, Mr Gordon had at last resigned himself to Hope's diagnosis and placed himself at Miss Gordon's side, insisting that he would watch over her first. They had each taken a turn while the others slept, and now, as she pulled herself upright, she saw Samuel was still at his post, his gaze intent upon the patient. For a moment she simply looked at him, taking in every detail from his dishevelled sand-coloured hair to his rumpled white shirt, long bereft of either a coat or cravat.

Memories of those heated moments in the library came rushing to the fore, her fingers tingling with awareness as though her skin itself could recall the feeling of the fine fabric of his clothes, of the outline of the muscles which hinted at their presence beneath them, of the warm softness of his hair. She felt her face grow hot as her mind lingered on how she had responded to his embrace, how she had kissed him back with reckless abandon. It had been an entirely new, entirely terrifying and entirely thrilling experience—to be held like that, to be touched like that. To be kissed like that.

The abruptness with which he'd ended the embrace had astonished her, but not as much as the tortured, guilt-ridden look on his face as he'd begun to speak of things he ought to say, of not being what she thought he was.

What on earth had he meant by that? That question, and all its possible answers, had circled around her mind throughout the long night. She'd replayed his words over and over, picking through them, searching for clues. He'd told her that he shouldn't have kissed her—why was that? Was he, in fact, a married man? Or was he betrothed, with a fiancée tucked away somewhere? Her face heated again as she recalled the enthusiasm she'd shown for his advances— an enthusiasm which was as mortifying as it was curious, especially if the kiss, for him, had been a grave transgression. An act of infidelity, and something to be regretted.

Of course, she reminded herself, if he had kissed her under false pretences, then he wasn't the only one. Last night the master of Hayton Hall had believed himself to be kissing a runaway heiress, not the penniless daughter of an outlaw.

Samuel had promised that they would talk soon, and certainly they both had much to say. Before that kiss had sent her thoughts and her wits scattering, she'd blurted out her intention to leave—an intention which now seemed more vital than ever. After last night, it was abundantly clear that her feelings for the master of Hayton Hall had grown beyond even her wildest imaginings, and it seemed from his actions that there was some attraction on his part too. An attraction, she reminded herself, which he felt towards Hope Swynford and not Hope Sloane. Extricating herself from this situation, and removing herself and her deceit from his life, was now essential. In that respect, whatever he'd been on the cusp of confessing to her last night surely could not matter.

But, God help her, she ached to know what it was…

'Good morning.'

Hope blinked, her whirring thoughts interrupted as she realised Samuel was looking at her.

'Did you sleep all right?' he asked, offering her a weary smile.

'Not too badly, considering.'

'In hindsight, it perhaps would have been best if you'd retired upstairs,' he mused. 'You are still recovering. It cannot have been good for your ankle, curling up like a cat in that chair.'

'I'm fine,' she assured him, resisting the urge to rub her throbbing foot. 'How is Miss Gordon?' She looked around. 'And where is Mr Gordon?'

'Charles is outside, smoking his pipe—as he does whenever he is vexed.' He glanced back at the patient. 'And Miss Gordon seems to be improving. Her breathing is steadier and she has stirred several times in the past hour. Maddie has just taken away the water and cloths as we agreed they're no longer needed.'

Hope smiled. 'You called her Maddie, not Madeleine,' she observed.

Samuel let out a small chuckle. 'I did. A perceptive and considerate lady once suggested to me that I ought to pay better attention to my servants' wishes, especially when they're in no position to challenge me.'

Hope inclined her head, acknowledging the compliment. 'Poor Maddie must get some rest too,' she reminded him. 'If she has been attending to Miss Gordon all night.'

Samuel nodded. 'I've told Smithson to give her the day off. I've also asked Smithson to arrange for some breakfast to be brought. I thought that if we can wake Miss Gordon, we may be able to get her to eat or drink something. And I do not know about you, but I am famished.'

Hope's stomach growled in agreement, and she remembered that they had never eaten the bread and meat which had been laid out in the library. Events, and passionate embraces, had intervened.

'Has there been any further word from the physician?' she asked, ignoring the heat which had crept into her cheeks once more.

'A message was left for him last night,' Samuel replied. 'I expect he will come today.'

'Good. Hopefully, he will confirm that Miss Gordon will recover well.'

'Hmm.' Samuel's gaze drifted back to the patient and gently he shook his head. 'It's a terrible business,' he said in a hushed voice. 'She could have died last night.'

'Laudanum is a terrible business,' Hope responded grimly.

'You sound as though you speak from experience.'

Those grey-blue eyes held hers once again. Hope could hear the tentative note in his voice, as though he had not been sure if he should broach the subject. But after last night, after seeing how she'd recognised what was wrong with Miss Gordon and taken charge of the situation, she knew he could hardly avoid talking to her about it. She knew too that she could not lie to him; she had offered too vivid a glimpse of the real Hope's life to do that. Only the truth, or at least a version of it, would do now.

'My mother,' she said at last, as evenly as she could manage. 'She began taking it for an ailment, to help with the pain. In doing so, she found that it could take away not just her physical pain but every other pain she felt too, and I think she rather liked the oblivion it offered her. But the rub with laudanum is that the more you take it, the more you need to take to achieve the desired effect. And the higher the dose, the greater the risk. My mother found this out to her great cost. She died a number of years ago, alone on her bed, an empty bottle of her beloved poison by her side.'

'I am so sorry, Hope. That must have been very hard to bear.'

Hope pressed her lips together, hoping Samuel could not sense how hard she was fighting to hold back her tears. 'I spent many nights watching over her, just as we had to do with Miss Gordon. And many days pleading with her to stop taking it. But that need she had to obliterate everything was just too strong.'

'Was there no one who could help? What about your father?'

'My father was the reason for much of her pain,' she replied bitterly, the words slipping out before she could prevent them. She should not have told him that. The last person she should be speaking to Samuel about was her father.

Samuel frowned, and she could see he was trying to make sense of her words. 'You do not have to tell me anything more, Hope,' he said in the end. 'Not if you do not wish to.'

But that was exactly the problem, Hope thought. She

did want to tell him. She wanted to break down and weep and tell him everything—about her mother, her father, her true self. About the childhood spent on that bleak hillside in Lillybeck, about her escape from a forced marriage and a life of crime. About her time on the stage, about those colourful years which had exposed her to so much culture and creativity on the one hand, and wickedness and debauchery on the other. About how her freedom had been snatched from her a second time, and how fate and fortune had conspired to send her into those woods, running for her life. Running, as it had turned out, into Sir Samuel Liddell's life, and into his warm, caring embrace.

An embrace, and a life, which she now had to detach herself from—to protect his feelings and to protect her own. Confiding in him was utterly out of the question; the hole she'd dug herself into with her deceit was now far too deep for that.

'I think that is quite enough misery for one morning,' she replied, forcing a smile as she rose carefully from her seat, ignoring how her sore limbs groaned in protest. 'If you will excuse me, I think I'd like to freshen up before breakfast.'

'Of course.'

Samuel too got to his feet. Hope could feel the heat of his gaze upon her as she walked towards the parlour door. She glanced down, feeling suddenly conscious of the state she was in. Her hair was hanging untidily about her shoulders and her clothes clung to her like a slickened second skin. She needed to wash, to breathe. To put some space between herself and Samuel and all that had been said and done. Perhaps then, she thought, her mind might not linger on the memory of his mouth pressed against hers quite so much.

'Hope? Can we speak again later? After last night…

well, there are some matters we need to discuss.' His voice sounded strained. 'Some things I need to explain.'

She glanced back at him, just briefly. 'Yes, of course.'

Hope hurried out of the room, reeling once more at the prospect of what it was he wanted to tell her, even while she told herself that whatever it was should make no difference to her now. The only thing that really mattered, she reminded herself, was leaving before any more harm could be done.

Chapter Fourteen

Samuel knew that he ought to have been exhausted, and yet he could not sleep. He'd spent the day dealing with the aftermath of the discovery of Miss Gordon's affliction, as Charles had rather euphemistically taken to calling it, in a daze brought on by his own lack of sleep. His turmoil over all that had occurred between him and Hope, and all that he had still to tell her, had conspired with his fatigue to leave him feeling thoroughly out of sorts. His stomach had churned almost incessantly, while every spare moment had been haunted by the confusion lingering in Hope's eyes as he'd uttered those most damning words.

'I must tell you that I am not who you think I am...'

More than once he'd given himself a stern talking-to, reminding himself that he had duties to perform, instructions to issue, and an unwell guest whose care required to be overseen. Miss Gordon had awoken properly by the middle of the morning, and the physician had turned up shortly afterwards. The good doctor had thankfully confirmed that Charles's sister was out of danger but had recommended bed rest and a lengthy abstinence from her tinctures.

Despite her weakened condition, Miss Gordon had protested at that. 'My headaches are severe,' she'd insisted. 'The laudanum is entirely necessary, to manage the pain.'

The physician, to his credit, was unmoved. Samuel had felt sure that Hope would have raised a knowing eyebrow at Miss Gordon's objection, had she been present. She'd gone to her bedchamber to rest after breakfast and he had not seen much of her since, although he knew from Charles's report that she'd spent some of the afternoon sitting with Miss Gordon while Samuel had been attending to estate matters at his desk in the library. She'd made only a brief appearance at dinnertime before retiring early, insisting she was still very tired. No doubt she was, but knowing that hadn't made Samuel crave her company any less. He still needed to speak to her, still needed to tell her the truth about himself. Kissing her had made his confession more vital than ever. And as for that kiss...

The memory of that had driven him to distraction more than once during his waking hours. Then there was her intention to leave and his promise to escort her to London—a promise he intended to keep, even if the thought of it made his heart sink and a lump grow in his throat. But he could hardly do anything else, could he? His duty was, and had always been, to protect her, and he would continue to do so, even after she learned he was merely Samuel Liddell. He would honour his promise, even if she despised him.

Even if he so desperately wanted her to stay.

In the ladies' absence, Samuel had spent the evening with Charles, although neither gentleman seemed to have much to offer by way of conversation. For his part, Charles seemed to be in shock over Miss Gordon's near-demise. He was clearly unwilling to discuss exactly what he knew about the extent of his sister's use of laudanum, although in his customarily clumsy way he did make some interesting admissions when referring to it.

'I suppose I ought to write to Mama and inform her of what has happened,' he'd said at one point. 'Although she will not be pleased. She'd put a lot of faith in Buxton's waters as a cure for my sister's many ills.'

'Many ills?' Samuel had repeated.

'I mean the headaches, of course,' Charles had blustered. 'My sister has for a long time been gravely afflicted. It affects her spirits too, as doubtless you have noticed.'

Samuel had nodded, deciding not to press his friend further but finding himself wondering if Miss Gordon, like Hope's mother, had pains beyond headaches which made the lure of oblivion too great to resist.

Once their brandy glasses were empty and their stilted conversation had all but evaporated, both gentlemen had retired. Since then, Samuel had tossed and turned in bed, unable to settle, and unable to quiet his thoughts. Everything he'd tried to push aside during the daylight hours had come racing to the fore, and now he found himself picking through the details relentlessly.

How delicate she'd felt in his arms, how warm her lips had been against his. How enthusiastically she'd kissed him back. How embracing her had felt so right, when in every sense it had been entirely wrong. Hope had sought sanctuary at Hayton, not seduction by its pretend baronet. How he could countenance kissing her when he was lying to her about the man he was… Well, he knew the answer to that. He couldn't. He could not countenance it at all.

Then there was the glimpse of Hope's past, which Miss Gordon's affliction had unexpectedly drawn from her. The thought of her losing her mother like that made his heart ache for her, even while he felt that now familiar protective urge burning within him at her veiled remark about her father and the pain he'd caused. Between her wicked uncle and the father she could not bring herself to discuss, it was clear that Hope had suffered at the hands of the men in her life. A fact which made Samuel's own deception of her even harder to swallow.

He had to tell her the truth, just as he'd begun to, in the library last night. He had to find a way to explain his actions, despite his fear that she would never be able to forgive him. That she would leave Hayton immediately and never look back.

Of course, leaving was exactly what she intended to do now, in any case! He pressed his fist into his pillow in frustration. It was clear that sleep would continue to elude him for some time yet, and his restlessness had left him hot and sweating beneath his sheets. Throwing off his bedcovers, he lit a candle, resolved to go downstairs and fetch some refreshment. Smithson could always be relied upon to keep the decanter of brandy in the library topped up for him; perhaps another small glass might see him on his way to slumber.

Stealthily, Samuel crept out of his room and along the wide, wood-panelled hallway. The house was silent, the servants having long since retired for the night. Just as well, Samuel thought, since he wore nothing but his drawers. For decency's sake he ought to have at least pulled a shirt on, but the cool air of the old house at night felt like a blessed relief against his bare skin.

Swiftly, he made his way into the library, closing the door so carefully that it barely made a sound. It was only once he was inside that he realised the room already had the dim illumination of a candle. Assuming that a maid had neglected to extinguish it before retiring, Samuel marched towards it furiously, muttering to himself about the risk of fire—in an ancient dwelling like Hayton Hall, filled with wood, the place would surely go up in flames in no time at all. It was only when he reached the table upon which it sat that he realised someone was there—someone who had curled up in one of the tall green wingback chairs which faced away from the door. Someone dressed in only a white linen shift and a shawl, with a book draped across her lap while she sat upright but fast asleep.

Hope.

Samuel swallowed hard, struggling to tear his eyes from the sight of her sleeping, her expression serene, her pink lips near-smiling, her dark hair loose and tumbling about her shoulders. Quietly, he stepped back, deciding to simply blow out the candle for safety's sake and leave her to rest. It was the proper and decent thing to do, especially given his own semi-naked state. Last night he'd all but seduced her in this very room; she did not need to spy him standing before her tonight, leaving little to the imagination in his undergarments.

Leaving was his plan, but fate—and Hayton's old floor—had other ideas. As he stepped away again, one of the wooden boards creaked loudly, betraying his presence, and waking Hope.

She jolted upright, blinking, then stared straight at him. 'Samuel?'

Sir Samuel Liddell in nothing but his drawers was a sight to behold. Even in her sleepy, confused state, Hope could not help but let her eyes rake over the details of him—from the broad shoulders and chest, sculpted by muscles usually buried beneath the finery of a gentleman's attire, to the trail of surprisingly dark hair which meandered down the lower part of his flat stomach and disappeared inside the white cotton.

Her fingers seemed to tingle with the urge to reach out and touch him; she fisted them, willing her mind, and her body, to behave. She had never seen a man looking like this before—at least, not a man she found so attractive. Like their kiss last night, this visceral, physical response was also a new experience for her. But that did not mean she should lose her head to the wanton and desirous thoughts currently racing through her mind.

'Samuel,' she repeated, almost choking on his name. Why was her mouth suddenly so dry? 'Is everything all right?'

He folded his arms across his chest in a manner which was endearingly self-conscious. 'You left a candle burning,' he said. 'I was just going to extinguish it, for safety's sake.'

His rebuke was gentle but clear enough.

'Forgive me,' she replied. 'I did not mean to doze off down here. I could not sleep so I decided to read awhile.' She forced a smile, trying to keep her eyes focused on his, and not the other, tempting parts of him, as she held up the book. 'You have a good selection of Mrs Radcliffe's novels. Have you read them?'

She watched as Samuel shook his head, those arms remaining stubbornly folded. 'Alas, no—gothic fiction is not really to my taste.' He continued to hover awkwardly for a moment, glancing down at himself. 'I should go. I only came down to fetch a brandy. I should not…well, should not be standing in front of you looking like this.'

Despite the fact that the way he looked was making her

heart continue to race, Hope found herself laughing. 'I've seen you now, Samuel, so I dare say the damage is done.'

'You may laugh, but what if Charles or Smithson walked in now and saw us together like this?'

Hope considered this for a moment, then carefully took off her shawl and passed it to him. 'Here,' she said. 'For your modesty. Now you can fetch your brandy.'

Samuel draped the shawl over his broad shoulders. In truth, its fine fabric offered little coverage, and Hope could still spy a great swathe of his bare chest and stomach beneath it. He looked ridiculous, and oddly more appealing than ever.

'Would you like one too?' he asked, holding up the decanter.

Hope nodded. Given her current state, a drop of something strong was perhaps not a bad idea. Although whether it was within brandy's capacity to dampen rampant desire, she had no idea.

'Have you finished reading Mr Hume then?' he asked as he poured two small glasses, handing one of them to her as he sat down in a chair opposite.

'No, but I was not in the mood for history tonight. Escaping into some fiction seemed much more appealing.'

'Too much on your mind?' he asked.

'Indeed,' she agreed, not daring to say more about the exact nature of the thoughts which troubled her. Thoughts about him, thoughts about leaving. Thoughts about all the lies she'd told.

Samuel held up his brandy glass. 'Same,' he replied. 'Hence the need for this.' He paused, taking a considered sip. 'Charles said you sat with Miss Gordon for a little while this afternoon. How was she?'

'In low spirits, if I'm honest. It's plain to see that she

fears the loss of her tinctures. I cannot say I blame her. Ceasing to take laudanum after the body has become accustomed to it can make you very unwell. My mother tried to give it up several times, but after days of fever and sickness she would always return to it.'

'Then we must keep a close eye on her, to ensure that does not happen. Tomorrow I will ask Smithson to ensure Maddie and one or two of the other maids take turns to remain with Miss Gordon throughout her recovery.'

Hope smiled. 'That is a good idea. I will assist them too.'

Samuel let out a long breath, clearly contemplating something. 'Charles seemed to suggest that Miss Gordon's headaches are responsible for her low spirits,' he said after a moment. 'However, I am unsure. He seems very evasive about the entire matter, which makes me suspicious that there's more to his sister's current woes than he's telling me. Has Miss Gordon said anything to you that might shed some light on what is going on?'

Hope shook her head. 'No, but, like you, I think whatever ails her could be due to more than headaches. Between her sombre countenance and cutting remarks, it is not difficult to see that she is deeply unhappy.'

'I suppose it is none of our business,' Samuel mused, before draining his glass. 'I dare say once she's well enough to travel, both Charles and his sister will be on their way. I spent an awkward evening with him earlier—it is abundantly clear this whole sorry episode has left him feeling very uncomfortable. And if I know anything about Charles, it's that his usual response to such feelings is to flee.'

Hope took a gulp of her brandy, steeling herself. 'Perhaps I should go then too,' she said, her heart pounding so hard that the sound of it seemed to echo in her ears. She did her best to ignore it, to remind herself that this was something she had to discuss with him. She had to make plans to leave, no matter how hard, how painful it seemed. 'I am well enough to travel now. Perhaps, if Mr and Miss Gordon would oblige me, I could travel as far as Lancashire with them, and make my own way from there.'

She watched with bated breath as Samuel's brows drew together in concern.

'I promised you that I would escort you to London, Hope.'

'But that was before the Gordons arrived and...' She faltered momentarily, her thoughts scattering as she saw the consternation growing on his handsome face. 'You have done so much for me, Samuel—truly, I am indebted to you. But I do not wish to cause you any more inconvenience, not when there is another possible solution.'

'But once you reach Blackburn, you will still be hundreds of miles from London, and you will be on your own,' he replied, shaking his head. 'Surely that is no solution at all.'

Samuel leaned forward, the shawl slipping from his shoulders and unveiling that magnificent physique once again. Hope swallowed hard, dragging her gaze back up to meet his.

'I do not wish to tell you what to do. Indeed, I am not your father, your brother, or...' He pressed his lips together momentarily. 'Or your husband. Therefore, as you once reminded me, you are not my concern. And yet I am concerned. I'm concerned about you going to London, about this uncle of yours, about you wandering straight back into danger. I'm concerned that there is so much more to your story than I know...'

'Well, that makes two of us,' Hope countered, giving him

a pointed look and trying to ignore how her heart lurched at the thought of how little he did know. How dreadful the truth was. 'Last night you told me that you are not who I believe you to be. What did you mean?'

Even in the dim candlelight his grim expression was unmistakable.

'What I meant was…' He faltered, his blue-grey eyes seeming to darken. For a long moment he pressed his lips together, steeling himself. 'What I meant to tell you was that I have lied to you. Hayton Hall is not my house. Its lands are not my lands. And I am not a baronet.'

In the night-time quiet of the library, Hope heard someone gasp. She presumed it was her own voice she'd heard, but the sound seemed somehow separate, somehow distant, as a maelstrom of sudden spiralling thoughts gripped her. Of all the possible explanations for his words last night, this was the very last one she could have imagined. To learn that he was not Hayton's baronet at all had shocked her and yet, as she sat there, her mouth agape as she regarded him, she realised that was only the beginning of her concerns.

A deathly cold chill crept up her spine as the full ramifications of his deceit flooded through her mind. If he was not a baronet, and if Hayton Hall was not his, then the protection she'd felt and the sanctuary she'd enjoyed was surely no such thing at all. Her father was a ruthless, dangerous man—if Samuel was not the prominent, important gentleman she'd believed him to be, then her father would think nothing of snatching her away from him and, worse still, perhaps even harming Samuel in the process. No matter who Samuel really was, she could not bear the thought that she'd unwittingly endangered him. She shivered, feeling suddenly exposed, as the illusion of her safe hiding place crumbled in the face of Samuel's lies. What if her father was drawing near? What if he'd already found her and was just waiting for the right moment to take her away?

'I am so sorry, Hope,' Samuel continued, clearly grappling with her stunned silence, with the look of horror she doubtless wore upon her face. 'Please understand that I only want to protect you, that I care about you. When I kissed you last night, I…'

'No,' she interrupted him, unable to bear her own thoughts or his words any longer. Unable to countenance hearing that he cared about her when her mere presence in this house might yet lead him into danger. 'That kiss was a mistake—a moment of madness.' She rose from her seat, hurrying now towards the door. 'I must leave Hayton as soon as possible. I must speak to Mr Gordon tomorrow.'

Hope hurried out of the library before Samuel could spy the tears which had begun to gather in her eyes. Tears of shock, tears of terror—tears which acknowledged that the safe haven she'd put so much faith in lay in ruins, and the protection she'd believed Samuel had given her had turned to dust.

Chapter Fifteen

'*A moment of madness.*'

Samuel replayed those words over and over in his mind as he sat at his desk, trying and hopelessly failing to concentrate on working through the pile of papers in front of him. He'd been like this for a couple of days now, attempting to bury himself in the business of running the Liddell estate, to avoid everything and everyone as much as he reasonably could. Mostly, all he'd managed to do, however, was revisit that night-time encounter with Hope again and again, picking over its details while he licked his wounds.

The sight of her sitting in the library, ashen-faced, eyes wide with horror as he confessed the truth seemed to have etched itself indelibly on his brain. He'd expected her to be shocked, angry even, but the fact that she'd appeared so appalled, so offended by the idea that he was neither a landowner nor a baronet, had devastated him. And then there were those words she'd uttered as she'd retreated from him, rejecting his affection for her so emphatically that he felt as though his heart had been trampled on all over again.

That kiss was a mistake—a moment of madness.

All he'd said was that he cared for her, and yet now that

she knew who he truly was she could not even countenance that.

Samuel groaned, burying his head in his hands. How could he have got it so wrong, how could he have so gravely misunderstood a woman's feelings for a second time? In the summer he'd wrongly interpreted Charlotte's flirtatiousness as genuine interest in him, and now he'd allowed himself to imagine that the way Hope had kissed him back might have been an expression of her affection for him. Perhaps it had—but it was an affection which had been easily extinguished as soon as she'd discovered that it held no promise of becoming Lady Liddell.

Of course, she would have known there was no prospect of that if he'd been truthful with her from the beginning. In that respect, Samuel knew he only had himself to blame for her evident disappointment in who and what he really was. He deserved every bit of her dismay, her ire, her swift retreat from his affections. He deserved to feel humiliated.

If only he had explained who he was straight away. If only he hadn't kissed her. If only holding her in his arms like that hadn't felt so perfect. If only he hadn't lost his head in that moment of madness in the library, then he wouldn't be on the cusp of losing his heart now too. Because he was, wasn't he? That was why Hope's rejection of him hurt so much.

And now she was going to leave him. She was going to step into Charles Gordon's carriage and never look back. It was the prospect of that, Samuel realised, which hurt most of all.

Despite being preoccupied by his sister's woes, Charles had not failed to notice that something was amiss between Samuel and Hope.

'Trouble in paradise, Sammy?' he'd asked after knocking on the library door yesterday and trying to coax Samuel out for some tea.

Miserably, Samuel had informed his friend that Hope now knew that he was not Hayton's baronet, and that she had not taken the news well. He had not been able to bring himself to talk about that kiss, or the way she'd rejected him—the wound that had inflicted was still too raw to be confided to anyone. But he had told Charles that Hope now intended to leave, and that she wished to enlist his help to do so— if she hadn't already.

'She'd talked of leaving before now, and no doubt learning the truth about me has made her more desperate to do so,' he'd finished with a heavy sigh. 'I've made a terrible mess of this, Charles. I have only myself to blame.'

His friend had sat down at the other side of his desk, an uncharacteristically serious expression on his face. 'Miss Swynford hasn't said anything to me about leaving,' he replied. 'Perhaps she's had a change of heart?'

'Somehow, I doubt that.'

'Well, even if she hasn't, do you not think you should talk to her about it, rather than skulking around in here? I'm not blind, Sammy. I've seen the way you look at her. You cannot possibly want her to leave. Why don't you just tell her how you feel?'

Samuel had winced at the thought of it. He'd tried to speak to her about his feelings once, he'd told her that he cared for her, and look where that had got him.

'So, I am correct then?' Charles had continued, taking his friend's silence as acquiescence. 'You are smitten with the chit?'

'I care very much about her,' Samuel had begun, his

voice sounding odd and strangled, even to himself. 'I want to protect her. I want to help...'

'Then I would suggest that you talk to her,' Charles had concluded as he rose from his seat. 'You've told her the truth about yourself, Sammy, but perhaps it's time for a bit more honesty. All cards on the table, so to speak.'

Charles's words rattled around Samuel's head as he tried once again to apply himself to his work. In the end he pushed his papers aside, frustrated. Samuel was more accustomed to being on the receiving end of Charles's teasing than he was to being the recipient of his advice. But for all that he was boisterous and more than a little ungovernable at times, his friend's heart was usually in the right place. Perhaps, Samuel considered, his advice was worth heeding. Perhaps he should try to talk to Hope, to explain himself properly. Certainly, it would be better than sitting at his desk feeling sorry for himself.

Surely it couldn't do any more harm. Could it?

Resolved to act rather than dwell any further on it, Samuel leapt out of his seat and hurried out of the room in search of Hope. He strode along the hallway, contemplating where she might be. Often she spent the afternoons sitting with Miss Gordon; if that were the case, he could hardly go bursting in. Perhaps he ought to find Maddie first, and request that she ask Hope to join him in the small parlour...

The sound of soft laughter coming from that very room reached his ears just as he placed his first footstep upon the stairs. Followed by two voices—a woman's and a man's—deep in conversation. Furrowing his brow, Samuel drew closer to the door, then turned the doorknob and walked in.

Hope's wide-eyed expression was what struck him first, as though his sudden intrusion had alarmed her. He watched as her lips parted in surprise, her teacup suspended in mid-air. Across from her sat Charles, that usual broad smile of his illuminating his face as he rose from the comfort of the sofa.

'Ah! Finally dragged yourself away from all that work, have you, Sammy?' Charles greeted him. 'Come and join us for some tea.'

Despite his friend's beckoning, Samuel found that he could not move. Instead, he seemed frozen to the spot, his gaze flitting between the pair of them, taking in the cosy scene. The teapot on the table, the small plate of neatly arranged slices of cake at its side. The way their conversation, and Hope's laughter, had ceased the moment he'd walked in...

'Sammy?' Charles prompted, frowning now.

But still Samuel could not answer. He could only look at the scene before him and think how it reminded him of the events of the summer, when another woman had decided he was not good enough for her and had sought out his older, titled brother instead. Charles might not be titled, but he was the heir to a tradesman's fortune—a better and wealthier prospect, to be sure. As he met Hope's eyes once more, holding her astonished gaze, his blood heated with an intolerable jealousy as it dawned on him that she knew this. That, having learned the truth of who Samuel was, she'd found him lacking and had set her sights far higher.

Just like Charlotte had.

'I think that I will go and get some air.'

Hope watched, aghast, as Mr Gordon made his excuses and hurried out of the parlour. Little wonder, she thought. The tension in the room was so thick that she doubted a knife could cut through it. Near to the door stood Samuel, his expression severe, his usually merry blue-grey eyes uncharacteristically stormy. Something was amiss, but she was at a loss to understand exactly what.

Since that last meeting with Samuel in the library late at night, and since learning who he really was, she'd managed largely to avoid him. She'd spent her time grappling with the turmoil his deception had caused, placing it with that gnawing guilt of knowing that she continued to deceive him. She could not possibly have done anything to offend him. Indeed, if anyone ought to be angry right now, it was her, wasn't it?

'Well, are you going to sit down and join me?' she asked, gesturing towards the chair which Charles had recently vacated.

'I wasn't aware you and Charles took tea together in the afternoons,' he said, ignoring her question.

She frowned. 'We don't usually. However, I wanted to speak to him about travelling with him and Miss Gordon to Blackburn. I believe I told you I would do so, the last time we spoke properly.'

He seemed to bristle at her reference to that ill-fated conversation. 'I see,' he replied, giving her a brittle nod. 'And what did Charles say?'

'He assured me that once they'd made firm plans for their departure, I would be included in them,' she replied.

In truth, Mr Gordon had been a good deal more noncommittal than that, professing a lack of certainty over when his sister would be fit to travel. Certainly, he would not wish to name a date, or so he'd told her. Indeed, he'd confided to her that he'd made the grave mistake of mentioning their return to Shawdale to Miss Gordon and she'd reacted terribly. He would have to tread carefully from now on, he'd said, which meant that Hope would simply have to wait. He'd changed the subject then, trying his best to amuse her, to occupy her with lighter topics of conversation. In response she'd smiled and feigned laughter in all the right places, whilst quietly wondering what on earth she was going to do. The longer she remained at Hayton Hall, the longer she risked bringing danger to its door. Not that she even knew who that door, and this house, actually belonged to...

'You both certainly looked very at ease in each other's company,' Samuel observed, snapping her out of her thoughts. 'Given that you were merely discussing travel plans.'

Hope felt the heat of indignation rise in her chest at his insinuation. 'What are you suggesting, Samuel?' she asked, getting to her feet and marching towards him as she challenged him to spell it out.

'I'm suggesting that the two of you seem to be getting along very well. Perhaps that is why you are so keen to travel to Blackburn with him and his sister...'

'Oh, for heaven's sake!' Hope threw up her hands in despair. She stood merely a foot away from him now, her hands planted on her hips as she glared up at him. 'That is completely ridiculous. I've no romantic interest in your friend, Samuel. None whatsoever! I must leave Hayton because my injuries have healed and it is time to do so.'

And because he'd lied to her, she reminded herself quietly. Because she could no longer trust that he was able to protect her, or indeed himself, from the malevolent men who sought her. And because she continued to lie to him too.

Samuel stared at her, unmoved. 'Charles has much to recommend him,' he began again. 'He is extraordinarily wealthy, for a start, although he has no title, which I dare say is the paramount consideration...'

'Not to me!' Hope prodded an angry finger against his chest. Why was he being so insufferable? Where on earth had all this talk of her and Mr Gordon come from?

Touching him, it transpired, was to be her downfall. Almost as soon as she had tapped that finger against the fine fabric of his shirt, her hand seemed to develop a will of its own, her fingers splaying out across his chest, the gesture dissolving from one of fury into one of tenderness. She felt her breath catch in her throat as beneath her hand she sensed his heart beating faster. She looked up at him, her eyes locking with his as he raised his hand, capturing her chin beneath his delicate touch as their lips drew closer.

The kiss which followed was as explosive as it was brief. Hope wasn't sure who deepened it first, such was the speed with which instinct and desire overcame them both. She pressed herself against him, her hands roaming and revelling in the promise of that masculine, athletic physique, hinted at beneath his fine clothes. For his part, Samuel seemed to have absolutely lost control too, his lips firm and hungry against hers, his hands similarly seeking out the curve of her breasts, her waist, her bottom. Then, somewhere within the recesses of her mind, a voice emerged, the one reminding her of his deceit, and of her own. Of the danger of falling for a man she could not have, a man who would be utterly horrified to know who and what she really was. A man she had to leave behind.

'Enough,' she breathed, stepping away from him, breaking the spell.

She hurried out of the parlour, reeling at what had just occurred. One moment they'd been arguing, the next they'd been kissing—how had that happened? How could she lurch from being in the grip of guilt and anger one moment to melting into his arms the next? She made her way up the stairs as quickly as she could, frantically straightening her hair and her gown as she determined to put a safe distance between her and Samuel.

Perhaps she would go and sit with Miss Gordon for a while. She'd passed many an hour at her bedside of late, relieving either Maddie or one of the other maids of their duties for a while, and finding a sort of refuge in the woman's prolonged silences as she either slept or stared vacantly towards the window. Occasionally, Miss Gordon would reach over and tentatively pat her hand, or offer her an appreciative nod of acknowledgement. It was plain to see that the lady's low spirits persisted, although she had said nothing to Hope about the reasons for her continued malaise. For all her suspicions that at the root of the lady's ills lay something more than headaches, Hope had not attempted to press the matter. After all, she knew as well as anyone what it was like to have things about herself that she was unwilling or unable to discuss. She had a veritable list of them, growing day by day.

Topping that list was her hopeless attraction to a man who had lied to her about who he was. A man who'd just as good as accused her of pursuing his friend! A man who did not even know her real name.

Hope drew a deep breath, composing herself as she reached Miss Gordon's door and knocked gently. It would do no good to torture herself with such thoughts yet again.

'Maddie?' Hope called softly through the door, frowning that as yet the maid had not come to answer her knock. Usually, Maddie took her turn to care for Miss Gordon in the afternoon, and was always a committed presence at the lady's bedside, just as she had been while Hope had convalesced.

Hope listened for several moments, surprised that she could hear no sound coming from within. Maddie must have been called away, but what of Miss Gordon—was she sleeping? Or had she taken ill once more? Hope's mind returned to her conversation with Mr Gordon, to his words about his sister's reaction to the prospect of returning home. What if she'd had one of her little bottles hidden away and had sought oblivion from it the moment her brother's back was turned?

Gripped by a wave of panic, Hope pushed open Miss Gordon's door and rushed inside. Her eyes darted frantically about, her heart thudding ever harder as she spied the room's damning details one by one: the empty, unmade bed; the pile of clothes abandoned on the floor; the large chest, all of its drawers wide open, as though someone had been looking for something in a hurry.

Hope heard herself gasp.

As though someone had left in a hurry.

But how? When? And where had she gone?

Hope rushed out of the door, her recently healed ankle throbbing in protest as she began to run along the landing and back towards the stairs. 'Samuel! Mr Gordon!' she cried as loud as she could. 'I need your help. I think Miss Gordon is missing!'

Chapter Sixteen

Samuel stared out of the window of his carriage, watching as the wind swirled the fallen leaves into a frenzy of red, yellow and brown at the side of the road. At least the rain had ceased for now, making the search for Miss Gordon easier. A short interview with a very tearful Maddie had established that the maid had left her charge to attend to some clothing upon which Miss Gordon had spilled her soup, giving the lady ample time to make her escape.

'I am so sorry, sir,' the maid had wept. 'I should have returned right away, but Miss Gordon was very concerned about the stain. She said it was her favourite shawl and that it was so fine, no lye could be used upon it. She insisted that I supervise the laundry maid myself while she cleaned it.'

Samuel had tried to comfort poor Maddie, reassuring her that she was only doing what the lady had asked. It was clear that the prolonged dismissal of Maddie by Miss Gordon had been deliberate, to allow her to get away unseen. It was clear too that she had not been missing for very long, and therefore could not have gone very far. Samuel had proposed searching for her in Hayton village, since it was only a short distance away and if she'd followed the road she'd have likely ended up there. Since the quickest way to search was on horseback, he'd informed Charles that he would ask his groom to ready two of his fastest beasts.

Charles, however, had hesitated, his gaze shifting back and forth between Samuel and Hope. 'I think we need Miss Swynford to come with us,' he'd said. 'My sister seems to like you, Miss Swynford. If—when—we find her, we stand a better chance of her returning with us if Miss Swynford is there to speak with her. And besides, we must take a carriage in any case. We can hardly throw dear Henrietta across the back of one of our horses, can we?'

Samuel had been forced to concede that his friend's logic was sound. For her part, Hope had insisted that she wished to help rather than sit in the parlour waiting for news, and the determined expression on her face was such that Samuel had not dared contradict her. And so, with reluctance and a few cautionary words about Hope remaining inside the carriage and out of sight, Samuel had agreed. An agreement which had left him in exactly the position he found himself now, sitting across from Hope in his carriage as it rumbled along the road towards Lowhaven. Charles had also insisted that he should ride ahead, leaving Samuel and Hope to follow together. For all his evident concern about his sister's welfare, Samuel could not help but wonder if his friend had contrived to throw them both into close confines.

They'd gone to Hayton first, and in the sleepy village where not much went unnoticed they'd quickly learned that a young lady matching Miss Gordon's description had pleaded her way on to the back of a local harness-maker's cart bound for Lowhaven docks. Samuel had made the enquiries while Hope had remained quietly in the carriage.

Indeed, since leaving Hayton Hall she had not uttered a word, apparently preferring to gaze silently out of the window or at the floor—at anything apart from him. Not that he could blame her, he thought glumly. Given his behaviour of late—deceiving her, reacting jealously to the sight of her sitting with Charles, not to mention losing his head and kissing her again—he wouldn't want to speak to him either.

He knew he ought to say something, to offer a proper explanation for what he'd said and done, for why he'd lied to her. Yet now, sitting in her presence, he found himself struggling to formulate the words. His feelings, he realised, were like those swirling leaves outside the carriage window—utterly all over the place, and completely at the mercy of a stronger, higher force. He clasped his hands tightly together, as though praying for some divine intervention, some guidance out of the mess he'd created. Some way to assuage the myriad of feelings which continued to assail him—the hopeless attraction to Hope, the burning desire to protect her. The sorrow and guilt which his deception of her had provoked. The humiliation and hurt of knowing that the real Samuel was once again not good enough for a woman he'd begun to care for.

As the rugged countryside finally fell away and the humble cottages on the periphery of Lowhaven beckoned, his unspoken turmoil finally bubbled over.

'I am so sorry, Hope,' he began. 'I know this is a terrible time to talk about this, while Miss Gordon is missing, but I have to say something. I...'

His words faltered as she looked at him squarely, those emerald eyes steely and challenging. 'Which part are you sorry for, Samuel?' she asked him. 'The part where you let me believe you were a baronet, that I was living in your home, or the part where you accused me of dallying with your friend?'

He flinched at her caustic tone. 'I didn't say you were dallying with Charles. I...' He shook his head at himself as another wave of shame gripped him. Shame at allowing jealousy to get the better of him. Shame at how he'd allowed his wounded pride to rule him so often of late.

That stern stare of hers was unrelenting. 'But you did suggest that, how did you put it, we were getting along very well, and that Mr Gordon's extraordinary wealth might be of paramount interest to me.'

Samuel grimaced to hear his words repeated back to him. To hear how cold, how mercenary they sounded. To realise just how much he'd let his hurt and humiliation poison his thoughts.

'You were right—I was being ridiculous, suggesting that you and Charles had formed an attachment.' He drew a deep breath, trying to order his thoughts, to swallow his damnable pride. 'In truth, Hope, I am sorry for all of it. For everything. For what I said about you and Charles. For leading you to think that Hayton Hall, its lands and the title that goes with it, was all mine. It was wrong of me. Indeed, it was unforgivable.'

'How on earth did you manage to pretend to have a grand house and a title?'

Hope continued to hold his sorrowful gaze as she finally gave voice to a question which had been swirling around her mind. Once she'd managed to quell her initial panic at learning she was likely not as safe as she'd thought, questions about the practicalities of Samuel's deception had plagued her. It was unfathomable—all these weeks at Hayton Hall, cared for by the man she believed to be its master. Convalescing in one of his rooms, being attended to by his servants, dining with him, enjoying tea with him in his parlour. How could none of that have been real? How on earth did someone pretend to have a grand house, to have a title? How could they have guests and servants in that house who all believed that to be the truth?

'Who are you, Samuel?' she continued, her questions flowing freely now. 'What are you—are you Hayton's tenant?'

'Not quite.' His tone was unmistakably grim as he stared down towards his boots. 'Hayton Hall is my home—at least, it is my family home and it is where I have lived since returning from my travels on the Continent. However, I am my father's second son. My elder brother, Sir Isaac Liddell, is the master of Hayton Hall and its estate. He married recently—eloped, in fact—and is travelling in Scotland with his new bride. I am caring for the estate in his absence.'

Hope frowned, her thoughts still racing. 'But the servants all call you Sir Samuel...'

'They do—because I instructed them to.' He paused, grimacing. 'As you once reminded me when you rebuked me for calling my maid Madeleine, masters and servants are not equals. Please do not blame them for deceiving you; they had no choice in the matter.'

'And Mr and Miss Gordon—what do they know of this? Have you been deceiving them too?' This question had circled her mind earlier, while she'd enjoyed tea with Mr Gordon. She'd wondered what he knew, if he was being deceived too. If she ought to say something...

Samuel's expression grew increasingly pained. 'No— Charles and his sister know exactly who and what I am. When they arrived unexpectedly at Hayton Hall, I begged them to play along with the lie. They agreed, although it's clear Charles thinks I'm an utter blockhead and of course he's absolutely right.' He looked up then, his grey-blue eyes sorrowful and heavy with regret. 'Please do not blame them either. I am so sorry, Hope. The fault for this deceit is entirely mine.'

For several moments, Hope simply stared at him, stunned by the extent of his deceit, a thousand thoughts whirling around her mind. Samuel had lied to her about who he was, and he'd involved everyone else in his deception too. The thought of Smithson, Maddie, and the Gordons all being privy to the lie made her feel foolish, gullible even. But then, how could she possibly have known any different? She—the real Hope—knew nothing of gentlemen, titles and grand estates.

That was another thing, she reminded herself yet again. Samuel was not the only one of them who was lying about who he was. Like him, she was not what she had appeared to be. Hope searched Samuel's handsome face, her mind racing with memories of their weeks together. Memories of cosy afternoons in the parlour, of candlelit dinners, of their meeting of minds over Shakespeare's plays. Memories of his embrace, of his kisses. Throughout all of this time, had they come to know each other at all? Or were they each only familiar with the role that the other was playing?

And if she did not know the real him, then who had she been in danger of losing her heart to?

'Why?' she said quietly. 'Why did you lie to me?'

She watched as Samuel dragged his hands down his face. 'Please believe me when I say that I did not intend to lie to you,' he began. 'The day after I found you in the woods, when we spoke properly for the first time, it was clear you'd assumed I was the baronet, that the estate was mine and…

and I could not find the words to correct you. The way you looked at me, like I was someone important…' He paused, shaking his head at himself. 'To my eternal discredit, my foolish pride got the better of me. I vowed I would tell you the truth, but then you told me how safe and protected you felt with me, how fortunate you'd been to find yourself in the home of a baronet. I couldn't bear to take away that feeling from you, to allow you to feel anything less than completely safe. I know it was wrong, but I decided then that I would keep up the pretence.'

'So why tell me at all?' she asked. 'Why did you decide to tell me the truth, that night in the library?'

She watched as he appeared to wrestle with her question. 'As I said that night, I care about you and, besides, after I kissed you, I knew I had to say something.'

Hope felt her cheeks colour at the memory of that first kiss. That was one thing he had not apologised for, she noted. Not that she was sorry for it either. Nor could she find it within herself to regret the way their passions had spilled over in the parlour earlier…

Her thoughts were interrupted by the sharp sound of the carriage door clicking open. Cold air raced in, laced with a spicy sweetness as the scents of rum, cocoa and coffee all mingled. Hope jolted. Until that moment, she had not even realised that they'd stopped. Had not even noticed the bustle and noise of Lowhaven's docks as they sat in the midst of them. She looked up to see Mr Gordon peering in at them.

'If we're going to find Henrietta, we'd best make haste,' Mr Gordon said, his gaze flitting between them both.

Samuel nodded. Hope saw how he swallowed hard, as though collecting himself, before he turned back to address her. 'Will you be all right here?' he asked.

'Of course,' she replied in the most reassuring voice she could muster. 'Please, just find Miss Gordon and bring her to the carriage. Tell her not to worry, that I am waiting here for her.'

Briefly, Samuel seemed to hesitate, as though there was something else he wished to say. If there was, then he decided to keep his own counsel, instead offering her a brisk nod before disembarking. Involuntarily, Hope shuddered as the carriage door slammed shut behind him, feeling a final blast of that cool, pungent air before she was cut off from the outside world once more. She fiddled with the large bonnet she wore to shield her face, before peering tentatively out of the window. From this vantage point she could see Samuel and Mr Gordon begin their enquiries, doubtless describing Miss Gordon to dockworkers and passers-by in the hope that someone might have seen her.

Hope sighed heavily, collapsing back in her seat. She wished that she could be out searching too, rather than stuck inside with only her spiralling thoughts for company. However, that was utterly out of the question. Lowhaven docks might as well be a lion's den. As a centre of trade, they crawled with associates of her father—people who might recognise her even disguised in a fine dress and wide-brimmed bonnet. As she'd learned to her great cost that night at Lowhaven's theatre, her years of absence had not left her quite so unrecognisable as she'd hoped. As much as she wanted to help, she could not run the risk. So instead she sat there, feeling useless, as she stewed over Samuel's lie and his explanation. An explanation which she had still to fully digest.

An explanation which left her with absolutely no idea how she should feel.

On the one hand, she still felt the joint sting of betrayal and anger as potently as ever, and on the other hand, she was acutely aware of the irony of feeling upset at all. Samuel had lied about who he was, but so had she, albeit it for very different reasons. Hope had deceived Samuel to protect herself—in a weakened state, riddled with injuries, and in the home of an unknown gentleman, she had done what was necessary to conceal an identity which, for all she knew, would have meant her being handed straight back to her father.

Samuel had lied to her to…what, exactly? Impress her? Or at least to impress the woman he thought she was—wealthy and well-bred. The thought of that made her groan aloud. How mortified he would be if he knew that he'd dragged his servants and his friends into a complex web of deceit to impress a mere actress and outlaw's daughter.

What a terrible mess.

Then there was his confession that he'd kept up the pretence to make her feel safe. Her heart had ached when he'd spoken of how he couldn't bear the thought of her feeling unprotected. After all, it was undeniable, wasn't it? She had believed in the sanctuary that a titled man and his grand home could offer her. Yet no matter how good and pure his intentions had been, his actions had ultimately fallen far short of being honourable and that was enough to make her question her judgement of him.

Weeks ago, she'd put her faith in a gentleman who'd been unfailingly kind and gentle, who'd seemed so decent and honest. It was Samuel's good nature, and her growing closeness to him, which had made her own deception harder to maintain, which had tempted her to share the truth of her situation with him. Now she wondered if she'd been wrong in her assessment of him. If he could lie to her so effortlessly, perhaps he would cast her out just as easily if he knew who she really was. If he knew she was no genteel heiress at all.

Hope huffed a breath, looking out of the window once more. Both Samuel and Mr Gordon had slipped out of sight now. In vain, Hope searched for them, her eyes skimming frantically over a busy scene of cargo, men and masts. Then, amongst the chaos of the quayside, a figure caught Hope's eye. A tall woman wearing a deep red cape, the hood pulled up to conceal her face. She seemed agitated, darting around and approaching men at random, seemingly asking them something, because each in turn shook his head at her. Miss Gordon—it had to be.

Hope searched again, trying to see either Samuel or Mr Gordon, but neither gentleman appeared to be near. Desperation burned in her gut and her heart raced. Leaving the carriage was an enormous risk, but so was leaving a vulnerable woman wandering alone around a port.

She had to act now.

With a deep breath, Hope pushed open the door of the carriage, hurrying towards the red-caped woman and praying that she was indeed Henrietta Gordon. Praying too that no one on that quayside would recognise the face of Hope Sloane beneath all her borrowed finery, because if they did she would be in serious trouble.

Chapter Seventeen

The scream Miss Gordon let out was like nothing Samuel had ever heard in his life. Even above the din of the port it rang out, a high-pitched yet feral, guttural sound. Part-banshee, part-bear. Across the quayside he saw her, a spectre of chaos in her dishevelled red cape, her arms flapping wildly, her hood falling down to reveal a veritable bird's nest of dark hair. Yet it was neither the sight of her nor the sound she made which horrified him the most. It was the smaller woman standing in front of her, clad in cream, her wide-brimmed bonnet insufficient to shield her face from all the attention which Miss Gordon's scene was drawing. Hope.

Samuel dashed towards her, his heart racing and his hackles slowly rising. What on earth was she thinking, leaving the carriage? After all these weeks in hiding, why would she put herself in such danger?

As he drew nearer, he saw Charles had joined them now, his gestures suggesting he was trying, and failing, to calm his sister down. If anything, the sight of her brother seemed to make Miss Gordon more hysterical. Samuel ran faster, his agitation growing at the woman's relentless cries. They needed to get her away from here. And, more to the point, he needed to get Hope back in that carriage and back to the safety of Hayton Hall.

'Oh, Sammy, thank goodness!' Charles called out as, finally, Samuel reached them. 'Is there a physician nearby? I think we're going to have to call upon the man and ask him to attend. Henrietta is unwell.'

Unwell? That was an understatement. Samuel's gaze shifted from Miss Gordon to Hope, who stood in front of her, speaking softly and calmly, trying her best to reassure her. It seemed to work as slowly the woman's wailing abated, replaced by quieter sobs. Around them he could sense the onlookers circling, their collective breath bated as they watched the scene unfold.

'We need to get you away from here, Hope,' Samuel said, not answering Charles. His thoughts were consumed now with only this—making sure Hope remained safe. 'Now.'

Hope glanced up at him, her green eyes challenging, her jaw set hard. 'I must help Miss Gordon,' she insisted. 'Besides, I dare say the damage has already been done.'

In breach of his usual calm temperament, Samuel felt his temper flare. How could she be so flippant about the threat she still faced? How could she be so obstinate when she was in such clear danger? For several moments he stared at her, her choice of words stinging him as though he'd been struck across his cheek. Words which could easily refer to more than her recognition, her discovery out here. The damage had indeed been done—by him, weeks ago, when he'd lied to her about who he was.

'Please, Hope,' he replied, swallowing down the fire which had risen in his throat. 'Please, go back to the carriage.'

'Not without Miss Gordon,' she replied, her voice quiet

but firm. 'I am not yours to command, Samuel. I am not your sister, or your wife.'

Samuel blinked at her, those words ringing in his ears and whirling around his mind.

'I am not...your wife.'

But what if she was—at least for now, in this moment? Would a new name and a husband be sufficient to throw any malevolent onlookers off the scent? Or, if she was recognised, would the news that she'd wed protect her, if it reached the ears of those who sought her?

No, he told himself, he could not countenance pretending that Hope was his wife, not under any circumstances. He'd quite finished with the business of telling lies, even for good and noble reasons. Even if he rather liked the idea of hearing the words *Mrs Liddell* fall from his lips...

Before he could say anything further, however, Hope turned away from him and back to Charles's sister, who stood trembling and sobbing quietly at her side. 'Come now, Miss Gordon,' she said softly as she took the lady tentatively by the arm. 'Let us return home. A little tea and cake, that's what you need. Then you will feel much better.'

It was hard to discern whether Hope's gentle words had the desired effect on Miss Gordon or whether she'd simply exhausted herself but, either way, Charles's sister submitted to Hope's coaxing without complaint. The audience which had gathered began to fall away as the four of them walked back towards the carriage, apparently losing interest now that it was clear that the scene Miss Gordon had made was over.

Inwardly, Samuel breathed a sigh of relief. Perhaps all would be well, after all. Perhaps no one there had known Hope for who she really was; perhaps word of her presence in the docks today would not reach her uncle's ears. Perhaps no damage had been done.

Except the damage he'd caused by lying to Hope, he thought glumly. He was not sure if that could ever be repaired.

Charles strode up beside Samuel, emitting a heavy sigh. 'Thank goodness that is over. I suppose I should be grateful that Henrietta's hysterics were witnessed here and not in Blackburn. The damage to her reputation there would have been irrevocable. At least here, no one is likely to know us.'

Samuel gave his friend a stern look. 'Frankly, Charles, I am more concerned about someone here recognising Hope, and about the danger that would place her in,' he replied, his voice hushed.

'Ah—of course. Indeed, Henrietta and I owe Miss Swynford an enormous debt for intercepting her like that, despite the risk to herself.' Charles gave Samuel a pointed look. 'Miss Swynford did not look delighted by your efforts to steer her away from danger, however,' he whispered. 'It's clear she's still angry with you. I presume you did not heed my advice about laying all your cards on the table.'

Samuel grimaced, watching Hope as she clambered into the carriage beside Miss Gordon a short distance away. This was a conversation he was not prepared to have— especially when Charles was partly correct. In the carriage, he'd begun to explain himself, but he'd not laid his cards on the table; he'd thrown them up in the air, leaving them to land wherever they might and leaving Hope to make of them what she would. And, of course, he kept one card hidden away—the one which told of the events of the summer, of his pain and humiliation. Of the hope he'd begun to harbour that, no matter who he really was, Hope might care for him too.

'As you said, Charles, you owe Hope a considerable debt for her actions today. I think you can begin by explaining exactly what is amiss with your sister, the moment we return to Hayton.'

'Ah…yes, of course,' Charles replied, looking suitably chastened.

Samuel strode towards his carriage, his heart sinking when he climbed in and saw how steadfastly Hope avoided his eye as she sat beside Miss Gordon. After all that had happened today, Samuel was not sure what tortured him more— the irrevocable damage that his lies had caused between Hope and him, or the uncomfortable, unexpected knowledge that he'd rather liked the idea he'd fleetingly entertained, of calling her his wife.

Throughout the journey home, it was this latter thought which his mind kept returning to. Along with another thought—that even if by some miracle a woman like her would have ever considered him, his deceit now meant that she would never trust him again, never mind consider marrying him.

Hope sat quietly opposite Samuel, sipping her tea and wishing she was a million miles away as they waited for Mr Gordon to join them. Samuel had asked her to come to the parlour almost the moment they'd arrived back at Hayton and put the ashen-faced Miss Gordon safely into Maddie's care.

'Charles is going to explain everything,' he'd said, leaning close and speaking in a hushed voice. 'After what you did for his sister today, he owes that explanation to you most of all.'

Hope had nodded obligingly, a flustered heat growing in her cheeks at her awareness of his proximity. 'Of course,' she'd replied, unable to bring herself to meet his eye.

In truth, she'd wanted to slip away into her room, to put some distance between herself and everything that had happened today. Between herself and Samuel, and that maelstrom of emotions she felt whenever she so much as glanced at him. Her confusion, her upset, and her anger. Her niggling worry that she should not trust him, even as she wished with every fibre of her being that she could. Nonetheless, she was still curious to hear what Mr Gordon had to say about his sister's behaviour. It was, it seemed, a day for honesty—from everyone else, at least.

What a strange day it had been. A strange and dangerous day. As Mr Gordon hurried in, looking flustered, Hope tried not to dwell on just how risky her actions at the docks had been. Neither did she allow herself to consider the sheer horror on Samuel's face at the sight of her standing with Miss Gordon in the midst of the gathering crowd. How tinged with fear his words had been as he'd pleaded with her to return to the carriage. How he'd once again sought to honour that solemn promise he'd made to her weeks ago, to keep her safe.

Samuel rose from his seat, interrupting her thoughts. 'Well, Charles?' he prompted. 'How is Miss Gordon?'

Mr Gordon gave a curt nod. 'She is resting.' His gaze flitted between Hope and Samuel, his agitation evident. 'I hope that you appreciate that what I am about to tell you must be treated with the utmost discretion...'

'Of course,' Samuel replied. 'I am not one to meddle in

the affairs of others, Charles. But this is my family's home and until my brother returns I am its master. I have a duty to know what goes on under Hayton's roof but, more importantly, as your friend I am concerned. Your sister's behaviour today was as alarming as it was reckless. It cannot be left unexplained.'

Mr Gordon gave his friend a pained look. 'I know,' he said in a tight, strangled voice. 'God, Sammy, if only you knew…' He paused, pressing his lips together in a clear effort to collect himself.

'Take your time, Mr Gordon,' Hope interjected, leaning forward and gesturing for him to sit. It was hard to see this usually jovial giant of a man so evidently perturbed. 'Did Miss Gordon go to the port today to try to procure more laudanum? I did see her talking to some of the men around the docks.'

Mr Gordon let out a bitter laugh as he slumped down in a chair. 'Worse than that, I'm afraid, Miss Swynford. It turns out that she was trying to buy herself passage on a ship.'

'A ship?' Samuel repeated. 'What ship? Going where?'

'Any ship, going anywhere,' Mr Gordon replied. 'Ireland, the Isle of Man, the Caribbean—it appears my sister cares not. Such is the strength of her desire not to return to Shawdale that she is willing to go anywhere in the world on any vessel which will take her.'

Hope's mouth fell open. The sea was a dangerous, often lawless place; she knew from bitter experience just what sort of rapscallions sailed its rough tides. A woman like Miss Gordon would have no idea if she was throwing herself upon the mercy of legitimate merchants or a crew engaged in far more nefarious activities. As desperate as Hope had been to escape her father's clutches—not once but twice now—she'd never even contemplated going to sea. Whatever had led Miss Gordon in that dark and potentially deadly direction must have been grave indeed.

'What happened to your sister, sir?' she asked.

Mr Gordon drew a deep, shuddering breath. 'She fell in love, Miss Swynford. A love which my parents forbade. That love is at the root of all that ails her.'

Hope listened as Mr Gordon finally told his sister's sorry tale. Several years earlier, he explained, his sister had become involved with a worker in one of their father's calico printworks. The young man had been about her age, and was known to be decent and hardworking. Miss Gordon, it seemed, had fallen head over heels in love with him, and by all accounts those feelings were reciprocated as the young man had proposed marriage. The pair had planned to run away and elope. However, before they could do so, word of their relationship and their plans reached Miss Gordon's father's ears. Mr Gordon senior had reacted furiously, effectively locking Miss Gordon away in Shawdale and dismissing the young man from his employment. Unable to find work because of the scandal, the young man had been forced to leave Blackburn, and Miss Gordon's heart had been broken. She'd not been the same since.

'I left for the Continent not long after the scandal broke. I hoped by the time I returned that Henrietta would have recovered from it. Unfortunately, she was worse than ever,' Mr Gordon concluded. 'She complained constantly of headaches, chest pains, stomach pains—pains of every sort. She was given laudanum by our physician but, as you know, that has only made matters worse. I've tried everything to help her, getting her away from Shawdale as much as I can. That was why I took her to Buxton to take the waters, and why I jumped at your invitation to come here. But I fear now that she is lost—if no longer to her tinctures, then to her despair.'

'Oh, dear, Charles,' Samuel said. 'You never breathed a word of any of this during our travels.'

'I confess, I was content to be far from my family's woes,' he replied glumly. 'I proved very capable of putting it all out of my mind.'

Hope, meanwhile, found herself overcome with sympathy for the lady who lay in bed upstairs. Little wonder that she was so prickly, so sombre, so prone to drowning her sorrows in the bottom of a laudanum bottle.

'Poor Miss Gordon,' she interjected, shaking her head sadly. 'To have been denied love like that... Really, could they not just have been allowed to marry?'

'What?' Mr Gordon just about leapt out of his seat. 'I am sorry for Henrietta's pain, Miss Swynford, but are you honestly proposing that my father should have consented to the match? With one of his workers?'

Hope felt her hackles begin to rise. 'I am proposing that Miss Gordon should have been permitted happiness, sir,' she replied, standing too. 'I am proposing that she should have been allowed to make her own choice.'

'Are you really?' he scoffed. 'Well, I suppose that having an uncle who tries to sell you off to anyone willing to split the proceeds would affect your judgement on these matters.'

'Come now, Charles,' Samuel intervened, getting to his feet now and standing close beside her. 'That isn't fair on Hope...'

'I'm merely pointing out that your mysterious heiress here might be as embittered by her experiences as my sister is. Not that any of us know much about what those experiences were. Indeed, Miss Swynford, it is odd that you have so much to say about my sister's story, and so little to say about your own.'

Hope's heart sank like a stone at Mr Gordon's pointed observation. The truth, as ever, bubbled not far from the surface.

'You are right,' she said, changing tack. 'I have said too much. It is not fair to discuss this when your sister is not present to talk about it herself. Indeed, with hindsight, I should have liked to have heard her story in her own words rather than yours, sir.'

Mr Gordon's nostrils flared. 'I suppose you think her wicked family has deprived her of those too,' he replied. 'Just as you clearly think we deprived her of the chance to marry so far beneath her.'

Hope sighed, wishing now that she'd held her tongue. It was clear that she'd provoked Mr Gordon and he was spoiling for a fight. She glanced at Samuel, noticing how he remained at her side, watching his friend carefully, every muscle in his body apparently tense. She knew she ought to back down, apologise meekly and extricate herself from this conversation. And yet, as she stood here, she felt the fire of indignation burning in her gut. Indignation for that young man and indignation for herself, her true self, and the way others looked down upon them when their rank in life was nothing more than an accident of birth. Who they were—who they truly were—was a matter of words and deeds, not wealth and titles.

'I just… I find it sad that people are considered above or beneath each other at all,' she said in the end. 'Surely, we love who we love and that should be all that matters. You said yourself that this young man was hardworking and decent, yet such traits meant nothing because he was not wealthy and therefore your sister marrying him would be viewed as an embarrassment or a scandal. Never mind that it might have made her happy.'

'Outrageous, revolutionary nonsense.' Mr Gordon's face grew a rather unbecoming shade of scarlet as he turned to address Samuel. 'Are you going to tolerate such talk under your roof, Sammy? Or are you going to tell us that you'd quite happily wed one of Hayton's servants?'

Hope watched as Samuel studied his friend, his expression unreadable. 'As a gentleman, I'd never presume to tell you your business, Charles. However, as your friend I sincerely hope that you and your family can find a way to ease Miss Gordon's suffering.' His blue-grey eyes shifted from Mr Gordon to Hope, growing serious as they locked with hers. 'If you are asking me my personal opinion, then I am sympathetic to Miss Swynford's view. I wish to marry for love, and nothing else. Frankly, I do not care if the lady in question is a maid or a marquess's daughter.'

'And yet, until recently you were pretending to be a baronet,' Mr Gordon countered.

Still Samuel held Hope's gaze, his eyes at once searching and sincere. She was in no doubt that his words, whatever they would be, were meant for her.

'I was,' he said after a moment, 'because even I, for all the many advantages life has bestowed upon me, know what it is like to be looked upon as less than someone else. To have the wind knocked so thoroughly from your sails that you wonder if your pride will ever recover. However, that is no excuse. I should never have deceived you, Hope, and I am deeply, sincerely sorry that I did.'

The hurt and the shame which clouded his expression

was palpable. Before she could stop herself, before she could remember that Mr Gordon was still in the room, Hope reached out and took Samuel's hand in hers. Surprise flickered across his handsome features in response to her touch, before melting into such an affectionate smile that it caught Hope thoroughly off-guard even while it seemed to warm every part of her. She wanted to place her trust in Samuel, and she wanted to understand the nature of what pained him. Of who or what had cut him down and caused him to feel so thoroughly diminished.

In spite of everything, she realised, she wanted his affection. She wanted Samuel to look at Hope Sloane the way he'd just looked at Hope Swynford. And above all she wanted to find the strength to tell him the truth.

Chapter Eighteen

Hope sat in front of the mirror, watching her reflection with a soft gaze as Maddie brushed her hair, teasing the tangles out of her curls with a look of pained apology. She had retired early, excusing herself not long after dinner and retreating to her bedchamber to wash and to change for bed. After the day's events, she doubted she would sleep easily, but at least the night-time hours alone would give her time to think. And goodness, did she need to think.

She understood now that Samuel's lie had been born of some painful, unspoken experience and not simply a desire to impress her or to make her feel safe. She wondered about the nature of that experience, about who would look at a gentleman who was so kind, so caring, so jovial, so undeniably handsome and draw the conclusion that he was not good enough. Whoever they were, they were wrong. If she could muster the courage, Hope would tell him so.

Courage. That was something she was going to need in abundance, if she was going to also admit the truth about herself. If she was going to find the words to explain why she'd deceived him, not only when she'd first arrived at Hayton but for all the weeks since. She had to hope that he would understand, that he could forgive her. At the same time, she had to acknowledge that telling the truth was the right thing to do, even if he could not. She owed him that much for his protection, for his generosity. For the affection he clearly had for her. She could not countenance allowing that affection to be directed towards a woman who did not exist for a moment longer. She cared about him too deeply to do that.

Nonetheless, the very real prospect of losing that affection, of watching it disappear along with the character of the enigmatic heiress which she'd inhabited for so many weeks was terrifying.

'I suppose it's all been a lot to take in,' Maddie said, meeting Hope's eye in the mirror and no doubt noting the pensive expression on her face. 'I do hope you're not too cross with Mr Liddell. He isn't a bad sort, I promise you.'

Hope acknowledged the remark with a tight smile. Hayton's servants had now been released from the obligation to keep up their caretaker master's pretence and, unsurprisingly, Maddie seemed relieved. Hope had rebuffed her attempts at an apology earlier, insisting that she had nothing to apologise for when all she'd been doing was following orders.

'I just wish I knew why he told you that he was the baronet,' Maddie continued to muse as she began to plait Hope's hair. 'It's not like he's ever appeared envious of his brother for inheriting all of this. No, I'd say he's always seemed quite content to be his own man, and his brother's heir, of course. Although I dare say he won't be the heir for much longer, now that Sir Isaac has wed again.'

'Again?' Hope asked, giving the maid a quizzical look. She knew that the true master of Hayton Hall was travelling with his bride, but she did not know that this recent elopement was not the baronet's first trip down the aisle.

Maddie nodded. 'That's right. Oh, my mistress, God rest her soul, was such a wonderful lady. So beautiful and so elegant. I remember the first time I saw her, I thought she looked like a princess. How I loved to help her dress! She had the best taste in gowns, although I don't need to tell you that, do I?' Maddie added, grinning at her.

'What do you mean by that?' Hope asked, furrowing her brow.

Hope watched as the maid's smile slipped from her face, her eyes widening in horror as realisation dawned.

'Forgive me,' she said quietly. 'I should not have said that. I just assumed that Mr Liddell had told you everything.'

Hope stared at Maddie's reflection, following her gaze as it slowly crept towards the mirror image behind them. When her eyes came to rest upon the bed, and the cream dress which lay discarded upon it, the penny finally dropped. The wardrobe he'd so easily produced for her—of course. He'd lied about that too.

'There was never a cousin, was there?' Hope asked quietly. 'There was never a trousseau, or a set of dresses left behind.'

Maddie shook her head sadly. 'I hope now you understand my reluctance to alter them for you,' she replied in little more than a whisper.

'Of course,' Hope replied grimly as she turned around and took her by the hand. 'You were being loyal to your mistress. You didn't decide to offer me her dresses—Mr Liddell did. And besides, for all your reluctance, you did take up a few of them for me.'

'Well, of course—you needed something proper to wear,' she said, blinking back her tears. 'And of course you should have worn them. But I think Mr Liddell ought to have told you who they'd belonged to.'

Hope bit her lip, the heat of her own tears stinging as they threatened to fall. What a fool she was! A gullible, thoroughly humiliated fool. To think she'd been sitting there, wanting to trust Samuel again, recognising that he'd been hurt and wanting to understand the painful experience which had led him to make such an error of judgement in deceiving her. To think she'd been agonising over going to him and confessing all, matching his honesty with her own, when all along he was still lying to her!

And why lie about the dresses? What possible reason could he have for spinning her a yarn about a cousin and letting her put on a dead woman's clothes without her knowledge? Was he laughing at her, or could he simply not help himself? Perhaps she really had misjudged him. Perhaps he was not the decent gentleman she'd believed him to be, after all.

Perhaps she was finally seeing the real Samuel Liddell. A serial liar.

Hope leapt out of her seat and hurried towards the door. 'Excuse me, Maddie,' she said. 'I think I need to have a word with Mr Liddell.'

'But…but he's retired for the night. And you're only wearing your shift!' Maddie called after her, aghast.

Hope, however, was not listening. She was already halfway along the hallway and hurrying towards a heavy oak door, beyond which lay the bedchamber of Hayton Hall's pretend baronet.

* * *

The sight of Hope standing in his doorway, feet bare, wearing only a shift, made Samuel sit bolt upright in bed. He blinked—once, then twice—convinced he must be dreaming. Convinced that he must have fallen asleep over the book he'd been trying his best to distract himself with after such an eventful, fraught day. A day in which they'd learned the truth about Miss Gordon, and he'd unfathomably allowed Hope to glimpse the hurtful, humiliating truth about him. A day in which Hope had taken hold of his hand and looked at him with such affection, such understanding. A look he hadn't deserved. A look which had occupied his mind ever since.

As Hope marched towards his bedside, however, her dainty feet stomping on the wooden floor, he realised that he was indeed awake. She really was here, in his room. And apparently, if the fierce expression on her face was anything to go by, she was very angry. Now there was a look he really did deserve to see from her.

'You lied to me!'

Samuel threw the bedsheets back, remembering just a moment too late that he wore naught but his drawers. Self-consciously, defensively, he folded his arms across his chest as he got to his feet and stood in front of her. She stared up at him, her green eyes wild and challenging, her plait half loosened in her fury, leaving several curls of dark hair to make their bid for freedom. He found himself overcome with a momentary urge to undo the rest of it, to run his hands through that lovely hair. Resisting temptation, he clamped his hand harder against his chest. Given her anger, any such move would be seriously unwise.

'You lied to me,' she said again, quieter this time.

'Yes—I know I did, and you've every right to be angry with me. I should never have told you that I was a baronet.'

'I'm not talking about that,' she replied pointedly. 'I'm talking about the dresses. The ones which belonged to your brother's dead wife. The ones I've been wearing.'

'Oh—yes. That.' Damn. His thoughts had been so pre-occupied with his enormous lie, he'd omitted to confess to the smaller one he'd also told. 'I'm sorry, Hope. I should have explained to you about the dresses.'

To his surprise, her face began to crumple, those earlier flashes of anger slowly replaced by the glint of tears as they formed in her eyes.

'Why would you lie about some dresses?' she asked, stepping back and turning away from him. 'Why would you lie about who they belonged to?'

He let out a heavy sigh, unfolding his arms and rubbing his brow wearily. 'If I'd told you the truth about poor Rosalind, then because I'd let you believe I was the baronet, I'd have had to pretend she'd been my wife. I couldn't do that—it was bad enough that I'd claimed my brother's title; I couldn't lay false claim to his wife and his grief as well.' He stepped tentatively towards her, though her back remained turned to him. 'Besides, you needed something to wear. I thought it was better for you to think that those clothes had come from a well-attired cousin who did not miss them rather than a lady who'd lived and died in this house. In my own foolish way, I was trying to make you feel at ease.'

'Surely that was my decision—whether to wear those dresses or not,' she countered, still not turning around.

'And if you had known, would you have worn them?' he asked.

'Yes. No. I don't know.'

He stepped closer again. 'I know I've acted badly, but it was never with mal-intent. Please believe that.'

He watched as her shoulders sagged. When, finally, she turned around, he was alarmed to see that tears streamed down her face. 'This is all such a mess,' she sobbed. 'So many lies. Do we even know each other at all?'

'Of course we do.'

The sudden urge to reassure her overtook him and, before he could stop himself, he pulled her into his arms. She didn't resist. Indeed, just as she had the last time they'd embraced like this, she tucked her head against his chest. Unlike the last time, however, she wore only a thin undergarment and he was naked from the waist up. The sheer intimacy of the moment meant that tender feelings quickly gave way to more carnal thoughts—thoughts he worked hard to suppress as he forced himself to focus on all that he still had to say.

'You do know me, Hope,' he said, softly running his hand over her hair. 'The man you've seen, the man you've taken tea with, the man you've discussed books and theatre with— that man is me. Calling myself a baronet and all the lies which sprang from that—it was all just costuming. All just foolish window-dressing by a man who, when you wandered into his life that evening in the woods, was feeling more than a little lonely and sorry for himself.'

'You said earlier that you knew what it was like to be looked upon as less than someone else,' she murmured. 'What did you mean by that?'

Samuel felt his breath catch in his throat. He'd been expecting that question ever since his remark in the parlour earlier, but that didn't make the events of the summer any easier to speak about. For a moment he pressed his lips to-gether, composing himself. Resolving finally to be entirely truthful, and to hell with the consequences.

'There was a lady in whose company I spent some time this summer,' he began. 'Her name was Charlotte Pearson. We seemed to get on well, and I thought—hoped, really—that it would progress to a courtship. However, Miss Pearson was very clear with me that she did not wish to continue our connection, and it quickly became apparent that she favoured my brother over me, on account of his title and estate.'

She glanced up at him, aghast. 'This woman is now your sister-in-law?'

Despite himself, Samuel laughed. 'Thankfully, no—Charlotte was never likely to succeed with Isaac. He only had eyes for Miss Louisa Conrad, who is now Lady Liddell.'

Hope leaned her head against his chest once more. 'Did you…did you love Charlotte? Did she break your heart?'

He drew a deep breath. 'I didn't love her, though I was more than a little captivated by her, at the time. And whilst she didn't break my heart, she did hurt me, and she certainly wounded my pride. I'd never been made to feel that way before, as though I was so unworthy.' He shook his head, remembering Charlotte's words. 'She spoke as though my affection for her was offensive—she even told me that things might have been different if I had been my brother.'

'Oh, Samuel…'

'I don't deserve your sympathy, Hope,' he said, inter-rupting her. 'Not after I've lied to you. But the damnable fact of the matter is that when you looked at me and thought you saw a titled gentleman with a grand house, I couldn't bring myself to contradict you. I liked to impress you, and I liked the way you looked at me. I couldn't bear to see your disappointment when you learned what I really am. And when I realised that it was the house and the title which made you feel so protected, telling you the truth felt completely impossible.'

'But you did tell me, in the end.'

'I did, but not soon enough. I should have told you right away. Indeed, I should never have lied at all.'

'Painful experiences make us do all kinds of things to protect ourselves,' she said, her voice almost a whisper.

He sighed into her dark curls. 'They do, but that is no excuse. I am so sincerely sorry, Hope. I'm not a man who is accustomed to telling lies, please believe that. Please believe me also when I say that if you cannot forgive me, I understand. It is enough for me to know that you will leave Hayton knowing who I really am, because the truth is, Hope, I care for you. When I kissed you in the library that evening, it was not a moment of madness for me. It was an admission of my feelings for you—feelings I had no right to feel, given I was deceiving you, but feelings which had grown nonetheless. Feelings which made telling you the truth about myself even harder. A cruel irony, but no more than I deserve.'

Hope looked up at him then, her emerald eyes still watering as they searched his. He became aware once more of her hands resting against his bare chest, of the warmth of skin on skin, of the feeling of her alluring form pressed against him. Of the proximity of his bed behind them, and the less than gentlemanly thoughts laying siege to his mind.

His heartfelt words surrendered to lust-filled passion as he captured her lips with his own, lifting one of his hands to brush her cheek whilst the other remained steadfast on the curve of her waist. His heart sang as Hope responded in kind, her mouth greeting his while her hands left the confines of his chest to explore his stomach, his arms, his back. He shivered at her touch, fighting himself to maintain control. He would not allow this to go too far. He would not take her to his bed.

Not unless she became his wife first.

The sudden thought astonished him, but not as much as Hope's swift action in breaking their embrace.

'No,' she breathed, stepping back from him. 'We must stop.'

He nodded, swallowing hard as he struggled to regain his composure. 'Of course. I'm sorry. I promise I have no intention of ruining you.'

If he'd hoped his words would be reassuring, he was to be deeply disappointed. Instead, he watched as her face crumpled once more, tears spilling unabated down her cheeks.

'Oh, Samuel, this is all such a mess,' she said, pacing about the floor.

He frowned. That was the second time tonight that she'd uttered those words. His heart began to pound in his chest as it dawned on him that all the obvious affection and ardour he had for her might not be enough. She might never be able to forgive him, to overcome the lies he'd told...

'I know the damage my lies have caused between us, but...'

'You're not the only one of us who has lied about who they are,' she sobbed. 'You cannot care for me, Samuel, and you could not ruin me, even if you tried.'

'What on earth do you mean?'

Finally, she stopped pacing. When she spoke again it was in a voice which sounded quite altered and which was laced, he was astonished to note, with a distinctly local accent.

'I am not an heiress. I am not wealthy. I have no uncle

and no inheritance,' she said. 'My name is not Hope Swyn-ford, it is Hope Sloane. I am an actress and the daughter of an outlaw. I am unruinable. I am the lowest of the low.'

Chapter Nineteen

Hope had never believed that telling Samuel the truth would be in any way cathartic but, even so, she was wholly unprepared for the depth of the shame which possessed her as she told the sordid story of her life. She watched the expressions of shock then horror cloud his handsome features as finally she unmasked herself, shedding Hope Swynford like a second skin and allowing Hope Sloane to walk free.

She told him about her childhood on that bleak Lilly-beck hillside, about the lack of food and warmth, about how, one by one, her siblings had perished until she'd been the only one left. About how her father had sought to solve their problems through a life of crime, allowing life on the wrong side of the law to corrupt him so thoroughly, whilst her mother had tried to drown her sorrows in a bottle of laudanum. That part of Hope Swynford's story, she said grimly, had been true.

She told him about her mother's death, how it had left her at the mercy of her father's cruelty and callousness, and how he'd tried to force her into marrying one of his associates. Despite herself, and despite knowing how unsavoury Samuel would doubtless find it, she could not help but speak fondly of running away and joining a theatre company. Those few years of freedom, she told him, had been the making of her, and for all the danger and vice which lurked at the periphery of such work, she'd been happy for the first time in her life.

Her lighter tone dissipated when she reached the final chapter of her tale: the story of her return to Cumberland, of her kidnap and her father's second attempt at forcing a marriage on her. She barely managed to utter the words as she spoke of how depraved he'd become, how sinister, how hateful. How ready he had been to condemn her to a life with a man who, she knew, had the same blackened soul as him.

'I've spent my life living on my wits, and when fortune smiled upon me for long enough to allow me to escape a second time I took the chance and I fled. I had nothing but the costume I'd been wearing the night that my father and his men snatched me from the theatre in Lowhaven. Nothing but that and my sheer determination to live my life on my own terms, and not his.'

'And then you found Hayton, and me,' Samuel added sombrely, slumping down on his bed with a look of unmistakable disbelief. 'So you're the actress Charles mentioned that day in Lowhaven. The one who went missing on the penultimate night of...' He shook his head, apparently struggling to remember.

'*The School for Scandal*,' Hope confirmed with a grim nod. 'I was playing Lady Teazle. Hence the beautiful gown I was wearing the night you found me in the woods.' She regarded him carefully, trying to ignore the tears which pricked at the corners of her eyes. 'You have to understand, Samuel, that I did not know you—I did not know if you were good or bad, if you knew my father or not. My father supplies his wares to many of the big houses across Cumberland, and has more than a few landowners and magistrates in his back pocket. For all I knew, telling you my true identity and story would have led me straight back into his clutches. So when I realised that my clothes had led you to make certain assumptions about me, I decided to play along. I created Hope Swynford and her story to protect myself.'

'Well, you are a consummate actress.' His grey-blue eyes were wide with dismay. 'Never for a moment did I think you could be anything other than a gentleman's daughter with an enthusiasm for the theatre. You certainly had me fooled.'

'Just as you fooled me into believing you were a baronet.'

'Fair point.' He offered her a grim smile as he got to his feet again. 'You were right—this is a real mess.'

She felt her lip tremble at his observation. 'Like you, once I'd begun my deception I found it so hard to end it, even when I suspected that you would have no idea who Jeremiah Sloane is and, even if you did, I knew you were too good a man to give me up to him.' She shook her head at herself, tears still threatening to overwhelm her. 'You said before that you liked the way I looked at you. Well, I liked the way you looked at me too. In truth, I felt ashamed of who I really was. I thought you'd be horrified if you knew who you'd allowed into your home. Gentlemen like you have nothing to do with low-born actresses with wicked outlaw fathers. The only time a woman like me encounters gentlemen is in the theatre, and believe me when I say that they are often anything but gentlemanly then.'

She watched as he flinched at her implication, and she realised then that she'd said far more than she should. It was bad enough that she'd spoken so frankly about the poverty and criminality which ran through her past like a poison, but to then confront Samuel with the sheer seediness and, at times, outright depravity of what she'd been exposed to off-stage and after dark—that was beyond the pale. Worse still, Samuel might believe that she'd been a willing participant in such behaviour—that she was, as Mr Gordon had once said of actresses, little more than a harlot.

'What I mean to say is…' she began, now filled with the sudden urge to explain herself.

'No—I understand,' he interjected, shaking his head again. 'Believe me, I know exactly what some gentlemen are capable of. But surely you know me well enough to know that I would not…' He strode towards her, and her heart sank as she saw him reach out a hand to touch her before retracting it. Of course, he'd thought better of it. He always would now. He shook his head, as though he was trying and failing to find the right words. 'I cannot imagine what you've had to endure…'

The look of horror which was etched in those wide, blue-grey eyes made Hope feel sick as it dawned on her that he was, indeed, trying to imagine it.

'I'm not a harlot,' she said quietly. 'I was never any man's mistress either. I'd run away from my father because he'd tried to trade me like contraband, and I didn't escape his clutches just so that I could sell myself to the highest bidder. I was determined that my life would be my own.'

'But that didn't stop well-dressed drunken wastrels trying their luck,' Samuel pondered.

Hope smiled bleakly at his observation. 'Quite. And some not so well-dressed wastrels, at times.'

An awkward silence descended between them as Hope waited for Samuel to say something—anything—more. But his words, if he had any, did not come. Instead, he simply stood before her, blinking, his sheer mortification and consternation etched on his face. His entire demeanour, from his wooden posture to the distance he'd placed between them, telling her that everything had changed. That what she truly was had shocked and appalled him, such that he might never recover. Such that he would never care for her again. Indeed, that he likely regretted ever saying that he did.

'It is late,' she said in the end, stepping towards the door. 'I should go.'

Samuel stared at her from across the room, but made no move to follow her. 'Yes, of course,' he said after a moment.

He conceded defeat easily—perhaps, Hope considered, too easily. He crossed his arms over his bare chest, and Hope's fingers tingled with the memory of exploring that part of him a short time ago. A profound sense of loss gripped her as it dawned on her that she'd never touch that skin again, that there would be no more embraces. The chasm wrought between them by the truth was simply too great. Looking at his astonished expression, Hope could see that Samuel knew this too. He knew that he could never look at Hope the actress the way he'd looked at Hope the heiress. There had been too much deceit on both their parts. Too many lies. At least now they both knew that.

'Goodnight, Samuel.'

Then, before he could utter a word in reply, she hurried out of his room. It was only when she reached her own and saw that Maddie had left that she allowed herself to weep in earnest—for all that had happened, and for all that could never be.

They'd both been lying. As he tossed and turned in bed, unable to sleep, Samuel's mind kept returning to that thought.

They'd both told stories, and they'd both had their reasons for keeping the truth from one another—some better reasons than others, but reasons nonetheless.

Hope's reasons, he knew, had been a matter of survival. Had he been in her position in those woods weeks ago, had he been injured and vulnerable and taken into a stranger's home, he might well have invented a tale about himself too. Hearing her confess the dreadful details of her past had been hard enough, but realising that it was shame which had motivated her to keep up the pretence of being Hope Swynford had been unbearable.

His heart had broken for her as she'd stood there and told him that she was ashamed of who she was and, in turn, he'd felt ashamed of himself too. Ashamed of the way he'd allowed his own wounded pride and misguided sense of honour to get the better of him, to lead him to pretend to be more than he was. Little wonder she'd felt unable to tell him her real story—between the baronetcy and the big estate, he must have seemed utterly intimidating. The bitter irony of this was not lost on him. In keeping up the pretence, he'd sought to make her feel safe and protected. Instead, he'd unwittingly placed a barrier between them.

If only he had been honest from the outset, he might have seemed more approachable.

Perhaps.

On the other hand, as she'd told him, in her experience, gentlemen were not to be trusted. His stomach had lurched at her remark about the so-called gentlemen at the theatre, at her implication as to how they'd often behaved. He'd desperately wanted to show her that he was not like them, that his affection for her was heartfelt and genuine, and that it endured—whether she was a wealthy heiress or an actress without a penny to her name. He'd wanted to gather her into his arms and kiss all her feelings of shame away, and yet he had stopped himself. He had held back from her.

Why? Because, despite those familiar tender, protective feelings he had for her, he'd realised he had to tread carefully. The last thing he wanted her to conclude was that he was just another rich rapscallion, seeking to take advantage of her. So he'd kept his hands to himself, and when she'd wanted to, he'd let her go, even when so much remained unsaid.

Such as telling her that she was still the Hope he'd come to know and care for, whether her surname was Swynford or Sloane, and whether her father was a gentleman or a common criminal. Whether she spent her life in drawing rooms playing cards or on the stage playing roles. Such as reminding her that her pretend heiress, just like his pretend baronet, had been a mere costume, that it did not alter who either of them were underneath.

The Hope who'd been on the run from her invented nefarious uncle was the same Hope who'd escaped the clutches of a very real, very wicked father—a woman who loved to read, whose knowledge of Shakespeare was second to none. A woman who'd lost her mother, and whose own pain had made her alert to and empathetic towards the suffering of others. A brave woman, and one who, he now knew, had carved out a life for herself, escaping the clutches of those who'd sought to drag her down not once, but twice. If anything, her runaway heiress story—a story which, notwithstanding the wicked uncle, had implied a certain amount of wealth and status—had meant that he'd not been able to fully appreciate the sheer amount of hardship and wretchedness which she'd overcome.

He did now.

He did, and the strength of feeling that knowledge provoked in him was overwhelming. As he lay in bed, sleep still eluding him, he realised that he wanted to protect her from all of it. From her father's cruelty, from a forced marriage, from men leering at her in the theatre. From cold, damp cottages and poverty and hunger. Weeks ago, he'd offered her sanctuary in his family home; now, he knew, he wanted to offer her love and security, with him. Because he did love her—he understood that now, and knowing that truth had done nothing to diminish how he felt about her. If anything, he loved and admired her more than ever. To him, she was beautiful and she was perfect, and honestly, the way she spoke in that soft local tongue had the ability to drive him wild. He wanted to hear that voice to the end of his days.

He would tell her so, he decided, squeezing his eyes shut. In the morning.

The indigo light of the autumn dawn bathed Hayton's gardens as Hope stepped out of the door at the rear of the house. She breathed in deeply, allowing the cold air to refresh her as the wind teased the shrubbery and tangled the branches of the tall trees in the woods beyond, warning of an unsettled day ahead. How fitting, since it had been a restless night. Hope had not slept a wink, her room growing more stifling and her thoughts more relentless as the hours wore on. Eventually she had felt the need to escape, and so she'd slipped on a day dress and shawl—or rather, as she now knew, Rosalind's dress and shawl—then put on her boots and wandered outside for some air.

She walked slowly along the path, acutely aware of

how heavy her weary limbs felt, and how her swollen eyes pricked and throbbed after so many hours of crying. For the first time in her life, she found herself at a loss. No matter what life had thrown at her, she'd always been able to formulate a plan or, at the very least, to take what she'd been given and run with it—sometimes literally. Now, she realised, she'd simply no idea what to do. No idea where she was going. Not to London—now that she was no longer Hope Swynford, there was no need for that. Back to Richmond? Back to her life in the theatre? Was that even possible? She didn't know.

All she did know was that the truth had changed everything, that Samuel would never look at her in the same way again. Her time at Hayton, her time with him in this blissful, peaceful sanctuary, was coming to an end.

The sound of stones crunching underfoot was the first clue that she wasn't alone. It was a clue which came too late, since by the time she realised a hand had already been clapped over her mouth, stifling any attempt she might have made to scream. The hand was dirty, coarse and all too familiar, as was the cold sting of the knife which was pressed against her throat.

'Time to go home, my lady,' he said mockingly, hissing the words into her ear.

Finally, after all these weeks of searching, he'd found her.

Chapter Twenty

She'd left him.

Samuel pulled on the riding coat which Smithson had handed to him, that same handful of words circling around his mind over and over again. She'd left him. The shame, the pain and the guilt she'd so clearly felt about all that she'd confessed last night had been too much for her to bear. And he, to his eternal damnation, had been thoroughly inadequate in the face of it, failing to comfort her, to properly reassure her. To tell her that none of it changed what he felt for her. Instead, he'd simply stood by as she'd walked out of his bedchamber and now out of his life.

She'd left him, and now he might never see her again.

Now, because of his hesitation, she was wandering the countryside, alone and vulnerable. God forbid she should end up injured again or, worse, find herself a captive of her father once more. If some dreadful fate befell her, it would be all his fault.

She'd left him, and now he had to find her. He had to make amends.

'She could be anywhere by now. This will be like searching for a needle in a haystack.'

Next to him, Charles gave voice to Samuel's niggling

fears as he fiddled with his top hat. Outside, the grooms were readying two horses as fast as they could, after Samuel had all but press-ganged his friend into assisting him in his search for Hope. In the sheer panic he felt following Maddie's revelation that Hope was nowhere to be found, Samuel had appraised his maid, his butler and Charles of what Hope had revealed last night. All three had expressed their surprise. Like Samuel, they appeared to have harboured no suspicions that she'd been anything other than what she'd said she was.

'We have to try, Charles,' Samuel implored him. 'I cannot just sit here, knowing that Hope could be in danger. What if her father finds her?'

'But where should we even begin to look?' Charles countered. 'We don't know where she's going. Try not to fret, Sammy, I dare say she can look after herself. Women like her are…'

'What do you mean, women like her?' Samuel almost growled the question.

Charles held up a hand in protest. 'I mean no offence, of course. All I mean to say is that she's hardly lived a sheltered life. Surely she's proven just how resourceful she is, considering how well she's pulled the wool over your eyes for all these weeks.'

'And surely you can see that she had her reasons.' Samuel wished the grooms would hurry up, so that he could end this conversation. So that he could begin his search.

'I can see that given the chance and the talent required to pull it off, any base-born woman would pretend to be a princess if it meant ensnaring a wealthy gentleman.' Charles fiddled with his collar in front of the mirror, his reflection shooting Samuel a pointed look.

'That isn't why Hope deceived me,' Samuel replied, bristling. 'She lied to protect herself. If either one of us could be accused of lying to impress the other, then it is me. I know what you think of her, Charles, now that you know she's an actress without a penny to her name...'

'It doesn't matter what I think, Sammy,' Charles replied, turning around. 'I'm not the one who is besotted with Hope Swynford or Sloane or whoever she is.' He raised a knowing eyebrow. 'Or perhaps this is something more than infatuation?' he added searchingly.

Samuel shrugged, having neither the will to deny his feelings nor the desire to elaborate upon them. What he felt for Hope had gone beyond mere infatuation, but Charles did not need to know that. The only person in the world who needed to know the depth of what he felt was Hope herself. If he found her.

When he found her.

'Richmond,' he said after a moment, answering Charles's earlier question. 'Her theatre company came from Richmond. Perhaps that is where she is hoping to return to now. It would make sense, wouldn't it?'

'You want to go all the way to Richmond?' Charles stared at him, incredulous. 'That is several days of hard riding across the dales.'

Samuel put up a hand in protest. 'I'm saying that is the direction we should head in,' he said. 'It would appear that Hope is travelling on foot and, whilst she has recovered from her injuries, her ankle in particular will still be delicate. She will not be moving quickly. On horseback we stand a good chance of catching up with her.'

'If we can correctly guess the route she has taken,' Charles pointed out.

'To find her way there, she will surely have to follow the roads,' Samuel replied with a confidence he did not feel. He glanced towards the door impatiently. Where in damnation were those grooms with their horses? The longer they delayed, the further Hope would have travelled from Hayton, and the harder it would be to find her...

'Excuse me, sir.'

The soft, wavering voice of Maddie interrupted Samuel's spiralling thoughts. He spun around to see the maid standing in the middle of the hallway, tears spilling down her cheeks, clutching a delicate swathe of cream fabric in her hands. She held it up towards him, revealing that it was in fact a shawl. His heart lurched in recognition—it had belonged to Rosalind, and had been one of the items he'd given Hope to wear.

'I found this in the garden,' she explained, her bottom lip trembling. 'I was attending to Miss Gordon when she spotted it out of the window, stuck to one of the shrubs.'

'So she has fled via the woods then, and lost this on her way,' Charles interjected.

Maddie shook her head. 'I'm not sure about that, sir. You see, when I went outside to retrieve it, I noticed that the stones covering the path have been disturbed as though...as though there may have been a struggle. As though someone has been dragged along.' She turned her gaze to Samuel, looking at him imploringly. 'Oh, sir, what if her father has taken her? What if he's found her after all these weeks?'

Samuel's heart seemed to sink like a stone into the pit of his stomach. He'd been so wrapped up in the events of last night, so consumed by his own shortcomings in the face of her revelations, that he'd neglected to remember the danger Hope was in. The danger she'd always been in.

She had not run away from him at all. She'd been taken.

'I fear this is all my fault.' A faint voice crept into the brief silence which had descended in the hall, and Samuel glanced up to see a pale and frail Miss Gordon making her way gingerly down the stairs. Immediately, Maddie stepped forward to help her, but the lady waved the maid away.

'I don't quite see how any of this is your responsibility, Henrietta,' Charles said.

Samuel watched as a small frown gathered between Miss Gordon's dark eyes. 'That day at the docks in Lowhaven, when I…when Miss Sloane, as Maddie tells me she is in fact called…when Miss Sloane left the carriage to intercept me, she must have been recognised. If I had not gone there that day, then this might not have happened.'

'Miss Sloane's father is a common criminal, sister,' Charles replied. 'I dare say he would have gone to any lengths to locate her. I am quite certain this is not your doing.'

Miss Gordon put up her hand. 'From what I hear, her father is a smuggler, amongst other things. The notion that she was not recognised by someone at that port is therefore laughable. No, brother, I must take responsibility for the consequences of my actions.' She turned to Samuel. 'I implore you, Mr Liddell, please find her and bring her safely back to Hayton. Whoever she is matters not a jot. She has been good and kind to me, even when I have not deserved it.'

Samuel gave her a solemn nod. 'You have my word,' he replied. 'At least now we know where we need to look for her, and it is much closer to home than Richmond.'

'Where?' Charles asked, frowning.

'An isolated hamlet called Lillybeck, a few miles north of here,' Samuel said, stepping along the hallway towards the library, the semblance of a plan starting to form in his mind. 'But first I'm going to fetch a couple of pistols. If we're going to get Hope away from that villain of a man once and for all, then I dare say we ought to be armed.'

Hope's eyes flickered open, and for several moments she struggled to fathom where she was. Her head was pounding, and she felt sick and dizzy as she tried to focus on her surroundings. Before she'd awoken she'd been dreaming—she could recall that much. She'd been in Samuel's bedchamber, just as she had been when she'd confessed to who she truly was, except that in her dream, Samuel had not appeared frozen in horror, and she had not left. Instead, he'd told her that he loved her, he'd taken her in his arms and embraced her, before taking her to his bed, where she'd spent many hours wrapped up in his crisp white sheets. Wrapped up in him.

It had been a wanton, desirous dream, and one which ought to have brought a blush to her cheeks at the remembrance of it. Instead, as her blurry vision and sleep-addled mind finally gave way to clear and grim reality, she felt the colour drain from her face. Having relished her dream, she'd now awoken to a nightmare.

'Welcome back, my lady. Sorry about the sore head. You weren't for co-operating so I'd no choice but to knock you out cold.'

Hope blinked, trying to force her eyes to focus. 'How did I get...'

'Here?' Jeremiah Sloane finished her question for her. 'In a cart, lass. Roddy's cart. You remember Roddy, don't you?'

Hope grimaced at the memory of her father's long-standing accomplice. His had been one of the few faces she'd recognised that fateful night outside the theatre in Lowhaven, all those weeks ago. Now she thought about it, it had been his cart in which she'd been conveyed, bound and gagged, to her father's cottage that time too.

Jeremiah Sloane sat across the table from her, his customary mug of his strong brew clutched in his hand. Around them the cottage was dim and damp, the light of a single tallow candle doing little to ward off either the shadows or the creeping chill.

Gripped by panic, Hope tried to move, only to realise that she'd been tied to the chair upon which she sat, her hands and feet tightly bound.

'Oh, aye, I wasn't taking any chances this time,' he said, his eyes narrowed at her even as he chuckled. He took a long drink from his mug before wiping his mouth with the back of his filthy hand. 'Hayton Hall then, eh? You did well for yourself there, lass. And, judging by the look of you, you've not been working as a scullery maid neither. Aye, quite the lady. George will love that. He likes nothing better than to spoil fine things.'

'Still intent upon marrying me to one of your disgusting associates, then?' she asked, trying to ignore the bile which rose in her throat.

Her father simply shrugged. 'Marry you, not marry you—George can do as he sees fit. It's naught to me what happens to you, not after all the trouble you've caused.'

Hope stared at him. 'What on earth are you talking about? I've done nothing to you, Pa. Nothing at all.'

She tried her best not to flinch as Jeremiah Sloane launched himself towards her. 'Done nothing, have you?' he repeated, his face mere inches from hers. 'You cost me dearly is what you've done.' He slumped back down in his chair, reaching immediately for his mug and taking another large gulp of its potent contents. 'If only you'd wed five years ago when I arranged it, then all this unpleasantness could have been avoided. Instead, you ran away, and I had to pick up the pieces. Malky was not happy, you know. He'd taken quite a shine to you, so much so that he'd agreed to write off my debt to him as soon as you'd wed. Instead... well, as I said, you cost me dearly.'

'Malky?' Hope repeated, grimacing as her head continued to pound. Five years ago, her father had kept her in the dark about exactly who she was to wed, and she had fled before she'd had chance to find out. She did not recall anyone called Malky, although apparently he'd known her. 'Who is he?'

'Was,' her father corrected her, before draining the contents of his mug. 'He lived on the Isle of Man, traded from there. Died a couple of years back—drowned at sea during a storm. Always a risk-taker was Malky. He wasn't the worst sort, though. A better man than George, to be sure. The man's a beast.'

'A beast you're forcing me to wed,' she goaded him.

Jeremiah Sloane slammed his mug on the table. 'And for that you have only yourself to blame! Unpaid debts don't go away, my lass. They grow and grow. Things started to get desperate, and I had to pay Malky somehow so...'

'So you borrowed from Peter to pay Paul,' Hope said, the penny finally dropping. 'And kept on borrowing, from the sounds of it.'

'Aye, except these men aren't the apostles. In George's case, more like the Devil himself.'

'And let me guess, when word reached you that I'd been

spotted in Lowhaven theatre, you saw a chance to settle your debts for good this time. You offered me up on a plate to this George and he was willing to take me instead of payment, just like that?'

Her father shook his head. 'No, George insisted on seeing you first. A man like that wants to know what he's getting. I knew he'd want you though, the moment he saw you on stage.' He smiled bitterly. 'You got your mother's good looks, after all.'

Hope shivered at the thought of that beastly man surveying her like a prize heifer at a market. 'I'm not goods to be bartered and traded,' she said quietly. 'How could you, Pa? Your own daughter?'

'Sold yourself, though, didn't you?' he retorted, not answering her question. He filled his mug again, then took a self-satisfied sip. 'I wonder what fine clothes like that cost you, Hope? What price the master of Hayton Hall put on dressing you up and letting you parade around his grand house and gardens like a duchess? He must have thought all his Christmases had come at once. An actress? No better than a bawd.'

Hope felt the heat of indignation rise in her chest as she strained against the ropes which bound her. 'Samuel is not like that!' she snapped. 'He has been faultlessly kind to me and never asked for anything in return.'

An amused smile crept slowly over Jeremiah Sloane's face, showing off an incomplete set of brown teeth. 'Samuel is it, eh? You really did get your feet well under his plentiful table. He certainly kept you well hidden. A shame you got careless and went wandering about the port with your fancy gentleman.' He began to chuckle, although quickly it gave way to a terrible hacking cough.

Hope felt a solitary tear trickle down her face and wished with all her heart that she could swipe the evidence away. The last thing she wanted her cold and callous father to see was how much his words hurt her, or how much she cared for Samuel. She was all too aware how capable he was of using even the merest hint of emotion against her and turning it into a weakness to exploit. So she bit her tongue, forcing herself to remain silent rather than letting him know how wrong his sordid view of her relationship with Samuel was. Rather than telling him exactly what sort of gentleman she'd been living with, or just how blessed she felt to have spent time in his company.

Because truly, she thought now, Samuel had been a blessing, and not just when he'd come to her rescue that night in the woods. He'd been a blessing every day since, treating her with a kindness and gentleness she'd never before known. He'd welcomed her into his life and whilst he had lied about having a title, in every respect that mattered he'd shown her who he was. He was a considerate, thoughtful man who was interested in the world, and interested in her, listening to her and talking to her as an equal.

But of course, she reminded herself, she had been pretending to be his equal. The truth of her lowly birth had brought an end to that and, with it, an end to his affection for her. Perhaps, she reasoned, that was what had really brought tears to her eyes, and not her father's insults.

Perhaps she was crying for the loss of a future she'd almost fooled herself into thinking she could have. A future with Samuel. A future where he loved her and she loved him.

Because if she was honest with herself, that was what she felt. She did love him. But that love was as futile as it was unwanted. Samuel could never love her—that much had been plain in his horrified gaze and his distant demeanour last night. No doubt her disappearance from Hayton would come as something of a relief, marking the end of an embarrassing episode in his life when he'd been fooled into caring for an actress and an outlaw's daughter.

'Pity you won't find life with George quite so comfortable,' Jeremiah Sloane continued to taunt her, his fit of coughing abating. 'I sent Roddy to tell him that you're here. Word is that he's in Lowhaven finishing a job, so I dare say it won't take him long to come for you. If you know what's good for you, you'll wipe that sour look off your face and try your damnedest not to provoke him. He's been in a foul temper since you ran away as it is.'

He began to cough again, uncontrollably this time, forcing him to rummage in the pocket of his breeches and fish out a filthy rag with which to stifle the rasping, barking sound. From her restrained position Hope could do nothing but watch and, as she did, she began to study the man, to really look at him as though she might be laying eyes on him for the first time. As a girl she'd been terrified of his ferocity, of his temper, of the power she believed his life of crime had granted him. Now, watching him, she saw an ageing man, his skin sallow, his dirty clothes hanging from his emaciated frame, his would-be handkerchief bloodstained and betraying the illness which gripped him. She saw a man who was no longer in control, whose fate rested in the hands of monsters like George. She saw what all the years of corruption and vice had wrought, saw how it had hollowed him from the inside out.

'You're afraid of George, aren't you?' Now it was her turn to goad him. 'I used to think you weren't afraid of anything—not even the gallows. But now I see there's a lot that frightens you.'

'There's a lot that should frighten you too,' he snapped, breathless, before draining his second mug as though his life depended upon it. As though the potent contents could cure whatever canker had taken hold in his lungs. 'You'd just better hope that George sees fit to make you his wife, because otherwise I dare say he'll take whatever innocence you have left then drown you in the Eden river.'

The stark threat was like a punch in the gut. Unable to bear the sight or sound of her father any longer, Hope looked away, her eyes drifting towards the little window and her thoughts wandering across the rugged countryside to Hayton Hall. To afternoons drinking tea in the parlour, and to gentle promenades in the gardens. To conversations about Hume and Shakespeare. To passionate kisses in the library, in the parlour, in his bedchamber. To the feeling of being safe and cared for. To the happiest weeks of her life.

And, above all, to the man she loved and who, she felt certain, she would never see again.

Chapter Twenty-One

'Should we not alert the local constable?'

Samuel shook his head at Charles's question as they made their way along the rough track which led to the cottage where Hope's father lived. Information about the precise whereabouts of Jeremiah Sloane's abode had been difficult to come by. No one living in the scattered collection of low stone dwellings which made up the hamlet of Lillybeck seemed particularly willing to acknowledge that they knew the man, much less part with the details of where he might be found.

The offer of a few coins, however, had sufficiently loosened tongues, leading Samuel and Charles to an isolated spot on the very fringes of an already remote community. Although Lillybeck lay only miles from Hayton, it was far enough beyond Liddell land for Samuel to feel quite unfamiliar with this corner of Cumberland. Quite simply, it was a place he'd never had reason to travel to—until now. His scant knowledge of the area made him feel decidedly uncomfortable, as did the warning he'd received from the frail old man who'd taken Samuel's bribe for information. A warning which now rang in his ears.

'Have a care, sir. From what I hear Sloane is sickening,

but I dare say he's still a dangerous man. Whatever your business is with him, if you know what's good for you, you'll keep one hand on your pistol.'

Samuel had thanked the man for his advice, before enquiring if he knew anything about Jeremiah Sloane's daughter. 'Perhaps you've seen her recently,' he'd probed. 'I heard that she'd returned to Lillybeck.'

'If she has then I pity the poor lass,' the man had replied, shaking his head sadly. 'She ran away from him years ago—no one knew where she went. If she's come back then I doubt it'll have been willingly.'

Samuel shuddered at everything those words implied before glancing at Charles, who looked at him expectantly. 'No constables,' he said, finally answering his friend's question. 'From what Hope said, her father supplies his wares to some of the so-called great and good around these parts. If he's got magistrates in his pocket, then he's likely got a few constables in there too. I think we have to proceed without the help of the law, for now at least.'

'I don't like the sound of that,' Charles replied.

'Neither do I. But needs must.'

'So, what is the plan, Sammy?'

Samuel let out a long breath as he drew his horse to a halt. They were near the cottage, although now that he'd laid his eyes on it, Samuel felt that calling it a cottage afforded it too grand a title. It was a crumbling, ramshackle place, barely fit to house livestock, never mind people. Around it the grass grew tall, its days as grazing pasture for sheep clearly a distant memory. Near the rough track on which they now stood, lay the detritus of what would have once been needed to run a small farm: the rotting wood of abandoned carts, the remnants of broken fences and pieces of scythes and other tools, long since forgotten. The whole place reeked of neglect and decay. Samuel swallowed hard as his gaze wandered towards the tiny windows of the cottage. He prayed to God that Hope was indeed inside, and that she was unharmed.

'We leave the horses here,' he said, dismounting and leading the creature to a nearby tree, before tethering him carefully to its thick trunk. 'We approach quietly on foot and try to get a look inside the cottage first. We need to assess exactly what we're dealing with.'

Charles nodded his agreement, and together they crept towards the decrepit building, using the tall grass to shield them. If the situation had not been so grave, Samuel would have found the sight of the pair of them laughable. Well clad in fine riding coats and Hessian boots and sneaking towards a place which was the rural equivalent of the slum houses found in larger towns and cities, they looked just about as out of place as it was possible to be. As he tiptoed along, it struck Samuel again just how acutely aware Hope must have been of the difference between their worlds. The poverty and hardship she had known stood in such sharp contrast to the sumptuous comfort of his life at Hayton Hall.

A fresh wave of guilt washed over him. His life, and by extension the life he'd offered her these past weeks, must have seemed utterly intimidating. She must have spent every day feeling like a fish out of water. Little wonder she'd struggled to bring herself to tell him about it. Little wonder she'd felt the need to pretend to be someone else.

Well, there would be no more pretending now, on either of their parts. When he reached a little window, he made a silent vow. He would find her and bring her safely back to

Hayton, and he would offer her a life, with him, for ever. A life they would share and build together.

He just had to find her first.

'I can't see her,' Charles whispered as he peered tentatively through the window. 'The place is deathly quiet. I don't like it.'

Samuel found himself bristling at his friend's poor choice of words, before taking a look for himself. Sure enough, Charles was right—even in the dim light of the single-room dwelling it was evident that Hope was not inside. He cast his eyes around, taking in the simple, sparse furnishings, the bare stone walls, the last remnants of a single tallow candle, left burning in the middle of a table. Someone had been there, and not so very long ago from the looks of it.

'If this place is anything to go by, I'd say crime doesn't always pay,' Charles whispered. 'I always thought smuggling was a lucrative trade, but it seems not.'

'It's a cut-throat enterprise,' Samuel replied. 'Some win and some lose. It looks like Jeremiah Sloane has been on the losing side for some time. Hope said he runs some illicit stills from nearby caves too. However, that old man told us that his health is failing. Perhaps his business has been failing at the same time.'

Out the corner of his eye, Samuel caught sight of something, like a flicker of movement on the ground. 'What's that?' he hissed. 'See there—behind the table? It looks like a boot.' He squinted, trying to peer through the gloom and murk to see more clearly. 'I think it's…it's moving. Someone is in there, lying on the ground.'

Instinctively, he darted away from the window, rounding the cottage and heading towards its single wooden door. If it was Hope and she was bound or, God forbid, injured, then there was no time to lose. He'd detected no other signs of life within. If she was alone, then he had to rescue her before her father returned. He had to get her away from this dreadful place—now.

'I think it is a boot,' Charles hissed, scurrying behind him. 'But Sammy, it might not be...'

Charles's words were cut short by the loud thump of Samuel's boot as it made contact with the door, followed by the brittle crack of the old wood as it gave way feebly to his force. Samuel hurried inside, Charles still following him, to be confronted by a scene which made them both gasp loudly. Beside the table, a man was lying on the floor, groaning softly, his limbs twitching and his eyes rolling as he seemed to drift in and out of consciousness.

Samuel bent down, his gaze immediately drawn to the large bloodstain which was growing across the man's filthy shirt. 'It looks as though he's been shot,' he called, looking over his shoulder at Charles, who lingered behind, looking distinctly pale about the face.

'Should I send for a physician?' Charles asked.

Samuel looked back at the man. He suspected there was no time for that—the man was in all likelihood mortally wounded and would be dead by the time a physician arrived. However, Samuel decided, they had to at least try.

'Yes,' he began. 'Perhaps ask that old man...'

'No...' The man's voice was raspy but insistent. 'I'm done for.'

'Are you Jeremiah Sloane?' Samuel asked, his shock at the scene he'd uncovered abating, and the urgency of finding Hope gripping him once more. 'Where is your daughter? You must tell me, man. Tell me now!'

A sliver of a smile appeared on the man's weathered face. 'You must be Samuel,' he croaked. 'She really must have been like a harlot between your sheets if you want her back.'

Samuel felt the heat of indignation rise in his chest at such a remark—uttered by her father, no less. The man really was the lowest of the low. It was a mystery to him how such a person could have sired such a lovely, brave and intelligent daughter.

'Where is she?' he repeated, through gritted teeth this time. Samuel was not a man to allow his temper to get the better of him but, even so, he could feel himself close to losing it.

Jeremiah Sloane coughed weakly, causing blood to bubble up and trickle down the side of his cheek. 'George has her,' he wheezed, his eyes rolling again. 'They've gone north.'

'North?' Samuel repeated, his heart lurching as all that those words implied became clear. 'You mean to Gretna? To wed her?' he asked. Hope had never named him, but he realised George must be the terrible forced fiancé she'd described.

'Doubt...he'll...do that.'

Jeremiah Sloane's breathing grew laboured now, and Samuel realised they were almost out of time. If Hope's father would not part with his knowledge before slipping away to meet his maker, then their chance of finding Hope might be lost. She might be lost to him, and that was a thought he truly could not bear.

'Then where?' he prompted, hearing the desperation in his own voice as he shook the man by his shoulders in an effort to rouse him one final time. 'Damn it, tell me!'

'Rockcliffe.'

The word was a whisper, barely audible. Jeremiah Sloane

choked again, then let out one more whistling, agonising breath. His bloodied body grew still and limp, his grey, leathery face freezing in a contorted expression, eyes wide, lips parted in an O shape, as though death had come as a shock. As though, perhaps, he'd glimpsed something on the other side that he had not wanted to see. A gruesome testament to a lifetime of wickedness, law-breaking and cruelty, indeed.

Samuel got to his feet, turning away from the grim scene at last. 'Let's fetch the horses,' he said to Charles, hurrying towards the door. 'You must find the local constable. It's clear Jeremiah Sloane has been murdered, and we have a duty to report it. Do that, then return to Hayton, to your sister.'

'I thought you said not to involve constables, that Sloane had the law in his pocket around these parts?' Charles asked, frowning.

'Then if that's the case, hopefully they will be motivated to bring the killer to justice,' Samuel quipped. He sighed heavily. 'Honestly, I don't know, Charles. I only know that we must report what we have found here, immediately. To do otherwise might bring the law's suspicions down upon us.'

Charles grimaced. 'All right, point taken. And what will you do?'

'I must ride for Rockcliffe at once.'

'But where the devil is Rockcliffe?' Charles asked him, following behind. 'And who is this George her father spoke of, anyway?'

'A monster, Charles,' Samuel replied, recalling again Hope's words about the man her father had tried to force her to marry. Shuddering, he glanced back into the gloom of the cottage. 'One monster is dead, and now Hope is in the clutches of another. I must follow the road north, find Rockcliffe and this George, then I will find her. There is no time to lose!'

Samuel ran along the uneven track and back towards his horse, the same silent prayer circling around in his mind.

Please God, let me find Hope, he prayed. *Let her be safe and well. Let her come home with me, so that these malevolent men might never try to harm her again.*

Hope winced as the cart jolted on the road, the sudden movement making her already pounding head ache all the more. Despite herself, she let out a sob, partly at the pain and partly at the shock of it all. Tears ran unabated down her cheeks as her mind replayed all that she'd witnessed once again.

The way George had waltzed into the cottage so casually, as if he owned the place. How he'd licked his lips when he'd looked at her, an unmistakably greedy look lingering in his dark eyes. The way her father had scurried over to him like a beggar asking for his supper, pleading for reassurances that his debt was now settled. How George had refused to answer him, laughing and shoving him out of the way as he'd marched over to claim his prize. The way her father had begun to wail and yell like a man overcome by the realisation that he could never win. How that screaming had caused something in George to snap. How George's cheeks had flushed with anger, a cloud gathering over the already foreboding features of his angular face before he swiftly drew his pistol, took his aim, and fired.

How Hope had watched as her father tumbled quietly to the ground, his desperate wailing replaced by the soft moans of a man whose life was ebbing away.

When they'd left the cottage, Jeremiah Sloane had still lived—just. As George had untied her from the chair, unbound her feet and hands and dragged her away, Hope had been gripped by the most overpowering urge to run to her father's side. To remain with him in his final moments. To not let him die alone. It was strange. After all he'd done to her, Jeremiah Sloane deserved neither her concern nor her care, and yet both feelings had plagued her. His cruelty and callousness were unforgivable, but in the end the brute he'd become had been subsumed by an even greater monster—a leviathan who'd enfeebled him, who'd preyed on his weaknesses as age, debt and misfortune consumed him bit by bit. She would not mourn her father but, inexplicably, she realised that she did pity him. Better that, she supposed, than pitying herself. She would not surrender to such feelings. At least, not yet.

'Stop weeping, or else I'll give you something to weep about.' The monster spoke without even looking at her, his eyes intent upon the road ahead. He sat close by her side on the bench at the front of the cart, his hands firm upon the reins of the single horse which pulled them along. He'd left her feet unbound but had tethered one of her wrists to the cart, subtly enough that it would not be noticed by anyone else on the road, but firmly enough to ensure she had no chance of getting away. Not that she had any intention of trying to leap on to the road and run—she'd already seen what a good shot he was, and any such attempt to flee would undoubtedly be answered by a bullet from his pistol.

Hope straightened herself, fighting back the last vestiges of her tears. He was right; she did need to stop weeping. The options for escape, she knew, were vanishingly small as it was, and would certainly be undetectable if she was too busy crying.

'You already did—you killed my father,' she retorted, mustering a feistiness she did not truly feel. Better that, she decided, than allowing him to sense her fear.

'Ha!' He glanced at her, baring his yellow teeth and grinning in amusement. 'I've done you a favour there, trust me.' He reached out, placing his hand upon her knee and giving it a firm squeeze. 'Do as you're told, and you'll have a better life with me than you ever did with him.'

Even through the fabric of her dress, the feeling of his fingers made her skin crawl. Hope shivered, partly at his unwanted touch and partly at the cold which seeped increasingly into her bones. She wore only the plain blue day dress which she'd been wearing when her father had snatched her from Hayton Hall, and although its sleeves were long, its fine fabric was insufficient against the autumn chill. She was sure she'd been wearing a shawl in Hayton's gardens too, but when she'd awoken at her father's cottage it had been nowhere to be seen. Obstinately, Hope stiffened—against the monster's touch, and against the cold. She would not allow this man to detect even a hint of her discomfort, lest he perceive it as a weakness to exploit.

'And what does this better life entail?' she asked him. She gave him a haughty look, once again masking her fear as her father's warning about being drowned in the river rang in her ears. 'Because I had a perfectly good one, without my father and without you.'

'Which life would that be?' Briefly, he took his eyes off the road, looking at her with a gaze so dark it appeared almost black under the gloom of the surrounding trees. 'The one you spent on stage, or the one you spent at Hayton Hall, playing the harlot for its master?'

Hope scowled at him—better that than allowing the fresh tears which pricked in the corners of her eyes to fall. When her father had made similar insinuations, she'd protested. Now, she decided, she would hold her tongue. Allowing this dangerous, evil man to know anything about Samuel, about how much she'd adored her short time with him or about how much she cared for him, could put him in danger, and she would not be able to live with herself if anything happened to him. Better to let George believe that she'd spent these past weeks being ill-used than letting him know she'd spent them falling in love. A love, she reminded herself, which was lost to her now, even though she would feel it deeply to the end of her days.

'My life in the theatre, of course,' she lied, meeting his eye. 'A life in which I did no man's bidding.'

'Aye, well, you'll do my bidding now,' George snarled at her.

'As what?' Hope challenged him, although she hardly dared to ask. 'Your wife, or your harlot?'

George returned his eyes to the road. 'I've not decided,' he said coldly. 'But, either way, you'll be running contraband and having my bairns, Hope. That's what I've got planned for you.'

Hope looked away, biting her lip so hard that she might draw blood. All the pity she'd fleetingly felt for her father simply disappeared as she faced up to the sort of life the man had condemned her to, and in its place her anger grew. She'd spent her formative years living with a man who used fear, threats and sometimes violence to get his own way, and she was damned if she was going to spend the remainder of her life with another such man. She was damned if she was going to be forced into committing crimes or going to bed with a man who repulsed her. Frankly, she decided, she'd rather he did just drown her in the river and have done with it.

But first, she vowed, she would defy him every step of the way. She would use every opportunity she got trying to regain her freedom. Starting right now. Hope wiggled her bound wrist, straining against the rope, carefully trying to tease it loose without him noticing. She would bide her time, she would play the hand she'd been dealt, and when the right moment came along she would seize it—just as she always did.

Chapter Twenty-Two

Hope grimaced as George directed the horse to slow down and turn into the courtyard of a coaching inn. She'd long since lost any sense of where they were or how long they had been travelling. She knew from the scant details George had offered that he was taking her north, and since he'd admitted he had not decided whether or not he planned to wed her, she presumed they were not going directly to Gretna—a small mercy which she was thankful for. She also knew that the farm from which George ran his nefarious operations was somewhere near the Scottish border, not far from the Solway Firth, where the rivers Esk and Eden meandered out to sea. She had to assume, therefore, that that was where they were headed.

Realising that, however, served only to make Hope begin to panic. Despite her best efforts, she'd had little success in loosening the rope which bound her to the cart, and with each passing mile she felt the weight of her fate bearing down upon her. If she could not escape now, while it was just the two of them on the road, what chance did she stand once she'd arrived at his farm, no doubt living under the watchful eye of his many criminal accomplices? She had other, more immediate concerns too, such as what George had planned once darkness fell. Surely, he could not hope to travel all the way to the border today; they would have to stop somewhere tonight. At this, Hope shuddered—the thought of spending the night anywhere with that monster, and all that such a night might entail, did not bear thinking about. Which was why, when he turned into the coaching inn, she felt her heart sink.

'Why are we stopping here?' she asked, trying her best to sound curious rather than fearful.

'Because I need a drink, and so does the horse.' He glanced at her, a knowing smirk spreading across his face. 'Sorry to disappoint you, Hope, but I don't plan to take a room here for the night. I know you've been used to living like a duchess as Hayton's harlot, but you'll have to make do with a straw bed tonight—unless we forgo that and sleep under the stars,' he added, giving her an unpleasant wink.

'And where is this bed of straw, exactly?' Hope asked. If she could draw some specific information from him, she might better understand where she was. Information which she needed, if the opportunity ever arrived for her to make a bid for freedom.

'A friend's cottage,' he snapped. 'That's all you need to know.'

Hope suppressed a sigh as the horse drew to a halt in the courtyard and George climbed down from the cart. He was never going to tell her anything useful; he was far too cunning for that. She glanced down at her wrist, which was red and raw-looking from all the wriggling she'd done in a vain effort to free herself. Sitting next to him, she had not dared use her free hand to try to remove the shackle; to do so would have surely drawn his attention. However, if he left her to fetch a drink...

'I'll remain on the cart,' she said quickly. 'I can keep an eye on the horse while the stable boys attend to him.'

George began to laugh, walking round to her as he shook his head. 'You must think I'm stupid.'

'No, I'm just not thirsty, that's all.' A lie, of course. She was thirsty, hungry, tired, terrified—all of it. She was running out of options, running out of opportunities. If she was honest with herself, she was beginning to despair.

'I don't care what you are,' he said through gritted teeth. 'You're not leaving my sight.'

He untied the rope, liberating her poor sore wrist—another small mercy, she supposed, although likely useless to her whilst ever she remained under his watchful eye. Unceremoniously, he hauled her down from the cart, all but dragging her along as he approached two wide-eyed stable boys and handed them some coins to attend to the horse. His thirst for beer clearly growing, he hurried her around towards a small kitchen at the rear of the inn, coins again crossing palms—this time those of the innkeeper, who looked at Hope with some concern when he observed George's rough handling of her. However, he said nothing, instead wordlessly pointing them both through a weather-beaten wooden door and into a humble room, where they found a table laden with bread and beer mugs and a handful of other travellers crowded around it. Several male faces glanced up briefly to see who had joined them, before returning to regard their fare once more.

'Here. Sit.'

George pushed her towards a wooden stool, forcing her to sit down. He remained close at her side, still standing as he grabbed a hunk of bread and a mug and ate and drank as though he'd had no sustenance for years. Hope tried hard to ignore her dry mouth and empty, groaning stomach;

she'd sworn she was not thirsty and, besides, she would take nothing that he'd paid for. As her father had learned to his cost, this was not the sort of man you wanted to owe a debt to. This was the sort of man who would always want something in return.

Unlike Samuel. Generous and decent Samuel, who had wanted nothing from her. Kind and loving Samuel, who had given her so much more than sanctuary. If only she really had been Hope Swynford. If only she really had been a gentleman's daughter and an heiress. Then, perhaps...

She did not realise that she was crying until one of the other travellers, an older, stocky man with a round, kindly face, remarked upon it.

'Now then, lass, I'm sure it's not so bad,' the man said, offering her a small smile. She watched as he glanced warily at George, who was still devouring his bread and beer. 'Do you want to eat something? There's plenty to be had.'

'She doesn't want anything,' George snapped, his mouth full.

Hope watched as the man's keen gaze continued to flit between them both, as though he was trying to work something out, and a seed of an idea began to grow in her mind. She raised her sore, rope-marked wrist above the table, giving it a rub so that he could clearly see the marks upon it.

'I'm afraid I'm not very keen on plain bread and beer,' she said softly, putting on her Hope Swynford voice as she eased back into character. 'I much prefer tea and cake, you see. Two of the very best things in life, I can assure you.'

Next to her, she sensed George cease chewing. One by one, each pair of eyes around the table seemed to settle upon her captor, and for several moments no one moved.

'I dare say they are, miss,' the older man said, although

he barely tore his gaze from George. 'But those are things you'll find in the parlour, not the back kitchen. Perhaps if you went in there, you'd find something more suited to your tastes.'

'Don't you dare move.'

George gripped her arm so tightly that it made her cry out, and stools scraped in unison against the stone floor as several of the men rose to their feet.

'What is this man to you, miss?' the older man asked, his kindly expression long gone as his eyes blazed thunderously at George. 'Are you in need of some assistance?'

At that moment Hope saw her chance, and she seized it with both hands. 'This man has kidnapped me!' she cried out, getting to her feet. 'He has stolen me away and means to marry me at Gretna against my will so that he can steal my inheritance. He is a villain and a scoundrel!'

Together, the men rounded on George. Apparently startled by what was unfolding, he took several steps back, his eyes wide with something which almost resembled fear. As the men drew nearer, Hope moved away, finally out of George's grasp. What happened next was as confusing as it was alarming —a frantic scramble of limbs as punches were thrown and angry, expletive-ridden words were exchanged between George and the men. At one point George launched forward, clattering into the table and sending bread and beer flying about the room. For several moments Hope simply stood there, frozen, until three simple words spoken by the kindly older man brought her back to her senses.

'Run, miss. Run!'

Of course—there was nothing else for it. Without another moment's hesitation, Hope hurried towards the door, and towards her freedom. Towards her life, towards the unknown. Towards whatever lay ahead of her. This was it, she realised—she would not get a better chance. Indeed, she would likely get no other chances at all.

Quickly, Hope turned the knob on the door, poised to flee. Then a gunshot rang out.

Samuel was a good number of miles into his journey before he realised that he hadn't quite thought this through. Rockcliffe, he had managed to ascertain, lay to the northwest of Carlisle—reaching it within the day would be pushing the endurance of both himself and his horse, especially at the speed he'd so far travelled. He had indeed been riding hard; his best chance of finding Hope was to catch up with her and her abductor on the road, although how likely he was to manage this, he did not know. He'd no idea by what means this man was taking Hope away with him, and therefore how many miles they would manage to cover before darkness fell. He prayed it was by old horse and rickety cart—the more elderly and ramshackle, the better.

Unfortunately, despite covering a good number of miles of road and making brief enquiries at every inn on the way, so far there'd been no sign of either Hope or the dreadful George, and riding so fast was quickly wearying his horse. Stopping to rest was the last thing he wanted to do, but as he rode towards the latest coaching inn he realised it was a necessity. The poor animal needed water and sustenance at the very least, and if he was honest with himself, so did he. He'd barely eaten or drunk anything that day, such had been his complete preoccupation with finding Hope. With a heavy sigh, he turned his horse into the inn's courtyard, catching the eye of a young stable boy and giving him a beckoning nod. Perhaps, he reasoned, it would be best to change the poor creature while he was here.

Samuel climbed down from his saddle and the boy walked forward. He glanced around briefly, suddenly struck by how eerily quiet the inn was. It was not so much that there were no carriages or coaches—indeed, he could count several, sitting stationary at the far end of the courtyard. It was more that there were no people standing outside—no ladies or gentlemen hovering, waiting to depart, no carriages being readied, and no drivers checking their horses or the position of their passengers' luggage. It was, without doubt, very strange.

'Where is everyone?' Samuel asked the stable boy who, it struck him now, looked a deathly shade of white.

'Most are in the parlour, sir.' The boy's voice was barely a whisper. 'A few have gone behind the stables. They dare not come out.'

Samuel frowned. 'Why?'

'There was a sound like a gunshot. It came from the rear kitchen not so long ago.' The boy paused, swallowing hard. 'The master went to see what was afoot and…and there's a man in there, sir, waving his pistol about. Says anyone who comes in will get their brains blown out. The master's sent for the constable and says everyone's to stay hid—except us, on account of the horses we've to attend to, but everyone else.' The boy looked at the horse, reaching out to give him a gentle stroke. 'You could go, sir. He's tired but the next inn's only a few miles away. He could manage it at a trot.'

Samuel pressed his lips together, absorbing the details of the boy's story. Could this murderous and unpredictable man be the one he was looking for?

'This man you mentioned—do you know if there is a lady travelling with him?' he asked.

'Aye, sir, although if I had to guess, I'd say she's not come with him willingly. Poor lady was shackled to the cart when they got here. The master reckons he's taken her from a fine house somewhere. Says the man's trying to hide it, leaving her looking grubby and without a bonnet, but there's no mistaking that her dress is quality.'

'And the lady, what does she look like?' Samuel tried to remain focused on ascertaining the facts but, despite himself, he felt his fists curl. The thought of any woman being so mistreated made him angry, and the idea that it might be Hope was frankly unbearable.

The boy frowned, apparently recalling. 'Small. Dark hair, all matted and hanging loose like she's been in the wars. But very pretty—meaning no impertinence, of course, sir. Just an observation.'

Any lingering doubt in Samuel's mind was immediately blown away by the boy's description. It was Hope, he told himself, his heart beginning to race. She was here, and she was locked in a room with a madman wielding a pistol. A room, and a man, he had to now work to free her from.

Samuel gave the boy a nod and a tight smile before pressing a shilling into his palm. 'Be good to my horse,' he said. 'Hopefully, this won't take too long.'

'But sir, you can't surely…'

Samuel did not hear the rest of the boy's protest. He was too preoccupied, creeping towards the kitchen which sat at the back of the inn. As he reached the building he ducked down, tentatively edging towards the single small window which offered the only view into the room, and to understanding what was happening inside. Cautiously, he peeked in, surveying the scene swiftly from a low position and praying he would not be noticed.

Immediately he spied Hope, the sight of her making his heart fleetingly lift, before the gravity of the situation she was in made his pulse begin to race with trepidation. She was perched on a stool, her eyes cast down and shoulders slumped in an expression of utter defeat. Near to her was a man with sharp features, pacing to and fro, waving a pistol around menacingly. George—it had to be. On the other side of the room, furthest from the door, stood a handful of men, all looking glum, their hands raised in surrender. Samuel frowned. Clearly, something had happened to provoke this potentially deadly scene, but he was damned if he could discern exactly what.

No matter. All that counted now was rescuing Hope from George's grasp, and ensuring no one else was hurt in the process. Samuel reached into his pocket, placing a careful hand upon his pistol. On the one hand, he felt relieved at having the presence of mind to come armed; on the other, he felt alarmed at the prospect of having to use his weapon. No matter, he told himself. He could not afford to deliberate on this; even a moment's hesitation could prove costly. He would do whatever it took to rescue Hope. If that meant aiming his pistol at her captor and pulling the trigger, then so be it.

He continued to watch at the window as George's pacing slowed and he came to a halt with his back to the door. This was his chance, Samuel realised. He had to act—quickly and decisively. He had to take a leaf out of Hope's book and live on his wits.

It was this thought which spurred him on as he hurried towards the door, launching himself at it with such force as to render turning the doorknob entirely unnecessary. He was aware of a deep, guttural roar coming from the depths of his throat as the door gave way, a sound which was so ungentlemanly and so unlike him that it would have taken him by surprise, had he not been so thoroughly consumed by his mission. Out of the corner of his eye, he saw Hope leap to her feet.

'Samuel? Samuel!' she breathed, part-question and part-affirmation.

A shocked-looking George turned. As Samuel threw himself towards the man he saw him move to raise his pistol but, mercifully, he was not quite quick enough. Overwhelming him with the element of surprise combined with sheer brute force, Samuel wrestled George to the ground, holding him with his face and stomach pressed to the floor while he tried to get the pistol out of his grasp. But his adversary was not about to give up so easily. He flailed about, yelling obscenities as he tried to fight back with a considerable strength of his own.

Thankfully, around him, Samuel sensed the reinforcements begin to assemble. The cluster of men whom George had been holding at gunpoint now sprang into action, several of them joining Samuel in pinning George to the ground, while another, burly man managed at last to prise the pistol from George's firm grip.

Disarmed and overwhelmed, George finally seemed to concede defeat, his limbs growing still, his breathing rapid and exhausted. For several moments Samuel and a couple of his assistants continued to hold him down, apparently not quite daring to move. One of the other men ran outside, returning swiftly with a couple of lengths of rope and offering them to Samuel.

'The stable boys say that the constable is on his way,'

the man said. 'We can use this to restrain him until he gets here.'

'I'll do that.' The burly man grabbed hold of the rope. 'It'll be my pleasure to shackle him like he shackled that poor miss over there, judging by the state of her wrist. You go and attend to her, sir. She's had quite the ordeal.'

Samuel nodded obligingly before hauling himself to his feet. He heard George groan as the burly man took over, holding him down with his considerable weight while tightly binding his hands behind his back.

'You must have been very worried about her,' the man continued. 'Is she your sister, or…?'

But Samuel was not listening. Indeed, his attention was no longer on the burly man, or on Hope's abductor, at all. Instead, his gaze had wandered across the room, towards the woman who stood there, frozen with shock, her dress filthy, her long dark curls mussed, her face drained of all colour. She lifted those emerald eyes to meet his and his heart stirred, just as it had the first time she'd gazed up at him from the floor of her bedchamber, all those weeks ago. Perhaps it had been love even then—it was hard to say. All he knew for certain was that he loved her now.

Wordlessly, Samuel strode towards her, reaching out and enveloping her in his arms. She melted into his embrace, clinging to him tightly as though she too had feared that she might never see him again. For several moments he simply held her, running his fingers gently over the knotted tendrils of her hair. Then she stirred, lifting her chin to gaze up at him, meeting his eyes with a look which spoke of tenderness, of admiration, of affection. Of love. A look which told him everything. He leaned down, his lips capturing hers in affirmation as he poured his heart and soul into that kiss. Everything she felt, he sought to show her, he felt too.

Behind them, an amused voice intruded. 'Not your sister, then,' the burly man said.

Against Hope's lips, Samuel smiled. 'No,' he murmured, breaking the kiss to see that Hope was smiling too. 'Not my sister,' he said, caressing her cheek as he gazed intently into her eyes. 'But I hope, one day soon, she will be my wife.'

Chapter Twenty-Three

Hope collapsed on the bed, completely exhausted. Outside, the afternoon had given way to evening, the sky darkening rapidly as heavy drops of rain began to fall. Given the coming night, the change in the weather and their weariness, not to mention that of Samuel's poor horse, Samuel had suggested that they should remain at the inn overnight before travelling back to Hayton Hall the next day. Hope had nodded her agreement; indeed, in her shocked state, nodding was all she seemed able to do. Samuel appeared to sense this, and with a reassuring smile he'd taken charge, requesting everything from rooms and food to a bathtub and some clean clothes. Once the constable had arrived and George had been taken away, Samuel had escorted her upstairs before leaving her to wash and change with the assistance of a maid he'd managed to secure for her.

'It's all over now, Hope,' he'd said, cupping her cheek with his hand. 'You're perfectly safe. I will just be downstairs in the parlour and will check on you in a little while.'

Now, lying on the bed and listening to the soft crackle of a small fire burning in the hearth, Hope pressed her eyes shut, replaying his words in her mind. She was perfectly safe, and it was all thanks to him. Samuel Liddell had been her rescuer, not once but twice. Weeks ago, he'd saved her from probable death in the woodland near his home, and today he'd saved her from a fate worse than death—a life spent with George. He'd ridden across the country to find her, and put himself in harm's way to save her from George's awful clutches. Then he'd taken her in his arms and he'd kissed her—a kiss which had told her in no uncertain terms that he loved her, before speaking words which left her in no doubt that he meant to ask her to be his wife.

But how could he mean to marry her, when she'd lied to him about who she was? How could he, a wealthy gentleman, want to wed a low-born actress and the daughter of an outlaw?

A knock at the door caused her eyes to fly open and her heart to race. Her head might know that she was safe, but it was clear it would take some time before her fight-or-flight instincts realised that too. Hope forced herself to take a deep, calming breath. More than likely, it was the maid returning, having left a short while ago to take the bathtub away.

'Come in,' she called out, pulling herself upright. She glanced at the plate of food the maid had left for her, a veritable platter of cheese, cold meats and bread which she'd barely begun to pick at. Her stomach, it seemed, hadn't realised that she was safe either, if the way it continued to lurch was anything to go by.

To her surprise, however, it was not the maid's face she saw peering round the door, but Samuel's. He smiled at her somewhat sheepishly. 'Sorry—the maid said you were dressed,' he said. 'But I will go if you're resting.'

'No, it's all right. Please, Samuel, come in.' She offered a smile to mirror his. 'I doubt I will manage to sleep anyway.'

Samuel slipped inside the room, closing the door softly behind him. 'It doesn't look like you've managed to eat much either,' he observed, nodding towards the almost full plate. He pulled a chair up to the bedside before sitting down next to her. 'How are you feeling?'

'Like I've been hit over the head, kidnapped and shackled, so, all in all, I think I have had better days,' she replied.

'What? He hit you over the head?' Immediately, Samuel leapt to his feet, gently brushing her still-damp hair back from her forehead and looking for signs of injury.

The feeling of his fingers against her scalp did strange things to her insides. 'My father did,' she explained. 'Apparently I wasn't a very cooperative kidnap victim so it was all he could do to silence me.'

'You were unconscious? I will summon a physician at once.'

'Samuel—' gently, she captured his hand with her own, lowering it and bringing it to rest at her side '—I will live. I do feel somewhat better after bathing and putting on clean clothes.' She smoothed her other hand over the skirt of a grey dress which felt about two sizes too big for her.

Samuel raked his eyes over her attire. 'Ah—yes. I'm afraid it was all the innkeeper's wife had to offer.'

She grinned at him. 'It is fine. I have grown accustomed to borrowed clothes.'

Samuel shook his head in embarrassment. 'Please, do not remind me.' He squeezed her hand ever so gently. 'When we return to Hayton, Hope, we shall visit a dressmaker in Lowhaven and you shall have a complete wardrobe of your own—I promise you that. And, despite your protestations, I am going to have a physician attend to you before we travel. I cannot believe your father did that to his own daughter.'

She felt her smile fade. 'George shot him—my father. He shot him, just before he took me away. He will be dead by now.'

Samuel nodded gravely. 'I'm afraid he is,' he replied. 'I went with Charles to his cottage, to look for you. He was near death when we got there. He just about managed to tell us where George was taking you before he…before he passed.'

For a long moment Hope pressed her lips together, putting her feelings in order. Holding back her tears. She would not weep for that man—not after all that he had done.

'At least he told you that,' she said in the end. 'And at least he did not die alone.'

'Oh, Hope.' Samuel slid on to the bed beside her, wrapping his arm around her shoulder and drawing her near. 'You really are a remarkable woman, do you know that? Truly remarkable. The life you've lived…the things you must have seen…'

'My life has been no worse than the lives of many men and women across England, Samuel,' she countered softly. 'Most people's experience of life is closer to mine than it is to yours. Not everyone grows up with a free trader for a father, but most know something of hardship.'

He nodded. 'You're right. It reminds me that I am fortunate but also…well, very sheltered. I have not had to be brave like you.'

She chuckled. 'I wouldn't say that. Just hours ago you wrestled a pistol-wielding madman to the ground, or have you forgotten about that already?'

He pulled her closer, placing a kiss on the top of her head. 'Oh, I haven't forgotten. That was probably the bravest and the best thing I have ever done.'

'Probably the most reckless too. You could have been killed.'

'I confess I wasn't really thinking about that. When I saw you through that kitchen window, all I could think about was getting you away from that monster and back with me.'

She looked up at him then, meeting those lovely grey-blue eyes. 'I'm glad you did, Samuel. I'm glad you found me.'

'I almost didn't.' His expression grew serious. 'When I first realised you were gone, I thought you'd left of your own accord, that after our conversation the night before you'd decided to leave. I wouldn't have blamed you if you had. You poured out your story to me and, instead of comforting you, I held back. I hesitated. Then I let you leave without saying all that there was to say.' He shook his head at himself. 'It was unforgivable.'

'No, it's not. It must have come as a shock to learn that the person you'd welcomed into your house wasn't who she said she was at all.' She paused, swallowing hard. Preparing herself for complete honesty. Preparing herself to face up to what she'd seen in his eyes that night. 'It must have been disappointing too, to learn that I am so far beneath you in status. Indeed, you'd have every right to be angry with me.'

'I cannot deny that it came as a shock, but I'm not angry, and certainly not disappointed. You hid your true identity for very good reasons, Hope—reasons far better than the foolish ones I had for borrowing my brother's title. Indeed, you're the one who ought to be angry with me. As for disappointment, surely you know me well enough by now to understand that neither wealth nor connections are of much interest to me. It is companionship, it is the meeting of like minds, it is love—those are the things I want.

Besides, you do yourself a disservice to speak about yourself in such a way.'

'I'm an actress, Samuel,' she reminded him. 'No better than a courtesan or a harlot, as I recall your friend Mr Gordon once saying. And, even worse than that, I'm the daughter of a criminal. I doubt it's possible to have a more dubious background than that.'

He caressed her cheek, lifting her chin gently and placing a brief, soft kiss upon her lips—a kiss which, despite their heavy conversation, left her wanting more. 'You're a beautiful, intelligent, strong and resourceful woman,' he replied. 'You are admirable, Hope—truly. You have survived everything that life has thrown at you. Indeed, against all the odds, I'd say you've flourished. You are clever and you are cultured and you are brave. That is what I should have said to you when you told me your story.'

She raised her eyebrows at him, trying to ignore how her heart sang at his words. She would not get carried away, no matter how sincere his sentiments sounded to her ears. 'So why didn't you?' she asked.

He sighed. 'Partly because I felt ashamed of myself. If I hadn't been so busy pretending that I was a baronet with a big estate then perhaps you'd have found me more approachable. Perhaps you would have told me the truth sooner.'

She smiled sadly. 'I doubt that very much, Samuel, although I do wish I had.' She frowned, searching his gaze. 'You said that was part of the reason. What was the other part?'

Samuel breathed out an embarrassed chuckle. 'The other part was the fact that we were in my bedchamber, late at night and only half-clad. You'd made some remarks about how gentlemen had treated you in the past, about what they had expected, and…and I did not want you to think I was just another gentleman seeking to take advantage of you.'

'You would never have done that,' she replied. 'You've always been impeccably good and decent towards me.'

Samuel nodded. 'Nonetheless, Hope, I was still a man standing in his bedchamber with a beautiful woman. Believe me, it took all my self-restraint not to kiss you or take you into my bed.'

Such loaded words made her cheeks colour, as did the realisation that she wished he had. She tried to suppress the thought, reminding herself that there were a hundred other matters they ought to be discussing. How he couldn't possibly wish to marry a base-born actress being top of the list.

Before she could say another word, however, Samuel sat upright and released her from his embrace. 'I should probably leave you to rest. We can talk more tomorrow. You need to sleep if you're going to be fit for the ride back to Hayton.'

'Don't.' She touched him lightly on the arm. 'Stay awhile—please. I know I am safe here but I'd rather not be alone.'

For good measure she shuffled over, patting the sheets where they lay over the space she'd made. She watched Samuel hesitate, his gaze switching contemplatively between the bed and her. He was a gentleman to a fault—a true, proper gentleman. That was one of the things she loved about him. It was also one of the reasons why she knew that in the cold light of day, when the dust had settled on the chaos and terror of today, he would realise that he could not marry her. If, indeed, he had not realised that already. After all, he had not broached the subject again. Hope pushed the thought from her mind; there was little point in dwelling upon that now. Samuel was right—she needed to sleep and, whether it was wise or not, she wanted to have him by her side.

After several moments of deliberation, something apparently made up Samuel's mind. 'All right,' he said, sliding back on to the bed beside her and taking her into his arms once more. 'I will stay, just until you fall asleep.' He kissed the top of her head as she nestled under his chin. 'I love you, Hope.'

'I love you too, Samuel.'

Hope closed her eyes, overcome by the comfort and reassurance she found in this intimacy, as well as the myriad of other, less familiar feelings she felt stirring within her. But even as she relished his warm embrace, her doubts and her fears continued to niggle at her. He loved her and she loved him, and yet she feared that would not be enough. She would not be enough and, sooner or later, Samuel would come to his senses and see that whilst Hope Swynford could have been his wife, Hope Sloane never could.

Chapter Twenty-Four

The ride back to Hayton was torture, almost as much as the previous night had been. The feeling of Hope sitting on his horse, nestled against him, continually reminded Samuel of their night spent in the bed at that inn. Indeed, it had been a full night. Despite his insistence that he would leave once she fell asleep, he had fallen asleep too and had remained there, holding her in his arms, until the first hints of the sleepy autumn dawn slipped through the thin fabric of the curtains which hung at the small window.

Nothing improper had happened, of course—they had both been far too exhausted for that and, besides, he was a gentleman. But still, the experience of waking beside her, of feeling her warm, petite form pressed against him, of burying his nose in those dark curls while he kissed her good morning had been overpowering. It was more than lust—although God only knew he had felt plenty of that. It was a sense of rightness, of belonging. A sense that if he was fortunate to spend every morning waking like that, with Hope in his arms, then at the end of his life he would die a happy man.

It was love, but then he knew that. He'd known that for some time. Now, as he caught first sight of Hayton Hall's castle-like roofscape, he knew he needed to make things formal. To ask, in the proper way, the vital question. In the aftermath of Hope's rescue and George's apprehension, he'd blurted out his intentions in the heat of the moment, and yet he had not actually asked her.

Last night he'd gone to her room intent upon proposing, but one look at her pale, weary, worried face was all he'd needed to understand that it was not the right time. It had been clear to him that Hope needed to talk about what was on her mind—her ordeal and the death of her father, not to mention her clear and persistent worries about what Samuel thought of her, now that he knew the truth. What she'd needed from him, he'd quickly realised, was comfort and reassurance. Proposals, he'd decided, could wait.

Although, he realised now, not for much longer. He wanted her to know that his intentions were serious and sincere. And he desperately wanted to know whether she would accept him or whether, in the cold light of a dismal, damp autumn day, she would decide that she wanted to return to Richmond and to the stage. To that life she had so admirably carved for herself against all the odds.

His horse drew to a gentle halt outside the grand front entrance to Hayton Hall, prompting a flurry of activity from all directions. Samuel was vaguely aware of the simultaneous approach of his groom, his guests and two of his household servants as he climbed down, before reaching up to assist Hope. Gently, he lifted her down, once again overcome by the feeling of holding her in his arms, the heightened awareness combined with those more desirous emotions which were absolutely not appropriate with so many people nearby. As he drew her level with him, Hope's eyes met his and he gave her a smile—one which she returned with just as much affection as he hoped his would convey. A good sign, if ever he wished for one.

Composing himself, Samuel turned to greet the assembling welcome party. He would ask her soon, he told himself. He would find the right moment, and until then he would simply have to be patient.

'Well done, Sammy,' Charles declared, patting him on the back. 'You've brought her back. I do hope there was no harm done, Miss Swyn—Miss Sloane,' he corrected himself swiftly as he turned to Hope.

Samuel watched as Hope nodded, a look of uncertainty momentarily clouding those lovely green eyes as she regarded his friend. 'I am quite well, thank you, Mr Gordon, all things considered. Samuel tells me that you went with him as far as Lillybeck, to look for me. I am grateful to you. I know what you must think of me, now that you know who I really am...'

'Ah, yes. I'm afraid that in the past I have been far too adept at judging books by their covers, Miss Sloane,' Charles replied, a deep blush rising from beneath his collar. 'Such opining will cease henceforth. As a rather spirited young lady once informed me, I'd do well to pay more attention to the character of my acquaintances rather than other, more avaricious considerations.'

Samuel smiled at his friend's words which, for all his embarrassment, were clearly heartfelt. Beneath that boisterous personality and propensity for outright snobbery lurked a good heart. Hope, meanwhile, inclined her head politely, the ghost of a smile playing upon her lips. 'I am glad of it,' she replied. 'Especially if you intend to extend such generosity beyond your own acquaintances and consider, perhaps, those of your sister's acquaintance by the same standard?'

Charles's beetroot visage was all the confirmation that was needed that Hope's message had indeed hit the mark. Samuel could have kissed her out of sheer admiration for the way that, despite her own ordeal and exhaustion, she did not miss the opportunity to champion Miss Gordon's lovelorn cause. Instead, he reached for her hand, threading his fingers through hers and giving them a squeeze in solidarity.

Miss Gordon, meanwhile, hovered beside her brother, looking somewhere between relieved and chastened. 'I owe you an apology, Miss Sloane,' she began, her lip trembling. 'If I had not run away to the docks, you might never...'

Hope shook her head. 'It was my choice to join the search for you, and to get out of the carriage when I saw you,' she insisted, touching Miss Gordon delicately on the arm. 'You have nothing to reproach yourself for. My father was determined to find me—if he hadn't then, he would have eventually. At least it is all over now.'

The brave smile Hope gave Miss Gordon made Samuel's heart lurch for her, and he squeezed her hand again before releasing it as Hope hurried towards Maddie. He watched as the maid gathered Hope into her arms, letting out a few heartfelt sobs of relief as she whispered words that Samuel could not quite hear.

Next to them, Smithson hovered, endearingly trying and failing to remain composed as he clasped his hands behind his back and grinned from ear to ear. Samuel could not help but think about the wily old butler's warning to him all those weeks ago, about lies and the way they could all too easily get out of hand. How right the man had been, although Samuel suspected that even the ever-perceptive

Smithson could not have predicted where Samuel and Hope's deceptions would have led them. Nor could he have known, that evening when he'd lectured Samuel on being truthful, just how close to the surface the truth had always bubbled between them and how, despite the disguises they'd worn, they'd come to know and understand each other's true characters nonetheless.

He knew the essence of her, and she of him. Everything else, as he'd once told her, was simply window-dressing. He could only hope and pray that she would agree. That she would consent to becoming his wife. As Maddie released Hope from her embrace he stepped forward, offering Hope his arm. He could bear the wait no longer—he had to ask her. The right moment, such as it was, could be created as well as found.

'Hope, would you mind joining me in the gardens for a few moments?' he asked her. 'There is something I'd like to discuss with you, then we can freshen up and dine.'

Hope's eyes widened briefly, before she nodded her assent. 'Of course.'

Samuel walked with her to Hayton's sprawling rear gardens, his heart hammering in his chest. The right moment could indeed be created, he told himself and, despite his nerves, this felt right. Hope deserved to be asked for her hand properly; she deserved to know just how sincere and honourable his intentions were. She deserved to know just how much he loved her. There would be no more secrets between them, and certainly no more lies.

They drew to a halt on the footpath, the earthy, damp smell of the surrounding shrubbery heavy in the air. Samuel drew a deep breath, hurriedly collecting his thoughts as he settled upon what he would say. He'd never proposed marriage before—he had to do it correctly, had to find the right way to express himself…

Before Samuel could utter a word, however, Hope relinquished his arm and turned to face him. 'If this is about what I said to Mr Gordon, about his sister's acquaintances, I was only trying to…'

Samuel placed a gentle finger over her lips, smiling at her. 'I know what you were trying to do, and I think Charles understood too. But this is not about Charles, or his sister's romantic entanglements,' he replied quietly. 'This is about us.'

She furrowed her brow, then looked away. 'It's all right, Samuel,' she began. 'You don't have to explain yourself. I understand well enough that whatever this is between us cannot go on. You are a gentleman, whereas I am an actress and a…'

'You are the woman I love, Hope,' he replied, still smiling. 'And you love me—you told me so, only last night. Surely that is all there is to understand.'

She nodded. 'I do love you, Samuel, but what if love is not enough? What if the circumstances make it impossible? What if there are simply too many obstacles?'

He gave her a knowing look. 'Like Romeo and Juliet?' he asked, recalling her words in the library that night when they'd discussed Shakespeare. That night when they'd first kissed. That night when everything had changed.

'Yes—like Romeo and Juliet,' she replied.

'But, unlike Shakespeare's lovers, the only obstacles for us are ones we make ourselves. And for me, Hope, there are no obstacles. When I look at you, I see a woman I cannot fail to admire. You are not shameful, you are remarkable. Being an actress has not made you a scandal or a harlot— it has made you a talented woman with a passion for the theatre, not to mention a knowledge of the Bard which is second to none. I love you, Hope, and I believe with all my heart that love is enough.' He took hold of her hand. 'As a clever lady I know once told a friend of mine, we love who we love and that should be all that matters.'

He watched as she pressed her lips together momentarily, suppressing a smile at hearing her own words quoted back at her. She regarded him carefully. 'Are you sure that it isn't Hope Swynford you've fallen for? How can you be sure you're not in love with a character?'

'How can you be certain you don't love Sir Samuel the baronet and not Samuel Liddell, the title-less younger brother?' he countered.

'Because they are the same...' she began. He watched with delight as a wry smile crept on to her face. 'All right — point taken.'

He held those lovely emerald eyes with his own. 'The night that you told me your story, you said you'd allowed me to care for a woman who doesn't exist, but that simply isn't true. Hope Swynford might be a character, but she is also you. Calling yourself Hope Swynford rather than Hope Sloane and an heiress rather than an actress didn't change who you are, Hope, and even while you kept your true story from me and everyone else at Hayton, it was always there, wasn't it? Indeed, I would venture to suggest that a sheltered heiress would have been far less likely to astutely point out the unfairness of me not heeding my maid's wish to be called Maddie, or to recognise and empathise with Miss Gordon's difficulties. Only you, the real you, could have done those things. I'm not in love with a character. I'm in love with you. Marry me, Hope.'

Her eyes widened and she searched his gaze, clearly

disbelieving. 'When you spoke of marriage at the inn, I thought it was only because of the situation—that it was the stress and the relief talking. Never did I imagine that you could be serious.'

'I have never been more serious,' he replied. 'Do me the honour of becoming my wife, Hope, and make me the happiest man alive.'

Samuel held his breath for what felt like an eternity, watching her as she seemed to consider his proposal. Then, to his sheer relief and utter joy, she leapt forward, throwing her arms around his neck and pulling him close to her. He responded in kind, wrapping his arms around her waist and vowing in that moment to never let go. To make her the happiest woman that ever lived. To build a life together, one filled with laughter and adventure, with family and fun. With afternoons sipping tea and eating cake in the parlour, surrounded by all the children they would have, and evenings out at the theatre or spent cosily inside, savouring the finest bottle of Bordeaux and poring over a good book. With nights curled up together, and mornings waking to each other's embrace. A comfortable, contented life which consigned hardship and heartache to the past.

He buried his nose in the thick curls of her dark hair, breathing her in, imagining the years stretching before them, filled with promise. Then he realised that he had not yet heard her answer.

'So, is that a yes, then?' he ventured, whispering the words in her ear.

Hope gazed up at him, an irrepressible grin illuminating her face. The best and most wonderful smile he'd ever seen. The smile he wanted to see until the end of his days.

She reached up, placing the briefest, loveliest kiss upon

his lips. 'It's a yes,' she replied, her mouth still close to his, inviting him to kiss her back.

Which he did, of course—thoroughly, and with wild abandon.

Epilogue

February 1819

'*If music be the food of love, play on...*'

Hope settled into her seat as the curtain went up, the many candles which illuminated the stage casting their bright glow over the darkened theatre. From her position in the box at Lowhaven's Theatre Royal she could see Duke Orsino strutting around, musing about his unrequited love for Countess Olivia. Next to her, Samuel reached out and took hold of her hand, giving it a tender squeeze. The irony of them enjoying a performance of Shakespeare's *Twelfth Night* together was not lost on him either. Indeed, he'd flashed her one of his amused smiles when he'd told her that the play was coming to town just after Christmas, pulling her close to him as he'd informed her that he planned to reserve seats.

'People in disguise, falling in love,' he'd remarked, kissing the top of her head. 'The Bard could have written that one for us, couldn't he? We must go and see it.'

Hope had laughed at that, reminding him that they went to see virtually everything that Lowhaven's theatre had to offer, a habit which would doubtless become fixed now that they had settled into their own home on the edge of town. They'd moved at the beginning of the new year, after spending the Christmas season at Hayton Hall with Isaac and Louisa. Hayton's real baronet had returned from Scotland with his wife in November, their travels brought finally to an end by the worsening weather and Louisa's delicate health.

The brooding older brother had been stunned to discover that in his absence his younger sibling had not only fallen in love, but had wed. Hope had observed Isaac's astonished expression as Samuel recounted the extraordinary tale, from their first meeting to their marriage in a private ceremony by common licence in Hayton's ancient, humble church, witnessed only by the Gordons.

The return of Sir Isaac Liddell had thrown Hope into turmoil, and her old fears about her base-born status and dubious past had briefly resurfaced. As Samuel's older brother and the head of his family had regarded her carefully during their introduction, she'd found herself fretting, convinced that he'd be horrified about their union. As it turned out, she need not have worried. Despite his serious demeanour and brusque manner, Isaac was a kind soul who'd welcomed her into the family without hesitation. When he'd learned about her lowly origins and her life on stage, he had not even flinched. Instead, he'd seemed to perceive her discomfort and had done his utmost to assuage it.

'You're a veritable woman of the world, Hope,' he'd remarked kindly, regarding Samuel with affection in his keen blue eyes. 'And therefore perfect for my brother, since he has seen so much of it.'

Recalling the memory, Hope smiled. Isaac and Louisa had joined them at the theatre this evening, although they planned to return to Hayton in their carriage as soon as the final curtain fell. Another thing Hope had quickly come to understand was just how besotted Hayton's baronet was with his lovely wife, and just how protective—even more so since they'd discovered that the fatigue and sickness which had been troubling Louisa did in fact have an altogether happy cause.

Hope glanced at Louisa. Even in the dim light she could make out the serene expression on her face, one hand resting firmly on her swollen belly as she watched the play. The baby's arrival was expected in the early summer. God willing, Hayton Hall would have an heir, and the Liddell brothers would greet the next generation of their family.

Although, Hope increasingly suspected, the child would not be the sole member of that generation for very long—not if her own morning queasiness and absent courses were anything to go by. It was a suspicion she'd not yet shared with Samuel, but with each passing day she felt more sure of it, more excited, and more anxious. Tonight, she was bursting to tell him the happy news, especially since it had already been a day for it. Earlier that day she'd received a letter from Henrietta Gordon, telling her that she was no longer Miss Gordon at all. Last autumn Mr Gordon and his sister had departed from Hayton on a mission to reunite Miss Gordon with her lost love. It was a mission which had taken them to the burgeoning mills of Manchester to find the man in question, and a mission which had ultimately succeeded.

Moved by the depth of their daughter's misery and their desperation to cure her of it, the Gordon parents had finally accepted the match. A wedding had followed, and the newlyweds had now settled back in Blackburn, where the new

Mrs Smith was, in her own words, blissfully happy. Her husband, she wrote, had secured a job alongside her father, and although it was early days, he was proving himself extremely capable in all that he did.

Hope had studied the letter several times, shaking her head in disbelief at such an incredible tale, committed to paper in the hurried hand of a woman who was clearly delirious with joy at the surprising turn her life had taken. It was a feeling which Hope recognised immediately, since it was one she knew only too well.

'If this were played upon a stage now, I could condemn it as an improbable fiction...'

Hope smiled at the familiar famous line in the Bard's play, a line which could just as easily apply to her own life of late as it did to a story written more than two centuries ago. A year ago she'd been a travelling actress, on the run from a terrible past. Now, here she was, sitting in one of the best seats in the theatre, married to the most wonderful man and probably expecting his child. Improbable— indeed, it was improbable. So improbable that sometimes she had to pinch herself to be certain she was not dreaming.

Perhaps Samuel was right. *Twelfth Night* could have been written for them.

On stage, disguises were dispensed with as, at last, all was revealed. In the faint candlelight Samuel's gaze caught her own and held it, even as all around them the crowd grew noisier, chuckling and murmuring in excitable anticipation. They were, for a moment, in their own little world, one of mutual affection and shared understanding. One which, Hope considered, was worthy of one last revelation of her own. Gently, she lifted Samuel's hand, bringing it to rest upon her stomach, and nodded slowly. She watched as those blue-grey eyes of his widened, and his mouth fell open in surprise.

Then he leapt to his feet, pulled her into his arms and embraced her as the final curtain fell to rapturous applause.

* * * * *

If you enjoyed this story,
then you're going to love Sadie King's
debut Historical romance
Spinster with a Scandalous Past

HARLEQUIN
Reader Service

Enjoyed your book?

Try the perfect subscription for Romance readers and get more great books like this delivered right to your door.

See why over 10+ million readers have tried Harlequin Reader Service.

Start with a Free Welcome Collection with free books and a gift—valued over $20.

Choose any series in print or ebook. See website for details and order today:

TryReaderService.com/subscriptions